SHADOWS OF TROY

SHADOWS OF TROY

M. J WRIGHT

Other works by the Author

Other works by the Author:

The Broken Child
The Lost Child
Millie or Lily?
When I made you smile

Print ISBN: 978-1-7643731-0-4
E book ISBN: 978-1-7643731-1-1

First Edition

Published by: Michelle Wright, Raymond Terrace, NSW, Australia
A copy of this publication has been deposited with the National Library of Australia under the *Copyright Act 1968*.

Electronic legal deposit submitted via the National edeposit (NED) service library.gov.au.

Dedication

This book is for my husband who has put up with crazy writing and research hours for nine years. For my beta reader Narrell for being my advanced reader in chief, co conspirator and suffering through multiple bad drafts of writing before getting to the good stuff. For my friends and support staff for never stopping believing that this project would have an end. This book is for those of us who exist in the real world, live in history and thrive in fantasy to cope with disability or illness-you rock.

Contents

Dedication   vii

Foreword   1

Part One   3

Arrival in Troy   7

The Priestesses of Eileithyia   12

Meeting Him   17

The Choosing   22

Part Two   28

Growing Tensions   36

Between Priestess and Princess   45

The death of Poseidon   52

Echoes of consequence   58

Ceremony   62

Poison   69

Shadows of Treachery   76

Part Three   81

Hektor's calculated command   89

A glimpse of the truth   95

Echoes of Hope   100

Collusion   112

First Blood	117
Retrieving the Amulet	127
The twin relics	133
A moment between sisters	138
Dragon Knowledge	142
The Mask of Deception	155
Isandros's Faith	157
Part Four	160
A night of loss	163
Hektor's Funeral	167
Betrayal Within	172
Alexander's Deception	181
Achilles Death	185
Grave Consequences	189
Part Five	193
Allies arrive	197
The Temple above the Sea	202
Troy's united front	208
The poisoned reckoning	211
Helena's true colours	215
Before the gates	221
The storm that came unbidden	226
Unseen Betrayal	229
Fire and Blood	232
In shadow and in song	236
Part Six	241
Dawn of the Phoenix rising	246

Afterword   251

Foreword

Foreword

When stars align and shadows fall,
A war will rise, consuming all.
Three sisters awakened through tragedy,
Their flames reborn, their power revealed,
A destiny shared, a fate unsealed.
Two relics lost, recovered through gain,
The amulet and coin, the ancient twin.
A Mycenaean power calls in an ancient debt,
To where flames and wings ascend, their fate is set.
In union, hope shall be restored,
Phoenix and Dragon, a single chord.
Through love, the world shall find its peace,
The endless war, at last, will cease.
Sacrifice shall mark the path,
Through fire's breath and dragon's wrath.
The hidden relics shall enhance latent gifts,
Bounded by love, no silence drifts.
The dragons follow the prophecy's call,
Protecting phoenixes, they stand tall.
A new foe shall rise, the fated chase,

Through time and space, a relentless race.
When peace is theirs, and the prophecy fulfilled
A new era of shifters emerges strong and skilled.
Their legacy, a future bright,
Born from fire, forged in light

Part One

Thera

(Theron)
Conclave. The inaugural summit of all Dragon kind from across the globe. We summoned all the leaders of ancient, powerful beings. A massive stone carved table built to seat 12 dominated the room. Twelve reclusive leaders, rarely seen beyond their nests. We were not known for our patience and so their words rose sharp in the air. Heat shimmered as I strode over blistering lava flows.

My brothers Seraphinus and Alexios sat flanking my throne. Alexios shuffled his notes into neat piles in front of him poised ready to take notes. Hebridean Blacks intimidated him-a stark reminder of his near fatal encounter. Seraphinus's lips curved in a subtle, defiant smile beneath his stern gaze, his eyes sharp as ice. 'Theron of Sparta.' he intoned. Stepping forward, I unleashed a vicious roar that swept over the assembly, rising to the gods.

'Welcome to the ancient hall of Drakaris. Once, as one nest, we burned with fierce purpose; now, scattered across the globe, our destiny calls. The prophecy demands our attention.' Our benediction weaves a golden net above us, guarding against the unseen. Venerated shifters shift in silent accord. 'I call on you now: stand with me and reclaim our legacy!'

"You speak of prophecy, boy. Summoned us all here like dogs to answer your call. What is this news that couldn't be sent with a messenger?" Growling out his challenge, the senior leader from the Hebrides thumped the table with his fist. Other thumps joined his in agreement, signalling that they agreed with Morvaeth. Before they could speak out of turn, Kai Long of the White Cloud dragon clan pulled his pipe from his mouth. "Hold your ire at being forced to make this trip, brothers. Let us hear Theron of the Thera Clan before descending into the chaos the mortals seem to love so much."

'Many of you know me. I have served as interim leader while my father suffered from Ember blight.' The room shuddered at the mention of the affliction that had stripped my father's flesh from his bones till he was nothing bar a skeleton surviving in eternal agony. 'Greece calls in her debt. We must send our strongest warriors or face having the decision taken from us. King Agamemnon holds the amulet of the ancestors mentioned in the prophecy.'

Roars erupted from the crowd surrounding the twelve chairs at the Council of Elders' table. Holding my hands up for calm, I waited for what seemed an age, allowing my glowing blue eyes to settle on Evander of Emberis. He was in partial transition, his midnight and gold feathers marking his phoenix heritage. The intricate patterns on his wings shimmered like the garment of a celestial warrior, adding an aura of majesty and power to his presence. The air crackled with violent ancient energy as I spoke. 'The prophecy in question,' I began, 'speaks of the deep relationship between our kind and yours, Evander. A war is on the horizon, far greater than this petty squabble between Menelaus of Sparta and Alexander of Troy. Our prophecy foretells a war to end all wars—a cataclysmic battle that will determine the world's fate.'

'I know it, Theron,' Evander replied, his voice heavy with sorrow. 'My people are not ready—my daughters are not ready to live in that time. Only one among them is versed in the ways of war, but even she is unprepared for what lies ahead. We are a peaceful people,' he said, his feathers rippling with agitation. 'Who would want to erase our existence from this world?'

'Who, indeed?' I echoed, feeling the weight of leadership settle heavier on my shoulders. 'We are bound by oath and by amulet to the Greek kings. Yet war is on the horizon and we must be ready. Who will supply warriors to this cause?'

'You speak of smoke hovering above ripples in the prophecy over the surface of time itself child. Your words hold more weight than you imagine.' She who had birthed me joined me at the table casting her gaze around the room, 'I have seen the war to come. You will be victorious.' A cheer echoed around the chamber before she held her hand up for calm, 'You will be victorious but you will be fighting this war for an age to come. Three will find their mates in a strange land not known to our kind. If you go on this quest to protect those etched into these very walls-you will not return to your mates. You will not see your children for a long time. You will have glory but it will come at a great cost. We believe in the decision of the conclave of Dragons and will support your decision.'

My Mother turned her sad eyes upon me knowing that my decision had already been made and I could not be swayed from my path. She kissed my brow before retreating into the shadows to stand with the other great mothers.

Evander planted both hands on the table, and as he stood, his wings unfurled, spreading wide for all to see. The midnight black and gold feathers gleamed under the chamber's ethereal light, a testament to his strength and resilience. Seraphinus and Alexios scrambled to their feet to join me showing a united front. 'We will send warriors,' Morvaeth conceded, smoke curling from his nostrils as the fire in his belly burned bright. 'As will we.' Kai Long added. The assurance from each clan that I could count on them for numbers had Alexios pushing one of his papers to me the minute we were seated. 'In my hand is an account of the war readiness of the clan of Thera.' Glancing down at Alexios scribbling a note to himself on a scrap piece of parchment made him the center of attention until I continued, 'In fact, it seems Alexios was overzealous—he has an accounting of the war readiness of the whole of Dragon-kind. We have much to do before we join Agamemnon, before the month is out. Evander, may I speak with you privately?'

Ending the meeting with the customary oath renewal, I waited until the chamber was clear before joining the lone figure studying the carvings surrounding the prophecy. The air was still thick with the remnants of ancient magic.

'My wife is pregnant again,' Evander opened without preamble. His salt-and-pepper hair, worn from years of responsibility and stress, framed a face marked by deep scars, a testament to his battles and losses. His wise blue eyes, however, shone with a spark of determination despite the weariness that weighed on him. His green tunic, intricately embroidered with phoenixes, clung to his lean frame, symbolising his heritage and the hope they all clung to.

'She has spent so long waiting between children in case the war comes, and now it is upon us.' He paused, his expression haunted. 'We held off having more children after the last great conflict that threatened our kind. The memories of that time and our losses linger in our hearts.' He ran a hand through his hair, revealing more of the scars that etched his skin. 'We always hoped for a safer world before expanding our family, but that hope is growing dim. I fear even with the warning you gave me, I may only be able to save a few.'

'And I will protect them.' Giving him my word was no light matter. I could only pray that he would be able to keep a remnant alive for us to protect.

Arrival in Troy

Arrival in Troy

(Selene)

My father, Evander of Emberis, had been right. His words shared with Theron of Thera in privacy after the great conclave had come to pass. Our people had refused to prepare for war. And yet in the dark of the night we were woken choking on fear and acrid smoke. Our people scattered in the destruction as did we, not knowing who may follow our flight path or whether we would survive...

I could feel the warmth sinking in through my pores as the last rays of the late afternoon sun kissed the horizon. We finally allowed our feet to sink into the golden sands we had spotted from the air. Waves crashed rhythmically along the shore, their sound merging with the rustling of leaves and distant wildlife calls. Sensing the presence of something extraordinary, the local bird life took flight in a flurry of feathers and alarmed cries, circling high above before seeking refuge further inland. Energy rising up through me from the earth echoed the promise of destiny wrapping around my inner soul.

Still partially in bird form, I cocked my head to the side, listening to the ambient sounds and scanning our surroundings for danger with quick, jerky movements. Strands of my messy, long, dark, curly hair blew into my face, loose from the simple, neat braid I had styled so long ago.

Flexing my azure and violet wings to ease the cramping muscles, I knew I was creating a spectacle for the humans on their beach. But heaven knows if I didn't stretch, I wouldn't be able to walk another step. My simple green tunic encrusted with sweat had once been embroidered with colourful flowers around the neckline over skintight brown leather pants. Boots were almost an afterthought as I never needed them when in flight.

I tucked my wings tightly against my back and took a few tentative steps, my gait still reminiscent of my avian form. The sands beneath my feet felt foreign and unstable, causing me to shift my weight from one foot to the other in a rhythmic dance, like a bird adjusting to a new perch.

Raya shifted beside me, still wearing the official uniform of the royal family's flight guard. Grief ravaged the faint lines of her face, and her gold eyes glowed dully as she pulled her rust-coloured feather cloak tighter around her to hide her leather surcoat embroidered with the gold emblem of office. She noted figures in the distance. 'We must shift fully.' she decreed, her voice firm, leaving us no room for arguments. 'This means you, Althea.'

My youngest sister Althea still had her face covered in the gold and green feathers she favoured. Her messy, long blond plait spilled out from the hood of her brown cloak, lined with soft fur trim. Clutching at the pouch of healing herbs she had rescued, she cradled it close to her chest. Her own devastation poured out of her like a signal for the humans. Her green dress shimmered with intertwining vines, and her cloak was embroidered with the traditional motifs of our land-making her seem less a myth, and more a memory made flesh. Over her shoulder sat a little bird, totally at peace with everything going on around us. 'Do you see him?' Her eyes scanned the skies as she obliged Raya's request by transitioning fully into her mortal form. She looked young in human years despite the wisdom that she had gained from our own.

'He was just behind me.' Raya assured her as I watched her long, dark cherry-red hair pull back in a soft half-up style. Henna tattoos rose up from her neckline, decorating the visible skin on her neck, and a henna phoenix graced her brow. Her mortal outfit was similar to ours. Forcing the last of my feathers to recede, my only thought was how to protect my family without Father to protect us.

'Over there.' They raced through the dunes to where she had spotted his inert body. He must have landed, still injured from battle and suffering too much from the strain of the long flight. He had transitioned upon touchdown. His once fierce visage is aged and careworn. 'Have we been sighted by the locals?' His voice rasped slightly after such a long period of disuse. 'We don't have long, Papa.' Raya turned to measure the distance of the mortals from us. 'They are but a few minutes away, and it seems they are bringing a priest.'

We exchanged long looks, and with a nod, I indicated that I would speak for our family while Thea tended to Father and Raya stood guard. 'Here, Papa—this will take some of your pain. Chew quickly and ignore the taste.' Thea had rationed out some of the precious herbs that would usually be steeped and mixed with honey. With no time to restyle my hair thoroughly, I gathered the wild locks and stuffed them under my hood to make myself look more presentable. 'They are here.' Raya warned us in a low tone. Thea's voice fell away entirely as she huddled with Father on the ground, tucked into his side.

I paused momentarily to pick non-existent lint off my clothes and stand up straighter because in that empty space between moments, Father was saying things about presenting oneself with decorum and poise. I straightened my spine, threw out my chest, and held my head high as I made my way to meet the delegation, my bearing more regal.

Glancing at Father, noting the caution in his eyes and then turning to face the group of soldiers on horseback.

They had placed the priest and another citizen at the centre of their formation—a classic tactic for protection. Familiar with such manoeuvres, I approached the soldier with the largest plume on his helmet. His dark hair was streaked with silver, and his chiselled face spoke of years of discipline. Stern eyes scanned us with caution. His build was robust, encased in gleaming armour marked with the insignia of rank. Around him, the delegation stood armed—spears and swords at the ready, prepared for any threat.

I stepped forward, and they had no choice but to see me. Then, as if I were invisible again, they overwhelmed the only male in our group with questions we couldn't answer. Our customs dictated one spoke to the designated speaker. Their customs seemed to be based upon whether or not I was male.

The horses, big and robust, were panting hard, their sides heaving from the weight of their travelling. They flinched slightly in our presence, realizing that we were not mortal. Standing slightly behind the heavily decorated captain was a priest, a thin, angular-faced man of advanced years whose skin ruffled and was so worn by wrinkled lines of worry and wisdom. His grey robe was flapping, and his eyes were like a hawk's. They should have noticed everything.

Standing next to him was a townswoman in her forties, perhaps, with no great pretensions apparent in her plain garb. However, her eyes sparkled with curiosity and apprehension. The priest beckoned her near. 'Go on, help him.' he said, trying to reassure her in as calm a voice as possible. The woman hesitated momentarily, steeling herself, then nodded and moved toward Father. Her hands were shaking a little as she concentrated on how to examine him, the weight of responsibility heavy upon her.

'I am Leon. You have no ship? No luggage? This priest of Poseidon says you just appeared on the beach almost as if the air parted itself and you stepped through from another world.' He stood directly in front of me, trying to assess if the group behind me posed any danger while his hand never left the pommel of his sword. I kept my movements calm and controlled, trying to appear harmless, human—just another survivor. 'I am Selene of Emberis. These are my younger sisters Nuraya and Althea, and my father Evander. We were shipwrecked somewhere along the coastline many days ago and have been on foot ever since. The journey has been harrowing on my father, and my sisters and I have done all we could, but our father needs a healer before blood poisoning sets in.' Gesturing briefly to the small group he was trying to assess behind me, I noted that they were doing their best to look suitably bedraggled to fit the narrative I was spinning.

'Please, sir, we have lost everything in this gods-forsaken voyage.' Raya begged, 'Our father needs a healer, or he will not see the next sunrise.' Her desperation was on display for all to see.

She knelt beside Father, pulling the edge of his tunic aside to reveal the wound. 'He has blood poisoning,' she said, barely above a whisper. 'The wound is encrusted with pustules, ripe to burst.'

The priest threw back his hood, his face grim as he surveyed the scene. 'Enough, Leon. We will heal the man, and then he shall serve Poseidon in his gratitude.'

His gaze shifted back to Raya, the recognition in his eyes deepening. 'The symbol on her forehead—she bears the mark of Eileithyia, a goddess whose temple and worship have almost been forgotten. Make no mistake with this family, Leon. They are destined for more than we know. They are tied to ancient prophecies and destinies the gods themselves oversee.'

'Excuse me, sir,' I waited until they had Father on a horse to ask the burning question in my mind. 'Could you tell me where we are?'

Leon pointed at the city high on the hill. My sharp eyes could make out the thick walls and large gates surrounding it, a testament to its strength and grandeur. 'We are in Troy, and Willusa is where we are headed, Selene of Emberis.'

The Priestesses of Eileithyia

The Priestesses of Eileithyia

I can hear my sisters soft whispers as we rise before the sun. I keep them close to me as we are the last of our kind. No more of our people arrived on the beaches of Troy in the days after we did. Still reeling in shock at our sudden change in circumstances we adjusted quickly from being royalty to serving the community with no real rest forthcoming. Explaining to Thea that we were no longer Princesses but a half step above servants was a little more than Nuraya could bear to sit through.

She was a protector first and she didn't like it when our sister cried. When the priests would separate us we clung together claiming that we could provide the sisterhood with a stronger leadership this way. We were always stronger together and together we made our way through the lower city on swift, silent feet, relying on our senses to navigate our way to the cliff. We were required to greet the dawn with rites dedicated to the goddess.

Stolen moments from our new responsibilities are all we have now to acknowledge our true heritage. Mourn our dead and remember Mother. Moments in which we take turns relieving the itch under our skin, transitioning into phoenix form, and finding freedom in the skies above the glistening ocean. Fleeting moments before the day breaks with a beautiful line of gold gracing the skies with lilacs, blues and pinks.

These ceremonies that we perform at dawn are in a way stolen moments as well to worship the goddess in all her forms. Turning my face toward the horizon I inhale deeply, feeling the cool morning air fill my lungs, I tip my head back, eyes closed, walling up the confusion and pain that we lived with before tending to the daily duties. Below us, the princes of Troy ride their horses with wild abandon before training in their swordcraft, the rhythmic clashing of blades echoing up the cliffs, triggering the unwanted memory of Father gathering us in the corner of Nuraya's room and leaving us to search for Mother. We cowered deep in the shadows behind Nuraya as we could hear a cacophony of terror rising from below.

'Breathe deeply of the fresh, clean air.' Nuraya murmurs into my ear, 'We are no longer there. Be in this moment, here, with me now sister.' Following her instructions the memories retract their claws from deep within me. Together, we raise our hands in unison, fingers splayed to capture the warmth of the early sun's rays, breathing deeply to ground myself in the moment before beginning the first chant of the day 'Great Eileithyia, bringer of life, we honour you at this sacred hour,' I keep my voice clear and steady as I continue, 'Grant us your blessings as we begin our day.'

Eileithyia reminded us of our deity, Aurelia, the goddess of rebirth and renewal. Thus, trading one name for another, we continued to worship our goddess despite the different name she wore in this country. Raya's soft, fervent voice continued the morning prayer: 'We offer gratitude for the light that guides us and the strength to fulfil our duties. May your wisdom guide us in all that we do.'

She loathed the life of a priestess. Stripped of her warrior status, she was forced inside to focus on womanly duties and the gossip that filled the day of the highborn. I knew my sister was unhappy, but I felt trapped in this new life, still too unsteady to find a way to help her. Finally, Althea steps forward, her eyes closed in deep concentration and devotion, 'We pledge to serve and protect, to heal and nurture. In your name, we greet the dawn and its promise.'

Thea had thrived in the change of location. Still a fledgling in our eyes, she had begun to learn the ways of Trojan healing. Mixing the new techniques with our phoenix tears had produced some truly startling discoveries that we prayed would aid someone in their final hours to be brought back to full health.

Unstoppering our vials of water from the sacred spring, we pour them into a bowl, symbolising the flow of life. Bowing our heads for show, we allow the moment's tranquillity to resonate within us and make our personal prayers to Aurelia before raucous voices rise from below. Many of these princes have never seen war, only training hard for the eventuality of one under the watchful eye of their war leader and their eldest brother. We can hear that training has been turned into a competition as usual. The war leader and Prince Hektor converse in urgent tones as they do not portray the same care free expressions as the younger princes. We were told by the priests to complete our morning rituals and not linger as watching a training session is forbidden to all commoners, displaced royalty included.

I steal glances beneath my lashes, remembering what it is like to have no responsibilities to the immortal gods. We had bartered our freedom for our father's health. Yet, I would not deny feeling drawn to the princes on the beach and wondering briefly what the expression in his eyes is like on this barely new day. Tossing the hood of my cloak back over my curls I feel my sisters gazes boring into my back. I was not free to look at any man, especially not one who was already married.

'Come sister.' amusement tinges Nuraya's words, 'We have much to do this day to earn a place to lay our head.' A softly spoken word helped guide a soul towards the sea god better than the harsh tones of the temple priests. Squinting up at the sun, I realise I have stolen more minutes than usual gazing upon the antics on the beach. It was fast approaching worship hour. Soft feathers rippled over my arms as

I hoisted the basket containing our tools onto my hip, ready to return to the temple.

'Your phoenix is showing.' Althea warns me before skipping ahead of us on the narrow path. Her bright hair glinted gold in the early morning sunlight. Craving the freedom of the air to dip and twirl where my heart took me, I knew I could not shift so freely in our new home. We were refugees in a land that considered the Phoenix bird a symbol of good fortune and luck. We were still waiting for one of our new hosts to try and shoot one of us out of the sky for a trophy to present to the King.

'Refugees and high slaves-could life get any better?' My thoughts took a solemn turn as we climbed through the nearest entrance to the tunnels, hurrying along the path. 'Better a place to lay our head and tasks to occupy our time than the memories of war and loss.' Raya guessed at my thoughts, her fiery hair braided firmly against her skull with the plait wrapped around her head. My dark hair was dressed simply with a few braids wrapped around to frame my face, whilst the rest fell to my waist in a mixture of straight strands and spiral curls.

Focusing on keeping my feathers contained beneath the skin we wore, I slowed my feet. It would not do for the head of our newly created order to be seen rushing through the lower city. 'You go ahead and open the temple to the petitioners. Princess Andromache requests audience this morning and I must go to the Palace to tend to her.' Directing them in their duties, I transfer the basket to Thea's arms before taking a different path, climbing higher into the city proper.

Hard-packed dirt roads gave way to cobblestones and clean stone houses in place of the mud brick cottages of the citizens outside the wall. Stopping at the nearest bath house, I took advantage of my visit to the Palace to indulge in the luxury of the warmth of the hot springs. Washing the grime of the last few days from my body allows me to settle my mind on the task ahead. Donning my ceremonial robes of a lightweight ankle-length deep emerald dress heavily embroidered with the flora and fauna of Emberis and a wide leather belt with our family crest of phoenix kind cinched at my waist. My hair is tamed by two combs decorated with finely wrought leaves of semi-precious stones.

Finally, I felt ready to continue my journey into the heart of Troy.

Meeting Him

Meeting Him

(Selene)

With each soft rustle of my ceremonial robes, I reminded myself: I had every right to walk these palace corridors. Now was not the time to draw upon the regal training my mother had instilled in me. They only needed to see what they wanted to see. Father had been sharing his wisdom after the temple had fallen silent for the night. *Walk with purpose.* I could do that. Slowing my heart beat and straightening my head I remembered to keep my gaze lowered respectfully in front of me.

Project an image of calm even if you do not feel calm inside. Adopting a serene expression on my face I continued down the endless corridors until I reached a secluded courtyard far from prying eyes. I was an outsider in this most sacred of family spaces. I suspected that these places were few and to have been invited to one was a high privilege indeed.

I ignored the blooming flowers and the soft ripple of the fountain behind me—a musical backdrop meant to soothe. The tree, ancient and sprawling, symbolized feminine energy. Its roots carved natural seats and alcoves into the earth, inviting reflection I had no time for. Statues of queens and deities lined the walls between manicured shrubs, each one pristine, each one forgettable. I hadn't been summoned to admire the decor. And yet I noticed it all—unmoved by its symmetry, unimpressed by its lack of soul.

Her royal highness, Princess Andromache of Troy was seated on a cushioned bench, her hand resting lightly on her pregnant belly highlighted by the light materials of her clothing. Her expression was calm. Too calm. She too was wearing a well practiced mask to hide her underlying worry. Dropping into a respectful bob, I rose quickly before approaching her slowly. 'Your Highness, you requested my presence this morning. I am grateful for the honour.' Keeping my voice steady with a warm undertone I was mindful of the minute politics that happened behind closed doors.

She offered a tired smile, 'High Priestess Selene of Emberis of the Temple of Eileithyia. The priests spoke highly of you in their last visit with my husband.' Before I could reply or resituate myself, Hektor strode into the courtyard, his armor glinting in the filtered sunlight, his face set in a frown. Alexander is unfocused as ever,' he grumbled removing his helmet and I sank into another hasty curtsy remaining there, 'This is not the time for distractions.' He must have known that this was his wife's place of solace when the palace around them became chaotic.

Andromache's gaze softened as she looked at her husband, 'Hektor, please join us. We were just beginning. You may rise Priestess.' She released me from the curtsy I was bound to acknowledge them with. Hektor's demeanor shifted slightly, noticing that she was not alone as he had supposed. 'Apologies, I did not mean to interrupt.' 'High Priestess Selene arrived mere moments before you my love.' There's an intensity about him as he focuses his entire concentration on his wife. His dark hair, still damp from training, framed a face that carries the weight of responsibility in every line, depicting an innate desperation to protect his people at all costs. Despite this exterior he greets his wife with nothing but love.

Love matches are rare in the world we live in. Deep respect for your chosen mate are even rarer still. Such was the affection between the two that I could not tell what sort of bond they shared. I watched their interaction from beneath my lashes trying to remain as unobtrusive as possible. A blush warmed my cheeks as he removed more of his armor, muscles glistening with lingering sweat. If Andromache's sharp eyes caught my cheeks heating she did not reprove me although the weight of her worries never left her gaze. Something was deeply troubling the princess, although she did her best to mask her worries from all surrounding her.

Hektor placed a gentle hand on her stomach, 'Is the babe troubling you this morning?' A silent conversation passes between them and the intimacy of the moment makes me feel more like an intruder than ever before, uncomfortable with the display of affection in front of me. 'He thinks to train with his father.' she smiles before addressing me again, 'Selene, I sought your presence not just for your skills but for your wisdom. The King...he has made it clear that Hektor must take another wife to ensure the line of Troy succeeds even if I do not survive childbirth. This is a burden I do not wish to bear, but I am left with no choice.'

Hektor's jaw clenches, his arms snake around his wife's shoulders silently supporting her in her grief. His arms encompassed his world. Touching her forehead lightly with his he promised her, 'You will survive Andromache. We will raise this prince of Troy together and the children that will follow after him.'

My heart ached for them. Childbirth was no small matter and often the will of the goddess contradicted the wishes of the husband. My mother-I could not think of my mother now or my lost ashen one. I refused to offer them empty platitudes as I knew the priests would have. Men had no clue about the true travails of childbirth. I could only offer her the words of my heart. 'Lady Andromache, you are strong enough for this moment in your life. I have watched my mother go through three childbirths. Despite this added stress the King has placed on your heart, I will do everything in my power to assist you and your family. Aurelia's light guides us even in the darkest times.'

The platitude was expected even if the honesty was not. I did not register time passing as I chose to offer Lady Andromache true comfort from the depths of my soul. Somehow, she subtly shifted the conversation to discover more about my background. I hesitated to describe the terror of being invaded in the night, the pain of the loss of my mother, and the horror of fleeing my homeland knowing that we were the last of our kind. She was pregnant, and such tales were not for those in delicate condition. I painted her a kinder version of the truth of who I was and how my family ended up in service to Troy.

'No matter the circumstances that brought you to Wilusa, it is comforting to have someone with such unwavering commitment in times of need.' She reached out to me, taking my hand in a gesture of solidarity.

Hektor nodded, but his focus was on the broader political implications. Caught up in my tale of political shifts and encroaching war, Andromache's eyes, however, were trained on me, silently conveying the weight of her hopes and fears in their liquid depth. Her fears were those of a queen in waiting. She feared for her husband's sanity should she die in childbirth. She feared for her people and the shift in public sentiment with whispers of war already in the air. She struggled with the concept that another woman might raise the child she carried, and she prayed for survival because that is what she desperately wished for.

She honored me with her kindness. I rarely felt such a connection with anyone other than my sisters these days. 'Thank you, Lady Andromache. I find purpose in serving the goddess and, by extension, the community in which I now live.' Remembering to respond, I bestowed upon her one of my rare full smiles. Although the answer was a political one she seemed to catch the underlying message. Andromache glanced at Hektor, then back at me. 'I hope, Selene, that you will be present at the Megaron during the upcoming event. I will arrange for my personal guard to ensure your presence. It is of utmost importance that I have you with me.'

Hektor, preoccupied with his own thoughts, did not catch the deeper implication. I could feel her unspoken plea, and it resonated deeply within me. What she was asking of me only the goddess knew. I had come to serve the princess, and she had a plan forming that I was not privy to as yet.

The Choosing

The Choosing

It had always been my habit to test the temperature by placing a finger outside of the warm blankets before the rest of my body was awake enough to care and then drawing it back to my body to assess it, and like a small child I had continued this habit. Cradling my cool finger close to my chest as I rose to offer obeisance to our chosen goddess, I reminded myself that the early hours should only be reserved for the drunkards stumbling home after a long night in their cups, the butchers sharpening their knives before dividing up their meat to sell, and for those of us who had too much on their mind to lay abed a minute longer.

I turned over the implications of my conversation with Princess Andromache in my mind. She had alluded to many layers, some personal and some political. She wished much from me, and I used the quiet of the early hours to prepare for the emotional onslaught that would come from being in the presence of the royal family as a whole.

By the time the sun had risen over the white sands of the beaches of Troy, the whole lower town knew that the King had sent his soldiers throughout the kingdom to search for a suitable second bride for Prince Hektor. His own personal guard had been entrusted with this duty, strolling through the streets catching the arms of any pretty girl who caught their attention.

Barring the doors to the inner temple complex, I exchanged long looks with Nuraya who gripped her staff calmly in one hand and had drawn her ceremonial dagger with her other. She deliberately stood in front of the door leading from the temple to the inner complex protecting our sister and the priestesses that I had ordered not to leave for any reason. Women were screaming in fear and the sound of it reverberated through the room.

Exchanging a steady look with Raya I pleaded with her, 'Do not engage with the soldiers. When they see there is no one here they will leave in peace. You must stay hidden and keep them safe.' Too aware of the gravity of the situation she replied, 'Do not get drawn into the games they play in the palace Sister if you can at all help it. Remember Father places his faith in the Dragons of Thera to rescue us.'

Theron was late. Father had been ill when we landed and had grown more despondent spending every spare moment he had on that cursed beach waiting for our supposed saviours. He was not present when the soldier came to escort me to the palace. We had spent the night preparing and planning. Nuraya did not wish me to be caught unawares without my essentials and Thea pressed a small packet of herbs into my hands silently. I knew they were praying that the guards would not strip me of my ceremonial dagger. Although it was tiny, it was the only weapons we were allowed to touch now.

The private guard approached me with a respectful bow, 'Lady Selene, your presence is requested at the Megaron. Shall I escort you?' He had a chariot parked slightly up the road from the temple. Two brindle horses chafed in their traces, impatient at the long wait. The scenery blurred as we made haste for the palace. He called out as we passed each checkpoint that there was one more maiden. Word passed ahead of us, and as we entered the palace proper, doors opened for me without question.

'One more maiden?' I stopped my escort deliberately outside the room. Anxiety gripped my heart as I realised what Princess Andromache had been silently begging me. I whispered urgently in a low voice as he bypassed the general court and positioned me with the maidens for consideration, 'Has there been a misunderstanding? I was asked to attend to observe not participate.'

The guard gave me a sympathetic look. 'Lady Selene, there has been no mistake. You are to be considered among the maidens today. Princess Andromache's request still stands, but your presence here is now twofold. Her words are as follows- please forgive me for my deception but you are more worthy to stand in his presence than any other.'

He then turned to address the Megaron at large, his voice strong and clear. 'There is one more maiden for your consideration today. She was found in the Temple of Eileithyia. I bring you Lady Selene of Emberis.' He bowed deeply to the royal family seated in front of us, prompting me to slip into a deep, sweeping curtsy, making note of the royals present through my lashes.

'Bring her closer.' A commanding voice called out, though I could not see who had spoken. Despite the lack of visual confirmation, I could feel all eyes turn our way. Heartbeat thundering loudly in my ears, I dropped my eyes to the floor. There were too many people looking at me. Memories of my parents' training flooded back. The graceful movements, the poised demeanor. Focusing on my breathing helped to control the trembling that had started within.

My outward appearance was calm but inwardly I cried for the injustice of that which was being thrust upon me. Father had said the Dragons of Thera were coming to our aid. Theron had promised us his protection and yet I was in a situation I was not entirely comfortable with. The murmurs of the crowd faded into the background as the weight of their gaze felt like a physical presence behind me. The honour of being chosen. My mind raced, trying to reconcile the conflicting emotions that pulled in different directions.

I could not refuse the direct order of the King nor of Prince Hektor without risking death. Did I want to refuse what fate had laid before me? He was a handsome man. Colouring prettily I blushed at my own thoughts and had the presence of mind to be in the present.

The guard gently urged me forward, and I found myself standing directly before the royal family. I dared a glance through my lashes, noting the stern faces and evaluating eyes that measured my worth. The Queen, dressed in the formal attire of Trojan royalty, wore a richly embroidered gown of deep blue, the color of the royal family, and gold. Her hair was elaborately styled and adorned with a diadem that signified her status. Her face was framed by dark, cascading curls, and her expression was one of regal authority. As she addressed me, her eyes narrowed with scrutiny.

'You stand before the rulers of Troy.' the guard announced, his tone both respectful and authoritative. 'Lady Selene, you may present yourself.'

Present myself... I can do this. Taking a deep breath, I raised my head, meeting the gaze of each royal in turn. 'Your Majesties, it is an honor to be in your presence.' Soft conversations ceased as I sensed their approach.

A sharp voice broke the silence. The Queen herself had spoken, 'I offer the daughter of my own sister. Crinos is maiden still.'

From the corner of my eye, I saw Crinos step forward, her expression confident and assured. Sun-bleached hair dressed in minute braids with a feathered headdress trailing delicately to the ground, she carried herself with an air of superiority. Her eyes briefly met mine, a smirk playing at the edges of her lips.

'Extended relative over a temple nobody. There really is no comparison, is there, cousin?' Her words were dripping with condescension and aimed to remind the court that I was not royalty therefore I could not compare with the status of she who stood sponsored by the Queen herself.

'Lady Selene comes from the Royal House of Emberis. She is more than suitable to be my husband's wife.' Andromache's calm yet firm voice interjected slicing through the palpable tension between us, 'Selene's life experience is what we need in these trying times. Her kindness and compassion will be a balm for our souls.'

My heart skipped a beat. Oh great lady no. The princess had just outed me to a room full of possible enemies. Any safety I had had in anonymity was now gone and with it so my sisters were no longer safe. I was a princess of a dead nation whose enemies were still at large. That simple slip of her tongue could cause multiple problems for my sisters before the night was through.

King Priam sat on a throne set higher than any other in the room. His eyes swivelled to explore the truth of Andromache's words by the expression she wore. His son needed a wife to continue their legacy. Would it be so awful if her possible predecessor were allowed to choose the replacement? If she did not die in child birth the two would have to learn to live with each other's presence for a long time to come. However it would not do to allow any female to believe they had a voice in a male led area of the palace. He spoke at long last keeping his voice gentle as he addressed Andromache, 'You have chosen your candidate wisely indeed daughter, however, Andromache, it is not your place to speak out of turn.' His kind words to her were a stark contrast to what followed as he turned his attention to Crinos. 'Sheath your tongue, girl. Children do not have a say in decisions belonging to men.'

'You were found in the Temple of Eileithyia.' the Queen reiterated, her tone less dismissive but still scrutinizing. 'Speak, Lady Selene. Why should the heir to the throne consider you?'

Panic bubbled up again and I decided that the truth would serve me best, 'Because I am prepared to offer myself to whatever is needed for the good of Troy.' My voice, though soft, held a firm conviction and while my answer had been brief none could deny it came from my heart. Crinos scoffed at my words, her beads and feathers dancing as she shook her head, and from the corner of my eye I caught Andromache's small nod of approval.

Prince Hektor stepped forward stopping shy of me still on the dais, 'Do you mean what you said?' he demanded in a low voice. 'That I give myself for the good of this country?' reiterating what I thought he meant I replied softly for his ears alone, 'You need a wife that Princess Andromache trusts. I was raised to serve my people not the other way around.'

'I cannot offer you my love. I can give you my respect and your family the safety of an alliance with our family.' His eyes gleamed as he continued our conversation quietly. 'Many marriages have been built upon less than that.' I agreed affably.

King Priam, who had been observing silently, finally spoke. 'If Helena is the sun of this court, then Selene will be its moon.' His words were thoughtful, weighing his opinion carefully. Hektor exchanged a long look with Andromache, holding a silent conversation. Unlike his father, who believed women should not speak in court and were merely there to be decorative, Hektor valued his wife's opinion deeply. After a moment, Hektor turned back to the court and announced his decision.

Barely a pause passed before Prince Hektor announced to the crowd, 'I choose Selene of Emberis to be my second wife.'

Hektor descended the dais, his footsteps echoing in the now silent hall. Each step brought him closer to me. His presence calming as his eyes met mine, holding me in place with the intensity of his gaze. I understood that this moment was for the court who had gathered to hear his verdict. The crowd watched in anticipation. I allowed a flush to rise to my cheeks as he leaned into me, drawing me into his arms his words carrying, 'I cannot promise you my heart Selene but I can promise you that I will protect you with my life and you will not want for anything.' His words were sincere and I could not help the timid smile escaping my solemn expression. I did not expect to hold his heart when he had another firmly in that place.

Part Two

P   *Women's Business*

What have I done? I promised Raya and Thea that I would be back soon. I left Raya in charge—goddess, she is even carrying the temple dagger to protect the sisters. My words are the binding oath that joins us together. No public ceremony. No day of celebration. Nothing of what my mother envisaged for the heir to the throne of Emberis. I need to resign myself to the fact that Emberis is gone. We must be who they see if we are to survive. I would forever be the 'other woman' in this marriage. Seen or unseen according to my Lord husband's whim. Would I ever see my two sisters again?

'Come, Selene.' I did not see Andromache descend from the dais in my introspection. She has made her way to the other side of Hektor, the perfect picture of the perfect wife. It is unheard of for the first wife to interact with any of the consorts or concubines. The Queen herself loathed her husband's mistresses. 'Come,' she reiterates softly, reaching for my trembling hand, 'We will find you something suitable to wear for the feast, sister.' She is being kind in front of Hektor. In front of the entire court. Andromache's compassion was the reason I was considered, though she does not know my true identity as crown princess. She only spoke that I was of the Royal House of Emberis. Perhaps she wants to set a positive example for all to see.

Something private transpires between them. I feel as if I am intruding on a match blessed by the gods, and suddenly the oath I just made in front of everyone seems so very wrong. 'Hold your tears a few minutes longer,' Andromache whispers her first order, 'Show them you are not afraid.' Squaring my shoulders, I raise my head and meet her eyes. 'I would be most grateful for your assistance, my lady.' Hektor is swept away by another male of the court already deep in his cups and rowdy with his well wishes. With his unruly blond hair and bright blue eyes, he is a sight to behold. His clothes, while once immaculate, are now slightly disheveled, and his breath carries the unmistakable scent of wine. He is a charming but untidy drunk, his gestures exaggerated and his laughter loud and infectious. Andromache notices my confusion and leans in to whisper, 'Prince Alexander.'

She draws me to the side of the room before warning, 'Watch out for Helena of Sparta and Crinos of the Amazons. Helena will not take kindly to being out of the centre of attention this eve, and you have taken away Crinos's deepest wish of a comfortable city life. She has been raised to think Hektor would always choose her should some tragedy befall me.'

Crinos's expression promises retribution and I turn my attention to the other *lady in question, Helena, with her strawberry blonde hair, sapphire blue eyes, and skin the color of cream, scowls fiercely in my direction before smiling prettily and dipping into a sketch of a curtsey to Andromache. Ignoring her pretence, Andromache slips her arm through mine and guides me out of the room. She leads me through the corridors into the Woman's Quarters to a chamber that overlooks the sea. 'Of all the women in that chamber, I'm so very glad he chose you.' She instructs the servants to find me something suitable to wear for the feast and my first night with Hektor before turning to face me again, 'You were the only one who acknowledged me.' Two strong men placed a tub in the centre of the room before a stream of serving women bearing large pails of hot water to fill it distracted me from the ornate bed covered in fine linen.*

She mistook my silence for awe, 'You will never want for anything again, Selene, not even hot water for private bathing. Hektor is a good man. A kind husband.' She motions for me to strip and step into the hot water. As I settled in, she took a seat on a low stool beside the tub.

'Here, let me help you.' Andromache dipped a cloth into the water and began gently washing my hair. Her touch was tender, and her presence brought an unexpected sense of comfort. She spoke softly, almost to herself. 'I asked the gods for someone who would understand our plight, who could bring strength and compassion to our family.' She looks at me, her eyes filled with a mixture of resolve and empathy. 'When I saw you, I knew you were the answer to my prayers.'

I sucked in my breath sharply as a stream of scented water fell over my hair. My ever-present wild curls seemed to disappear in the heat. Knowing that they would return as my hair dried lessened the shock of yet another change that I must get used to. I had become so reliant on protecting those I loved that my circle had almost become a noose around my neck, choking me from any kind of friendship outside of my family. Trust was something that we did not freely give, and in that moment, I knew I needed an ally in the palace. If I needed to extend my trust to include anyone, I decided in that moment to open my small circle to include Andromache.

'Yet you manipulated the situation to suit yourself. It was a skilled display of planning and chance my lady.' I felt that at this point if she could bathe me I could speak plainly with her. I did not wish a repeat performance with the lives of my sisters and, uncomfortable as the subject matter was, she had crossed a boundary that needed to be put into place. We were not game pieces to be shuffled around for the whims of my new family. Raising from the tub as gracefully as possible I wait while the women immediately swaddle me in a large towel. I wrap my dripping curls in another towel before drying off thoroughly.

'I did not do this without deep consideration for all parties involved.' Draping my body with a dress in the same dark blue linen as her own, Andromache ensures each piece fits correctly before cinching my waist with the belt I had worn to the palace that morning, stamped with the symbol of Emberis. She continues, 'My choices were not made lightly and in time you will come to understand the path we women must walk within these walls. Hektor promised the safety of your family and so shall I. Gods willing they will never know the sacrifice that you made for them.' The maid who had been putting everything from my bag away interrupted her train of thought, displaying my mother's jewels—lapis lazuli, jade, and turquoise. Precious items that no Temple slave should own, no matter how high ranked.

'They belonged to my Mother.' I did not offer any further explanation. What would I say? These are part of the royal jewels of Emberis. I was wearing them when we escaped a coup that slaughtered thousands of our people. Now was not the time to touch upon that truth, no matter what she thought she knew about me.

'Lady Selene will wear her own jewels and belt,' Andromache directed the women before addressing me, 'Your mother must have been loved by the gods and now so are you. Such a unique design.'

The collar and earrings were of old phoenix design it had belonged to the set that had been given to me when I had been deemed ready to take on the duties that went with the title of Crown Princess. My sisters and I all wore the jade set at every formal occasion and the belt was the last thing I had borrowed from my mother only hours before she died. 'The smith was an unknown who died after completing these pieces.' Layering truth in cryptic comments was becoming an art form in itself. So much to be explained away with an apologetic smile and soft words.

'The Queen.' Our guards announced her, giving us a scant few minutes to compose ourselves. Sharp words were whispered into my ear to sink low and only speak when spoken to. 'Queen Hekuba and Princess Kassandra.' Andromache's soothing tones greeted the senior Royal women of the house, 'You honour us with your presence.'

Fingers stroked my arm, a gasp followed by a soft exhale. The same fingers explored my chin and my features before I'm urged to stand.

Princess Kassandra, so young, about Thea's age. I wonder if it is a blessing or a curse to foresee the future. To bear such a gift at her age, what a burden it must be. Yet, it might be a blessing for Troy, a beacon of hope in these uncertain times.

'What do you see, Kassandra?' Andromache probed gently for an answer. The room tensed, preparing themselves for wildly prophetic nonsense to spew from the seer's mouth. Kassandra forced me to focus on her, adding pressure on her fingertips. I waited patiently I had heard the rumours that swirled around the city of her god-touched fate.

'I see you, little phoenix. I see the part you have to play in the war ahead. You will be a blessing to Troy in times of hardship. The dragons are approaching our shores. They have come for Helen of Sparta. They have come for you. There will be war such as we have never seen and bloodshed... so much bloodshed. Too much blood... royal blood. You must save as many as you can.' Her dark eyes had a fine film of white overlaying the sclera, and she whispered for my ears only, 'When you run from Troy, Princess Selene, you must keep going. There are those who will chase you that are far more dangerous than this war to end all wars. They will hunt you through the ages. Run hard, little Phoenix.'

Her minder tugged her gently away from me, and I longed to tell her that she wasn't going mad as she was led back to her room. 'Apologies, I hope Kassandra has not disturbed you with her words.' Kindness from Hekuba I did not expect, 'Even though you were not my first choice, your sacrifice for this family's survival will not be forgotten. This room is for the highest of the Royal consorts. You may not be married to my son in the eyes of the law, but you are married to him in the eyes of the people. Please child, let that be enough for you.' Hekuba shrewdly assessed my transformed appearance before placing one of her own gold bangles over my right wrist. 'Now you are a proper Princess of Troy.'

Crown and Duty

My head still rang from the formal dinner's noise—clinking goblets, ceremonial speeches, the weight of expectation. I sat on the wide balcony attached to my room, still dressed, letting the rhythmic hush of waves soothe the ache behind my eyes. Lantern light flickering over the stone work.

My fingers worked through the thick curls, tugging at the pins Andromache's attendants had insisted upon. The iron things clung stubbornly, biting into my scalp. Sucking a bleeding finger where one of the pins had pricked me I caught a shadow moving behind the curtain from the corner of my eye.

'Oh erm. I didn't mean to interrupt your disrobing.'

Hektor stood awkwardly, half in moonlight, half in gauze.

'Not disrobing,' I muttered, wincing as another pin refused to budge. 'Just trying to reclaim my head.' Shifting in my seat unsure whether to meet his gaze; Hektor rubs the back of his neck before speaking 'May I?'

He stepped forward, placing a skin of wine and two cups on the low table.

I hesitated. We'd never spoken alone. Not like this. But something in his voice-quiet and unassuming made me nod.

'Please. I never wear them. Andromache...' I let the sentence trail off.

He didn't press. Just began removing the pins, one by one, his fingers careful but unsure. He was gentle with me, cradling my head with one hand while the other worked methodically. Dropping them with a soft metallic clink as the pile grew ever higher with each pin removed. All stamped with a tiny symbol of the royal house of Troy.

'She wanted you to look the part,' he said eventually. 'Trojan tradition.' His breath ghosts over my brow choosing not to acknowledge it I respond honestly, 'I wasn't really given a choice.'

He paused, meeting my eyes briefly. 'You should have one.' His thumbs press gently on my temples, easing tension I hadn't realised

I had been holding. A small kernel of warmth stirred. Not affection. Not yet. But recognition.

'Thank you.' I murmured glancing away.

He nodded, then poured the wine. 'Would you like to talk?'

I looked out at the sea. 'I'm not sure where to begin.' He handed me a goblet that held the most tantalising concoction of spices amidst the scent of raisins.

'Anywhere.' he said. 'Or nowhere. I'll sit with you either way.' He lowered himself to the floor beside my chair. Taking a sip from his cup he waited for me to speak.

I told him, quietly, about my sisters. About my father's slow healing. About the Temple and the weight of dual roles—High Priestess and Princess.

He listened. Not interrupting. Not judging.

When I finished, he leaned back against the balcony wall absorbing my words processing my story. Have I said too much? Or not enough?

'My turn.' he said. 'I fear I won't be enough. That war will come faster than we can prepare. That my brother's choices will cost us everything.'

Silence stretched between us, soft and unbroken. Our fears are aligned. We both fear failing those we love and both carry burdens that have been previously unnamed. Recognition blooms deep within my soul.

'You are enough for me,' I said, the words surprising even myself. I hadn't planned to say it. But it felt truer than silence. Reaching out I touched his shoulder gently and he reached up to cover my hand with one of his own. He was enough for me. We would make this marriage work he and I. Not because it was a requirement but because we wanted to.

He looked at me then—not as a symbol, not as a second wife, but as someone trying.

'Thank you,' he said. 'That means more than you know.'

He stood, hesitating. "Would you... stay a little longer?"

I nodded. He held out his hand, and I took it, rising slowly. His calloused palm touching mine. The first touch that lingered. The difference in our height felt suddenly real, grounding. My heart beat loudly in my ears. His eyes met mine, luminous in the soft light. Unspoken need buried deep in their depths.

The evening chorus of crickets intruded on our private bubble. Hektor smiled, a little uncertain.

'Come share a drink with me, wife.'

Growing Tensions

Growing Tensions

Clanging bells had startled us awake in the small hours of the morning. Untangling ourselves, I followed Hektor out onto the balcony to face longships spread out across the ocean as far as the human eye could see. Using my far sight abilities I estimated we could be looking at ten thousand ships in the fleet. What would look like a thousand ants, in reality was a dark tide swallowing the horizon with barely a gap between each ship in the approaching armada. They had come with one purpose retrieve Helena of Sparta and destroy those who dared to steal that which did not belong to them.

Face blanching, I gripped the bedsheets I had quickly wound around my body stopping them from slipping in the early morning chill, thick with a stillness that I equated to dread. Ignoring my hammering pulse at the unwanted sight, I found solace in focussing on Hektor. He watched the longships, and quietly I observed him. Eyes darkening with anger. A muscle ticked in his face before he tightened his jaw, his chest muscles rippling beneath sun kissed skin. The warrior inside the man was rising, preparing for a battle that would come before the day was through. His stance automatically widened, bracing himself against the stone balcony before leaning over to observe frantic movement in the streets below us.

A small hitch in my breath alerted him that I had followed him out onto the balcony. I remembered the terror I had experienced when Emberis had fallen. Heart pounding wildly, I clutched it to my chest while the memories surged forward, breaking free of the box I'd sealed them in just to survive. Memories of that night, flames licking the sky. Screams piercing the air. Blood soaking the earth where our Mother fell. Our newest, unnamed sibling still clutched in her arms. The slick afterbirth still wet on his skin. The brother that we had longed for. The memory of his blue skin flooded in, merciless and unrelenting. *'Goddess, help me. I can't go through this again.'*

Suddenly, a faint, familiar voice drifted through my mind, like a whisper carried by the wind. It was soft, almost imperceptible, yet it resonated within me, stirring something deep inside. *'Your soul calls to me, dear heart. Are you safe? Are you well?'*

I shook my head, trying to clear the sensation, but the words lingered, an unsettling echo that refused to fade. 'Little love, are you alright?' Hektor pressed a kiss to my brow, his voice a lifeline in the darkness swallowing my soul. 'How long do we have before they're here?' Attempting to keep the dread from my tone caused a wobble that even he expected. The drums were faintly beating in the distance. 'Ah little love,' He cupped my cheek briefly in the grey morning light. Smoke was drifting on the breeze as more warning fires were lit along the coast warning us of their approach. 'We were both only discussing the war last night. Our fears are almost at the gate. I wish this had not marred our first night together.' 'It has not marred my memory.' I try to reassure him that flowery words and promises are not necessary in this moment. We had spent one night together and I prayed for more but as he stood facing me with stubble marring his chin, I did not care to hear these words.

He must retain his edge if he is to make it back to the palace this night. 'I know this will be the last thing on your mind today, but my family are in lower town in the temples of Eileithyia and Poseidon.' Father would be defenseless with the Temple of Poseidon sitting just outside the wooden walls nearest to the caves that led to the deeper mysteries. 'They've seen war but Hektor, if the invaders reach them.' If the invaders reached into the heart of Eileithyia I had no doubt that Nuraya would draw upon her training as leader of the Palace guard and slaughter all who dared to invade the inner sanctum. I could only pray that she would recognise the army of Troy and not injure the wrong men.

Following him inside, I linger, my touch trailing over his skin as long as I dare, desperate to keep him with me. Alive. My breath stutters as I fasten his cloak, fingers trembling. The clatter of armour echoes past the door, constant, urgent. Some footsteps pause as if waiting for the Prince of Troy to join them. One brave soul even has the decency to knock signalling their readiness. A flicker of doubt crosses his face as he realises that I am already saying my goodbye. The floor is cold under my bare feet and yet I make no move to warm them. The feeling of ice floods my veins. How could I not bid my husband goodbye? To have seen the challenge facing us on the horizon and expect to see him escorting Andromache to the supper table this evening would be a dreamer's vision. His hands caught at mine, stilling them after he processed what I had asked of him; to protect my family, to risk more than his life. Hektor took a deep breath before reassuring me, 'We'll protect them, Selene, but I must have your promise that you will stay safe also. Little love, we may have made a child of our own this night and you must think of yourself as well.'

Had we made a child this night? Would I be a terrible mother if I prayed that we hadn't? Kassandra had prophesied a war without end. A war that would devour sons and silence daughters. I could not bear the thought of raising a child in a world of rations, war and whispered betrayals. I did not want to stay safe while my sisters were in danger. Every breath, every heartbeat reminded me of what I had only just lost. But I had learned to wear my mask well. He was waiting for my promise and I hated that I could not give him more words. I knew I could not keep him with me any longer when Andromache would need his presence before he left the palace. 'I'll do what I can from here. But you, Hektor, be careful.'

'I will come home tonight.' His quiet assurance calms me. The sting of Hektor leaving our marriage night early to see to Andromache's comfort was a small wound, barely felt against the looming threat of war. He bends his head, pressing a memory of his mouth to mine, then slips from the room before I can open my eyes.

Anguished cries pierce the night and echo around the room, mingling with the flickering light of candles appearing in windows right across Wilusa. Around me, the palace stirred-boots thudding on marble, whispered prayers rising like smoke, adding to the cacophony rising on the coat tails of a night already slipping into my memory.

A voice-male, unfamiliar-echoed in my mind insistent, '*I feel you close by, dear heart. Are you safe? Are you well?*' '*I am safe. I am well. Who are you? Why do you call out to me?*' I feared for my own sanity. Dwelling on voices in my mind would only lead to a madness that would rival Kassandra's, god-given or not. And yet, deep within, I could not deny the pull of that voice. It made me feel cherished. Safe. A feeling that now belonged only to Hektor. Hastily dressing in the priestess's robes that I had brought with me in my bag, slightly crushed despite being hung overnight, grounded me to my duties as I made my way through the palace. The corridors echoed with hurried footsteps, hushed conversations, and the metallic clink of armor. Every face I passed was etched with fear and determination. It was as if the very walls of the city were bracing for the impending chaos.

Andromache had arrived in the courtyard ahead of me, her composure a stark contrast to the turmoil around us. Ignoring the small degree of awkwardness hanging in the air between us I maneuvered her to the nearest seat where she could hold court with those who wished to see her. I could not ignore the fact that spending the night with Hektor must have hurt her deeply, even though she sponsored me in the choosing. Her eyes, red and rimmed with exhaustion, softened as she reached out for me, pulling me into a brief reassuring embrace,

'There is much to do. He is your husband just as much as he is mine-we will wait for him together.' It was easy to see why she had been chosen as his first. Her grace in the face of heartbreak was almost unbearable. And yet, even in her honesty, I could not ignore the pain she must be carrying. The small almost-hidden tremor in her voice gave her away.

Queen Hekuba moved with practiced authority, assigning duties to the palace women, orchestrating the flow of people and supplies with ease. Kassandra stayed glued to her side, exactly a half pace behind her at all times. Her face was pale, eyes distant, like someone watching a storm only she could see. 'The gods have foreseen this,' she murmured, her voice trembling, 'We must be vigilant. The fate of Troy rests in our hands.' Suddenly, her hands flew to her hair, tangling in the curls as if trying to anchor herself to the present. I rushed to her side. Gently unwinding her fingers from the knots she had created in her curls. I glanced up at the Queen for permission to help with Kassandra, taking one more burden from her so that she might do her duty to the people in the palace.

I glanced back at Andromache, needing to reassure myself, she wasn't alone. Her ladies surrounded her, placing cushions against the stone bench and draping a shawl over her shoulders. Frantic, I searched my memories, there had to be something-anything, that might calm her without dulling her mind. I refused to drug Kassandra with milk of the poppy, not that I had any with me in the courtyard, so I begged for a piece of string from one of the slaves rushing through the once peaceful space. I tied the ends of the rough twine together, the fibres coarse against my fingers and looped it over Kassandra's hands in a simple puzzle as an effort to still them from causing harm to her body. Perhaps the texture would ground her and the puzzle's rhythm would draw her back from the edge. A memory surfaced- my mother doing the same in a crisis long ago. I could only entreat the goddess that it would work now. Kassandra's hands stilled briefly, eyes blinking as if waking from a dream, then lowered to the puzzle and a ghost of a smile tugged at the corner of her mouth. Content in her task, while the world around us spun into chaos.

As Kassandra's head drooped, her breath warm against my neck, the voice returned-louder, more insistent. *'Do not ignore me, dear heart. You must listen.'* The urgency in his tone sent a shiver down my spine. Who was this voice, and why reach for me now, of all times? *'Listen? To what? A voice inside my head, perhaps a shade that doesn't even exist? I will not go mad-not like the poor child resting against me. Now is not a good time in case you haven't noticed.'* Stroking Kassandra's tangled hair, her curls damp with sweat as she readjusted to a more comfortable position-I couldn't keep the irritation from my voice. Survival was paramount. Everything else, even gods and ghosts-could wait.

'You do not remember me?'

The wounded voice returned, wounded and persistent, refusing to leave me in peace.

'We were children, last we met. I will find you soon, dear heart-so you can see for yourself that I am very real.'

Only one person had ever called me 'dear heart'.

Theron of Sparta.

Oh, Goddess.

The dragons of Thera had come.

Theron had come-one day too late.

A fragment of memory surfaced-that last summer on Thera, when our parents spoke in hushed tones of alliances and trade, and we ran barefoot along the forest paths, pretending not to hear the low chuckles and whispers of bonding behind us.

That conversation that I had ignored too young to understand the implications.

That I must ignore now-for the sake of peace.

A hand shook my shoulder drawing me out of my introspection.

'Apologies for disturbing your prayers, Lady Selene. Your sisters have arrived. They are waiting for you in your chamber.'

The Queen's voice was soft, her presence commanding yet gentle. She slid a hand beneath Kassandra's head, allowing me to ease out from under her. With a nod, she motioned for one of Kassandra's minders to take my place.

'Thank you for devising a way to calm and occupy her mind.' she said. 'It has been of great help to me. If there is anything your sisters need, do not hesitate to draw from the palace stores.' Her gaze lingered on my face, searching, weighing-and in that moment, I knew I had earned her respect.

Kassandra speaks, with her eyes closed, her voice distant and hollow.

'Just because the sisters have been saved does not mean that Poseidon is satisfied. He requires the father still...perhaps for eternity.'

Her chilling premonition rooted me to the ground.

Was the cost of saving my sisters the loss of our father?

How much faith could I put into the visions of someone who needed constant care?

And yet...I had seen too much to dismiss her words entirely. She needed someone to believe in her-someone to see the divine thread woven through her life tapestry. I knew she was god-touched. I needed to see for myself that Nuraya and Althea were whole.

Gathering my skirts in my hands, I bolted through the corridors, my soft footsteps echoing off stone walls.

If Poseidon chose to take father there was little that I could do to intercede.

And still-I tried.

Breathless, I exhaled a desperate plea into the silence, 'No... not our father. Not after everything he's already endured.'

The expression on father's face when mother fell was heart rending.

He would have followed her into death if I hadn't forced him to flee.

Father's hand trembling as he closed her eyes.

Heart broken, I tore him from her side.

I had made him run.

I had forced him to take flight.

Had his extended life come at a cost?

Was this the price of survival?

Was this... my fault?

Bursting through the doorway, boots screeching against the polished stone as I finally lost traction. My entrance startling the guards posted on the balcony and one stepped forward just in time to break my fall. He released me quickly, stepping back with a nod. I spun around to face my sisters. Raya's eyes locked with mine, her expression urgent, eyes flicking toward the guards-whatever she had to say wasn't meant for their ears. Years of training kept her movements taut and deliberate, though her fingers twitched instinctively for the weapon she had been forced to surrender at Wilusa's temple complex gates. A small concession to the fragile peace that would bind us to Troy, a fragile pact that ensured Father's treatment continued under Troy's watchful eye. Thea's small body trembled as she huddled into Raya's side. Her arms clutched her satchel like a lifeline. The scent of crushed thyme and bitterroot clinging to its worn leather, along with bundles of partially dried herbs that she had collected around the cliffs of Troy, tied onto the outside. Relief flickered through me that she had the foresight to salvage what little remained of our sacred herbs before leaving the temple.

'You're safe.' The words escaped me in a breathless rush as I pulled them both into my arms. 'Are we?' Raya's low voice was a low rasp in my ear, 'The beach is over run. Lower town's in chaos. The rest of the sisters followed us-Hera's temple is sheltering them, for now.' Pulling back I studied her appearance. She looked every inch the warrior, her stance coiled and alert, despite the flowing priestess robes that clung awkwardly to her body. 'We are safe-for now.' I said it loud enough for the silent onlookers to hear. 'Obey the royal ladies without question and for the love of all that we hold sacred, do not cross Lady Helena or Lady Crinos.'

I drew her close, my voice barely a whisper, 'Keep the Temple daggers hidden. Use them only if Thea's life depends on it.' Then in a voice meant for the room, 'My station has changed. Yours has not. Do not let your conduct shame me.' Fear made my tone sharper than intended.

Observing the mayhem of lower town for myself, the flurry of activity on the walls and the sheer size of the invading army. I winced as I spotted enemy soldiers slipping into our sacred caves, one by one, burdened with supplies-settling in as if they meant to desecrate and dwell.. The hushed murmurs of the guards reached me-restless, distracted. Their thoughts already at the front line where their brothers were preparing to bleed for their country. 'Go.' I said quietly, 'We'll return to join the other ladies in the courtyard.' It wasn't my place to command them, neither was it right to chain them here while their hearts marched elsewhere. Their loyalty burned on the front lines. That's where they belonged.

Once back in the courtyard, I sent Nuraya to help with storing supplies and guided Thea over to Kassandra to keep her occupied. Hours dragged by. Each one thick with silence and the weight of waiting. The tension we were all feeling seemed to stretch the very fabric of time. Soft singing cut off as a young runner skidded into the courtyard, breathless. 'The Myrmidons have taken the beach.' he gasped, 'They slaughtered everyone in the path-even the priests of Poseidon.' His face paled as the weight of his words caught up with him-he had forgotten to soften the blow.

A wave of cold dread coiled in my gut. I couldn't breathe.

This was my fault.

Father was dead.

Between Priestess and

Princess

Between Priestess and Princess

Seclusion is what I craved more than the air my lungs were burning to receive. Latching onto the sharp pain in my ribs I gritted my teeth against the scream that was roiling throughout, threatening to break free. Dark spots shifted and pulsed in my vision as I struggled to work through the news we'd just been given. What utter savage would order the death of an entire religion in a country? It was a monstrous travesty of misjustice. I could not faint when all eyes would soon be upon me to lead a funeral of mass proportions. I could feel arms supporting me, steadying me. I did not feel firm on my feet as I threw off the comforting lure of blacking out. With sheer determination I turned to Andromache, 'I will be in my chambers preparing for what is to come.'

Silently Raya and Thea follow my lead. Our grief belonged to us alone. We would shed our tears privately and carry on with our duties. Like Mother had taught us. Like Father would have insisted on. Our safety in this strange land was paramount. Althea's emerald eyes were swimming with unshed tears threatening to spill over and shed the pain that engulfed her small frozen frame. Her sobs were barely audible, short, choked and fragile as she struggled to contain the pain on her own. It was hard to believe that this was my little sister who had been subtly teasing me about the crush I had had on a Prince not so long ago. Crushing pain enveloped my heart as I pulled her to me. She was young to lose both parents in such a short period of time. Panic rising forced me to face the fact that we were the last of our kind-what did that mean for us now?

The faint hum of palace sounds intrudes on my senses, scraping against the inside of my skull as I struggle to hold it together for my youngest sister's sake. Already the other temples are holding prayers for our lost family member and brothers in service. The evening breeze brings with it a cloying smell of incense as if the whole city is mourning with us, sharing our grief.

'Your Majesty.' Nuraya murmured respectfully. Her grief stricken expression overlaying her deep anger of not being allowed proper weaponry to protect her loved ones. Crossing her arm on her chest she dropped into a deep curtsey -holding it. Her fingers twitching against her chest, a phantom memory of the gold hilted ceremonial dagger she had hidden in her belongings in the corner of the room. Thea silently attempted to wriggle from my embrace to join her. Refusing to let her go she soon settled against me, tears continuing to soak the thin dress I was wearing that was clinging uncomfortably in the places where Thea's tears had soaked through the fabric.

A heavy silence descends between us, broken only by the fabric of Thea's robes rustling and her occasional muffled sob. Gesturing at Raya to rise, my automatic rejection of the throne, barely cooled, pours from me, 'The King is dead. Emberis is gone. You are my sisters not my subjects.' I paused barely able to restrain my body from shaking. All of my life I had been preparing to reign over our people but they were dead. The words felt as though they were ripped from my soul, 'Queen of what? We have lost everything.' Althea's blotchy swollen face studied me for a long moment before she reminded me, 'We have each other. Phoenix kind survives in us and we are all we need to rebuild stronger than ever.' Her fervent belief in my abilities floored me.

'Even if it is part of the nation of Troy?' I questioned them, exposing my fear that we were bound in this place by my oath to Hektor. The weight of it pressing in on me like chains tightening further around my chest. *Why had I promised to sacrifice myself for the good of Troy?* I did not regret my choice only the timing of my Father's death. 'We follow your lead Selene. You alone have the right to choose for us.' Raya's voice spoke with conviction as she joined us in a three way hug. Her added solidarity a sharp contrast to the aching hollowness rising within. Raya continued, 'We will support you any way you need us to. Please allow me to protect you the way I should have been allowed to protect Father.' she all but begged.

'We must tread lightly in our new home.' I warned her, 'I would expect nothing less from you then to do everything in your power to ensure we all remain safe. However, because of temple lore, you still may not carry a sword in public. Nor can you ignore the customs of my new family to protect me.' Feeling weary I sank to the floor, my sisters following as they had once done when we were hatchlings so very long ago. Hugging my knees to my chest, pressing my fingers hard enough to leave bruising so that the pain would ground me to this moment, I waited until they were settled to mention, 'We must lead the funeral rites for the lost souls of Poseidon. Eileithyia demands no less and Father would wish it were us above someone who did not know him.'

'We must coordinate with the other temples as well,' Raya reminded her in a sombre tone, 'Many will have families across multiple belief systems here. We will need runners and a scribe.' 'You will also need someone with expertise in holding state funerals.' Hektor's armour was dusty and covered with the blood of others, yet he had come to me straight from the battlefield. The muffled scrape as he moved towards me came from the dried blood cracking as he adjusted his stance. Beyond the open chamber door the muted hum of palace life continued despite our loss. The war would not stop for one death no matter how keenly felt. Acknowledging this with a slow exhale I could feel the tension lift slightly from my shoulders. A flitting feeling of comfort zipped through my mind at the sight of his sweat stained face.

Flickering torchlight on the walls cast dancing shadows, their steady crackle a stark contrast to the uncertainty in the air. We separated our untidy huddle as I asked, 'Thea fetch some water from that pitcher on my table. Raya...' my voice trailed off as Raya was already aiding Hektor in removing his breast plate and greaves. With practiced ease she ignored the dry stiff blood beneath her fingertips before searching my chambers for the means to clean the once bright armour. Brief happiness in a dark sea of despair by something so minor.

He joined me on the floor with his back to the wall, 'I'm sorry Selene for interrupting your planning. I thought you would have need to see me.' His eyes searched my face for the truth of my well being. 'I'm glad you came.' Sometimes the simplest words were the best ones. Leaning my head on his shoulder, exhaustion settled deep into my bones. 'You will get dirty little love.' he whispers for my ears alone. 'I don't care. I didn't realise how much I needed to see that you were safe as well.' Thea offered Hektor some water with a small forced smile and Raya...Raya had begun to clean and polish the armour in front of her with the familiarity that only one who had worn such an outfit would recognise.

'Your sister doesn't need to clean my armour for me. I'll have my manservant do it later.' He sounded half embarrassed and half impressed by the meticulousness of her work. A quiet clink of metal, like a metallic heart keeping beat adds to the city sounds creeping across the balcony as she continues to polish Hektor's armour. I knew for Raya this was one of her rituals for control when her world was overwhelming. 'It gives her something else to focus on. We were just beginning to sort out what we would need. Have...' I paused and waited till the tremblng in my voice receded and swallowed before trying again, 'have the bodies been recovered from Poseidon's temple yet?'

'My personal guard is standing watch there at this very minute.' He attempted to reassure me. 'Your personal guard is there...so who came back with you?' Nuraya looked up her brow furrowed, speaking with a clipped but measured tone heavy with unspoken questions about the battlefield before she remembered to tack on the appropriate honorific, 'Your Highness.' 'Your sister has the mind of a warrior little love.' He commented, 'An elite one at that. My brothers had my back Lady Nuraya.' He addressed her directly and included Thea also, 'Lady Althea you are welcome in my home. You both may stay with your sister whenever I cannnot. My Mother has had chambers prepared for you both across the hall so that you can remain close together. Father has asked that the ceremony be held on ..' His voice trailed off as I held up one finger at him to stop his flow.

It wasn't grief that made it hard to breathe—it was the certainty of what I must do. I could not allow this. Not this day. I would take orders from the King of Troy when it was appropriate to do so. My throat tightened as I realised what this moment would cost me. The king had been looking for someone forgettable, a woman who would follow the orders of her elders without question. Was I showing strength too soon? I hadn't even been married for more than 24 hours at this point.

'I must offer His Majesty my deepest apologies, but the chosen of Poseidon follow a destiny not dictated by royal decree. They will be buried on the day the Goddess has spoken of.'

I appraised Hektor, wondering if he belonged to the new world—one where a King's word eclipsed that of a Goddess.

'However, if His Majesty would be so kind as to send whichever advisors he deems fit to assist in organising the rites, we would gladly welcome their help—for the benefit of all Willusa.'

Across the room, Raya nodded imperceptibly, her fingers tapping her outer thigh beneath the table—a quiet signal that she remained armed. Her raised eyebrow turned briefly comical, her face brightening before she bent back to her task.

I nearly missed the shift in Hektor's expression—from consolation to quiet understanding.

'He will not like your answer.' Hektor warns, ghosting a kiss on my lips before allowing Nuraya to show him his freshly cleaned armour. Taking the warm hand he offers to me, I feel the coolness of the metal of the ring beneath my fingers, that he wears signifying that he is the heir to the throne. He steadies me on my feet before appraising the metalwork of his breast plate. 'I can be both Princess and Priestess but only one will submit to the crown the other serves beings far more powerful than he. You and I must find our balance Hektor, and so must your father and I.' Pausing briefly I wonder if the words I am about to speak are too soon but there is no time to play coy games. We were on a war footing and these were words I wished him to hear now in case there was no later, 'These points will not always meet in the same place but know that I am beginning to care for you deeply.' Hektor stills his movements and turns to face me. His expression was full of awe. Out of the corner of my eye I catch Raya drawing Thea out onto the balcony to give us a semblance of privacy, pulling at the sashes to close the curtains after them.

The flickering torch casts shadows across his face to mirror his shifting emotions, 'When Andromache mentioned that she wished me to pick you before all others I believe even she does not realise how deeply your kindness runs.' Running his hand roughly through his hair he met my gaze evenly, his face full of understanding, 'Gods you play a dangerous game. This is not the time to assert yourself Selene. My Father is King...' Inhaling sharply I couldn't stop the words tumbling from my mouth, 'And my Father just died.' I interrupt, voice wavering slightly, reminding him that this is deeply personal to me. 'He deserves so much more than quick platitudes before his pyre so that it does not detract from Alexander and Helena's wedding. Please Hektor do not make me tell my sisters that we cannot mourn our last family member with a little dignity.'

Leaning forward slightly I reinforce my stance refusing to back down on this matter. Hesitating less than a second before gripping my shoulders lightly, lending his aid and his strength, Hektor promises, his voice full of reassurance though carrying an under current of caution, 'I will speak with my Father but he will want words with you as well little love.' The weight pressing on my chest feels heavier-I could not afford to offend the King of my new nation. Hektor's thumb presses against my collarbone lightly reassuring me that he supports my decision.

The death of Poseidon

The death of Poseidon

Smile. Nod. Don't Cry. Not here. Not now. Pause and chat. Pretty words. Play to their whims. Keep it short. Move on. Repeat.

My mantra was keeping me sane in a room full of diplomats and leaders from across the country, and beyond, all wishing to pay their respects to the dead priests. I wished I could have hidden with my sisters in my chambers however they were meeting with the other sisters ahead of the ceremony to prepare the area for the sacred ritual we would be performing on behalf of our country. My heavy ceremonial robes only aided to the cloying heat sweeping through the room. Today, I was not a Princess of Troy or of Emberis. Today I must do my duty to the temple and be the High Priestess. Missing simpler times when all I had were learning how to rule a country and deal with difficult supplicants in court. I counted eight beats and bestowed a sad smile in another direction coupled with a polite nod.

Drawing myself to my full height I repeated my mantra to myself silently, 'Smile. Nod. Don't Cry. Not here. Not now. Pause and chat. Pretty words. Play to their whims. Keep it short. Move on. Repeat.' I wished one last time that I had had a chance to gather one of my father's feathers to wear in my hair. His feather would have been placed at my crown where all who mourned would recognise him. He had

had a magnificent plumage of midnight and gold. Maybe Raya had had the foresight to plan ahead for this moment. I would have to ask her before the ceremony. Mother's feather of silver with a lilac sheen was already wound into the top of one of my plaits. My little brother had been wearing pin feathers of the newly born. He was represented by the deep burgundy feather no bigger then my pinky feather. Despite the custom, we would remember our fallen with the traditions of Phoenix kind. The feathers we took from our loved ones were not mere tokens, their colours signifying a memory of the bright souls that had once graced this earth. Each placement in our hair considered carefully showcasing their importance to us and to others.

Feeling Hektor's eyes follow me protectively, his gaze narrowed slightly-a flicker of concern dancing briefly across his features. He stood beside Andromache on the dais, dressed in his full uniform. His golden chest plate was polished so brightly I could catch my own reflection in it from across the room. His armour clinked softly each time he shifted his stance. Andromache, hand covering her stomach protectively, wore a subdued expression. Her fingers tightened subtly over the gentle swell, shielding her child unconsciously from the unknown. She wore the same Trojan Blue as the other royal women, the colour offset only by the soft gleam of larimar at her temples, throat and wrists. They wore the ocean in honor of Poseidon. Fabric rippling like the water, an echo of the sea-based ceremony that we would be soon attending.

Smile. Don't Cry. Not now. Not here... Startled out of my internal mantra, I caught Helena shoot Crinos a meaningful look from across the room. Concern could wait. Right now, I didn't care. In retrospect, I should have.

'You are deeply saddened.' Theron's observation quietly pulling me from the conversation I was barely following. I offered a brief, apologetic smile before backing into the shadow of a column, away from the press of bodies.

The silence in this corner felt heavier than the crowd's noise. The stone on my chest growing heavier each minute we drew closer to the ceremony. Alone with the memories that threatened to engulf me, I closed my eyes, *'I am preparing to bury my father this night. He belonged to Poseidon.'* Smiling reassuringly at the guard who had been ordered to stay close to me trying to mask both the weight pressing on my chest and the telepathic conversation I was having with another outside of the city walls. 'You knew him.' The words echo silently in my mind.

The silence stretched, static buzzing in mind. Theron's stunned silence stalled the conversation briefly. *'I did?'* his shocked tone ringing in my ears before demanding, *'Who was he?'*

Who was he? The question echoed, absurd in its simplicity. He was so much more than a footnote in an ally's mind. Anger surged stinging at my throat, before I forced myself to breathe through the pain.

'Evander of Emberis.'

I was tired of playing games. *'Theron, you arrived too late to save him.'*

Cold horror poured through the link. It hit like a wave, sharp and breath-stealing. *'No warning-no news..'* the stuttered thoughts crept through my mind as he tried to process the truth, *'Misinformation...*

Who would ally with those wishing harm to the clan alliances?'

His thoughts focus on me again, sharper now. *'I thought I had time,'* he whispered across the link. *'Who else survives with you?'*

'My sisters and I...we are the last of the Royal House of Emberis.' The weight of truth settled over me like ash. Unbidden, a memory surfaced I hadn't meant to share of the capital in flames...our banners floating to the ground, disintegrating as they fell.

A silent sob caught at my throat as I added, *'We are the last of our kind.'* I knew the phrasing would give me away. I'd said it once before, the night we buried his cousin. He'd stood beside me on the dais gripping my hand tightly as he struggled to contain his sorrow and anger, comport himself with dignity and lead by example. We had been so young that day, too young to be touched by the horrors of death and yet our traditions celebrated death as a gateway to the greater mysteries.

'Oh gods, Selene, are you safe?' He demanded, compelling me to answer immediately, if somewhat evasively. 'I am protected.' I said, the words carefully chosen. It wasn't a lie. But it wasn't the truth he needed. He didn't know. Not yet. If he did, nothing-not distance, nor duty, would stop him.

Checking on the position of the sun in the sky, I promised him, 'We will speak again, Theron. But not now.' Duty called louder than grief now.

We gathered in the square where the pyres had been built. Each one topped with a priest, eyes bound with a strip of blue fabric, and two coins placed for the ferry man. Only one wore emerald green-the mark of the House of Emberis. Glancing at Thea, I saw her touch her covered sleeve, the ripped hem hidden from view. A quiet rebellion, a farewell stitched in fabric. Her way of acknowledging who we were-and saying goodbye to who we could no longer be. A black and gold feather displayed proudly at the crown of her head. She passed two more to Raya knowing how important they were for this ceremony.

I would not deny my little sister her right to grieve and I was grateful she remembered what was important to us also.

A bell tolls, echoing through the silent square. Another follows. Then another-until a unique hymn begins to rise, wending its way to the heavens made up of the tones of the priests who have passed.

'You are ready...' Father's voice whispers to me in the silence between the last chime and the breath of wind. *

'Light up my darling. Show them what you are made of. I'll be right beside you here. Always...'

'I'll show them. I promise. I love you, Pappa.' I whispered into the smoke. Then I stepped forward to lead the opening address, 'We gather here together to remember these brave men. Priests who as the mouthpieces of a god stood between all that they considered holy and tyranny. Let us remember them not only for how they died, but for what they stood for.'

My sisters sang for the dead, one final melody to fill their ears on their way across the river Styx while I gathered myself for the spectacle to come.

Let them see a daughter in mourning-

a queen of nothing,

a storm of their own making.

Let them be dazzled by the ritual, blind to the truth beneath the ash and incense.

We would farewell these men the only way we knew how, with song, with fire, with the weight of memory ending in a meteor shower that lit up the night sky with light. Countless whispered wishes filling the square for luck in the war to come, hope for the future and prayers from the lips of man to the pantheon of gods and goddesses above.

Flames licked at the air with fading hunger as the fires burned low, popping occasionally, and the songs faded into silence, broken only by the rustle of cloaks in the distance where Hektor and his men stood guarding over us. His shadow weary as we stood vigil. Holding true to his promise that he would be with me as soon as the public part of the ceremony had ended. Touching my shoulder with a gentle tone promising me that we could stay as long as I needed to.

The ritual masked the reality. While beautiful, it hid truths being buried with the dead. The truth that Father had begun his final transformation as his avian bone structure disintegrated. We stayed to watch the last of our father's ashes float away into the atmosphere, vanishing like breath on a cold night. 'We do not say goodbye.' I whispered to them, throat raw from smoke reminding them of our beliefs, 'We will see them again, in each other, in our children and in the stars at night.'

Gathering them into my arms, I turned to see Hektor already at my shoulder ready to wrap us in his warm cloak, 'You must be tired little love. My father would like an audience if you are ready.'

Was I ready to face the consequences of my quiet defiance? I didn't know. 'Can someone guide Thea and Raya back to their rooms? I don't have the energy to take them back and then see the King.' my vision blurred and legs trembling with fatigue, exhaustion hit hard. Letting go of my sisters I stumbled back into him. He steadied me against his body allowing me one last glance up into the early morning sky. Dawn but a gleam on the horizon reminding me that those who passed before us really did live among the stars watching over us. 'My men will see your sisters safe.' he murmurs, 'Come we cannot put this reckoning off any longer.'

Echoes of consequence

Echoes of consequence

Hektor led me to a warm royal chamber not far from the heavily guarded Royal couple's private suite. A slave brings us cups of warm mead and places them on the low table in the room. Flickering shadows danced across the stone walls, lit by the faint glow of embers in the hearth. I flinched each time the fire popped, my nerves too raw to ignore the sound. The scent of cedar filled my nostrils. I fought the urge to retch. The scent a cruel reminder of my father's body breaking down. I was seated in a heavily cushioned chair that I suspected belonged to Queen Hekuba. The weight of Hektor's hand on my shoulder prevented me from rising as the King entered the chamber tying the sash on his tunic. His grip is gentle and lingers in place, thumb rubbing softly, as if he can feel the bruising of my soul from this tragedy. Swallowing hard, they waited for me to settle back into the chair. 'No need to rely on ceremony so early in the morning, 'Hektor's father reassured me. 'You've had a trying time; we don't stand on honorifics here, this is a chamber for family and very close friends.'

He settles into the other over stuffed chair, waving Hektor away so he can stoke the fire. His gaze lingers on my face, measuring his words carefully before speaking again. 'You've had a trying few days and stepped into your role as High Priestess of Eileithyia with more skill than the Priests expected of you, my dear. With your own personal tragedy, you've done a remarkable job leading the country at their prayers. You did the right thing in obeying the Goddess in her wishes for the timing of the funeral. Who am I to question her?' Hektor's wary gaze softens into one of respect and realising that this was the King's way of taking care of his newest daughter. As understanding dawned, the tension in my posture eased. Exhaling softly it feels less like relief for my lungs screaming out for breath and more like involuntarily committing to the conversation I was too tired to have.

'And so the leadership of Emberis has passed to you.' Priam continues, his voice gentle as his fingers trace the embroidery on the cushion where his elbow rests. 'Selene, you are a Princess of Troy and Queen of a dead nation. You must decide who you will become moving forward.' That was the question wasn't it. My sisters wished for Emberis to live. Thea, adamant that our kind would rise once more in our children to come. Raya had promised to follow my lead and I trusted her to keep her word. But who was I? I had the flame of phoenix kind warming my insides, and I could no longer deny my true nature, nor the fact that I was a married woman with a soul mate hidden in the sacred caves on the beach. I catch my breath, steadying myself. I allow my fingers to flex against my lap, unable to bear the cramping pain from grasping them together so tightly. Studying the heavy gold band on my finger I know I can't return to who I was before my father fell. The shape feels unnatural to me now. I couldn't be who Thea wished me to be either. To be the Queen of Emberis would not fit my role here as the second wife. I could only hope that the words I was about to speak would allow me to forge a new path forward. Shifting slightly in the chair, I force the words through a tight throat. I know what I need to say, but words once said can never be undone.

'When I was a small child, my mother told me that I would one day marry someone from another nation.' My voice sounds worn out and raw. Rubbing my throat, I swallow some mead hoping that the lubrication would help. Resting it back on the table with the softest clink against the wood that I could manage. Goddess, I needed sleep, but I had to reassure them of my loyalties before I could rest. The hollow tap of Priam's finger against the armrest is an unspoken warning, his patience had a end that I was fast approaching. 'She said that...' I struggled to recall her exact words. The faint crackle of the embers in the hearth fills the gap in my mind, improvising slightly I say the words that come to me foreign to my own ears, 'She told me I would never truly choose who to be. Women do not have the luxury of choosing their own destiny.' Again my voice falters slightly, forcing me to swallow before continuing. 'My past, my family, my upbringing-woven into the fabric of my very being. And now my future is being written over it. Every piece of who I am, and who I will become, forming at Hektor's side for the benefit of Troy. I may hold a queen's title, but it is just a name. One that I do not claim and will fade with time as people forget Emberis existed. My father is gone, and I...I don't...' My voice breaks off as an icy tear rolls down my cheek. The subtle pressure of Hektor's familiar callouses against the skin of my hand grounds me to this moment.

The wisdom I offer them is precisely what they wish to hear. My mother's wisdom was a lesson etched into my mind-that I could never forget. She possessed the gift of foresight, and I truly believe the words I had chosen to share were fragments of a prophecy spoken in my tenth year. My mother told me that Emberis will never die as long as a daughter of Emberis lives. Royalty is not a metal crown that can be cast aside and melted down for gain. A kingdom cannot be erased with a single act. She told me that I would need to be strong for the future that destiny was creating for me. And she told me my destiny would be tangled in the affairs of men. Our kind-Phoenix kind, would survive at all costs even as other empires fell, for we had long lives and even longer memories. The subtle creak of Priam's chair punctuates his slow movements, each shift deliberate as he weighs my words for truth. He is deeply uncomfortable with the emotion that has escaped from my tight grasp. The weight of the gold ring on my finger presses over my heartline heavier than it should be as if this destiny foretold will be a tale of heroes, gods and men.

Priam's expression shifts to one of deep sympathy as he leans over to clasp my other hand, his chair scraping softly against the stone floor, 'You have spoken wisely. Your mother must have thought well ahead if she taught you these things. You have my support my dear but you should know that the world may not be as kind if they see you continually contradicting my wishes. Maybe we leave that for Priestess matters only, hmm? You should lean on Hektor during this trying time. Andromache has spoken highly of you to me. Troy is your home now and you are not alone in it.' His words offer reassurance, but the caution thinly veiled reminds me that we remain alone in a city of humans. *Theron is close.* My pulse quickens, not with fear, but with something deeper, instinctual, as the bond with Theron hums beneath my skin, reconnecting us after all these years. The weight of my words settles heavily on my shoulders. *Did the words I spoke at the choosing bind me to Troy forever? Would that one decision affect the rest of my life long past the death of my husband?* Keeping my expression carefully neutral, I tune out of the conversation, finally allowing my weariness to take hold. *Theron is close. We are safe. He had never left me alone.* His presence tugs at me, lingering on the edges of my mind-undeniably a force that refuses to be ignored.

A slave enters bearing a tray of fruit and cheese as well as more cups of the mead. My stomach protests at the imposition of being forced to eat at an unusual hour. Silence blankets us comfortably as we share the early meal together. I did not know what lay ahead of us but I should have been more prepared.

Ceremony

Ceremony

The scent of burning incense and funeral pyres clings to the air, yet Troy prepares for a wedding-an uneasy oversight, hastily rectified. Beyond the gates, the distant clash of weapons rumbles like distant thunder but no rain follows. Day after day, the dead, dying, and wounded flood through the city gates. The low wail of mourners rise from the temples, their lament carried by the wind. The cost of this war is already high. Outside the gates, one husband screams for justice, while inside...a married woman prepares to forsake her vows. Inside the palace, gossip swirls through the crowded halls, twisting the truth with each exchange-some eager for the match, others lost in grief. They swear that the scent of incense and decay mingling in the air is proof that Troy is already rotting from within. Soft laughter lingers in the air as the web of speculation is spun from the inside out.

From the first day, the senior royal family has assembled atop the highest tower, overseeing the battlefield, braving all weathers. Hot days carry fine sand particles, biting at exposed skin, while cooler evenings bring brief respite. Andromache's face is tight with exhaustion, forced to watch Hektor confront death over and over again. We worry for her child's safety. This relentless strain cannot be good for her pregnancy. We pass each other in the halls, feet scurrying in different directions-exchanging hurried words, passing on news the other may not yet know about Hektor. His comfort, his morale, his life-all are ours to safeguard, and we do the best we can. Yet no comfort will ever be enough while he stands for all Troy. Footsteps echo sharply on marble floors at all hours-hurried, purposeful, laced with silent worry as members of the court pray for peace in the midst of war.

How am I to care for an almost absent husband when my days belong to the temple? Widows come to petition the goddess-pleading to understand their loss, praying for their sons, begging her not to take another life. They search the still faces of the lost, hoping-desperate to find the ones they love among the fallen. But they never do. These precious few bodies-these are the forgotten deemed too unworthy for farewell, denied the pomp of ceremony. Their bodies lay rotting under the sun instead of placed on high piers and given over to the care of cleansing fire. No one pays the ferry man for their journey to Elysium so we care for them, whispering prayers on behalf of their families, knowing that-for their souls-that must suffice. The undertakers move swiftly and silently, ensuring Troy does not choke on its dead, that sickness does not take root among the living.

Healers petition temples, begging for cadavers to practice their arts-hoping to salvage life from death. Empathy is my boundary. I may share their sorrow but I cannot follow our grieving petitioners home. They are not faceless to me. I hear their screams to the goddess. I offer what comfort I am allowed to share. I cannot walk with them after being invited into their homes. These are our people and I am forbidden from lower town. Hektor's guards obey his words, not mine. These invisible boundaries between duty and freedom press against my skin like the iron grip of Hektor's guards, steering me through the crush of bodies in the temple at day's end. I wear these bruises with pride, knowing that they mark my service to those who need me most. Beneath my metal armbands, they remain hidden from Hektor's gaze. Not marks of devotion or of brutality-marks of safety. And what a beautiful illusion safety brings.

My sisters have been pressed into service as well. Thea with her skill in healing, works in the palace under the watchful eye of Queen Hekuba herself. She prays daily, hoping we might yet find a cure for Kassandra. She should never have looked upon the face of a god-once touched, there is no cure for one such as her. Thea spends her day tending wounds, hands stained with blood, whispering prayers when skill alone cannot save a life. Her face ages under the strain each death brings to her soul. She has begged more than once to mix her tears into the medicines she creates. Her hands tremble at the end of every shift. She too suffers from the soul-sickness creeping through the palace. I know her tears would save lives. Thea is a true healer-one that save lives at any cost. But that cost would be our freedom. I cannot allow her to expose us, not until we are ready for the humans' reaction. She forgets that the mask we wear is the only thing ensuring our survival.

Raya sharpens weaponry in the armory. I've heard stories of her working alongside metalworkers, forging newer, deadlier weapons-designed to maximise damage and prolong the life of the one who wields them. Even in her downtime, these lethal designs consume her-sketched onto parchment, carried with her into the next day's work. She does not design for glory. Nor does she crave recognition. She crafts for survival-for the ones who will fight beyond the city walls. Her skills are a shield for Hektor, and for that, I am grateful. These sketches are not plans. They are prayers-etched in steel, destined for our enemies. It is not a healthy obsession, and yet, Raya was raised to think like a bodyguard-to wield whatever she must in defense of her people. How can I deny her that right to use the skills she was born to use-especially when Thea and I are consumed by our own duties?

Fatigue lingers. The whole city suffers beneath its malignancy. Our people move with hollow steps, their bodies heavy with exhaustion. They clamour for relief-for their loved ones, for food, for an end to the blight consuming our city.

I do not believe we need such a distraction. The people do not want ceremony. They want survival. Yet I understand the political bind Alexander's actions have put Troy in. Even now, remembering the night King Priam announced it churns my stomach.

Priam called for the Priests of Zeus to consult with him during his war session with the leaders of Willusa. We watched them stride self-importantly across the square bearing their goats, birds and a snake coiled around the shoulders of one priest-all never to return. Snakes were considered sacred. To sacrifice a beautiful specimen meant the priests feared the gods had truly turned their gaze away. Or was it all just a cruel game? Were the gods of men merely playing with our lives, bored of eternity? Had they chosen Hektor, Alexander, Helena, Achilles and the Greek Kings-Agamemnon and Menelaus as their game pieces?

It was during the next family lunch that he announced with a smile that Zeus had requested Alexander and Helena formally marry, as if it would fix the fact that he had technically stolen another man's wife. They sat together on the opposite side of the table from us and I felt the bile rise in my throat at the self-satisfied smirk lurking at the corner of Helena's mouth. The Princes did not take the news well. Some of the elder ones had been in the war chambers and did not react but rather sat rigid, their silence heavier than the stone walls that enclosed us. Their inscrutable expressions concealing thoughts too dangerous to voice in the presence of the King. Others erupted, their voices crashing against the tapestries like rolling thunder. 'It is necessary.' Priam insisted sharply. 'We have offended a god somewhere to be suffering such heavy losses. The walls of Troy will endure, but my fear is that soon, there will be no one left to stand behind them. We need a distraction-to lift spirits, to appease the gods, to convince ourselves that fate still favours us. Alexander and Helena will be wed the day after Noumenia-a fresh beginning.'

Noumenia or the first day of the month when the sliver of a new moon hung over Troy. He hoped to wash the losses of the last month away by starting the next month with an auspicious occasion. We prepared-and beneath our dutiful silence, fury burned at the King's foolishness. How could they celebrate such a farce of a marriage when her true husband prepares to burn Troy to the ground? There was not a court in the world that would recognise the legitimacy of the wedding under these circumstances. People were starving, yet the resources squandered on giving Alexander a wedding fit for royalty were staggering. Did they believe that food would simply appear when the Greeks had entrenched themselves on our doorstep, surrounding us so completely that formal attacks had devolved into guerilla warfare? Did they grasp how easily Wilusa could be infiltrated by anyone with knowledge of the tunnels threading beneath the city streets?

Despite my personal feelings it would be my duty to attend at Hektor's side. Andromache was close to her due date, spending most of her time sequestered in her chambers. 'Do you begrudge them their day?' she asked softly then added, 'You had neither ceremony nor a proper feast to mark your wedding with Hektor.' No. That was not what unsettled me. How could I make her understand? She believed herself absolutely safe, while those of us with some foresight could feel the impending doom. I couldn't. Not till the child's first cry shattered her illusion. Not until she had passed the first flush of motherhood-and even then, she might still be too consumed by the child to notice-the child that would inherit Troy-whether it stood or crumbled.

'I do not begrudge Helena her ceremony.' I answer her at length after she prods me further from my thoughts for an answer. I only wondered if the ceremony was a bandage slapped over an already hemorrhaging wound. Too little too late.

She drapes a new dress over my arms distracting me further from the distraction of pondering the political implications of their actions. It is half a shade lighter than the deep Trojan Blue worn by the senior royal women. The fabric is embroidered with silver thread, twinkling in the bright sunlight like moonbeams on the darkest night. Yet, as I dress in it later, the reminder stings-I will always be half a pace behind her and Hektor, never quite equal-never fully belonging. Staring at myself in the mirror I forced myself to stop imagining what if and face reality. My bond with Hektor had been forged under different circumstances, and that had to be enough. But was it truly? This wedding also brought with it traitorous thoughts that questioned everything I knew. I had hardly seen him since the night we buried our father.

And suddenly he is here bearing a gift wrapped in the softest cloth. 'You look stunning little love.' His hands caress my collarbones, where a new necklace of sapphires rests. 'Yet there is one thing missing in your appearance.' He unwraps the gift himself, revealing a silver circlet adorned with sapphires. With deliberate care, he places it upon my brow-as if sealing the public vows we did not receive. Now, I was a true Princess of Troy. *Yet, could I truly step into this role with Theron's presence still lingering at the edges of my mind?* Theron never intruded-not unless the emotions surged too fiercely for him to ignore. Once I had woven a fragile barrier between us, he respected the space I needed.

'Thank you.' I touch the circlet, adjusting its position, then pin it securely among my curls. He is dressed in his highly polished golden armour, denoting his rank in the army and as heir to the kingdom. We make our way to the square under the multiple banners strewn throughout the city wishing the royal couple luck. The opulence of such an occasion astounds me although I recognise that I had never really seen Troy celebrate a royal wedding before. The first droplet of water sizzles against my overheated skin from the climb to the temple mount. The second and third fall in rhythm, no mere coincidence, but a quiet testament-a blessing on the union to be sealed in the city this day. Whether this was Hera's divine displeasure at Zeus's meddling I could not tell.

Priam had declared Helena was the sun from the first time that he had met her, and in this fleeting moment it was impossible to deny. Liberally adorned with golden accessories and a gown that complemented her hair perfectly, she was wondrous to behold. After the ceremony she approaches me in the Megaron. 'Lady Selene, will you not sit with me?' Hektor had claimed the place beside Alexander and it would not do to upset the newly married pair. Yet what did Helena seek from me? I had been warned to avoid her as much as I could from Andromache. I hesitate-just long enough to weigh my position, but not enough to offend. Duty wins. I incline my head, acquiescing to her request. Despite the quiet confusion within me, my role demanded obedience. I had made my choice and yet I found myself needing constant reminders. A quiet sacrifice, unseen but deeply felt.

Poison

Poison

As the evening wore on, my growing temper made it increasingly difficult to remain seated. How can I sit here, forced to play my part in this farce, while my father's body is dust among the stars? My sisters are now fatherless, and we are all that remains of a once proud people. Every polished insult, disguised as civility, felt like a deliberate mockery of the entire nation's suffering. Helena and Alexander had orchestrated our downfall, yet they dared to sit here, feigning serenity as if Troy would not demand justice for their actions. How can they be so oblivious to the chaos and suffering they've brought upon us?

My last memory of a dinner such as this was in Emberis, surrounded by my family, our hearts full of hope for my mother's youngest sister and her new husband. Our people were part of the celebrations that followed the ceremony. Mother had thrown open the palace halls, welcoming all who wished to share in our joy. I still remember how they placed tables two abreast in the hallways and even though they were not in the palace dining room our guests had been joyful to celebrate with us. Musicians had been placed strategically in every larger chamber, their melodies weaving through the halls, carrying meaning where words could not. They were more than slaves or servants or even faceless figures in the crowd. They were the heartbeat of Emberis and they were the very soul of our people. That world-rich with warmth, shared joy, and colour-is gone, replaced by this cold spectacle, dazzling in its emptiness. Queen Hekuba eyes Helena with carefully crafted mask, her gaze glittering with cold suspicion.

The contrast to this affair could not have been sharper. We were on a war footing, trying to mask a huge oversight that could cost my husband his life. Alexander-the boy fostered in the foothills of Mount Ida-had yet to grasp the true cost of his reckless passion. This long day of celebration, stretched thin by even longer days of service, weighs heavily, evident in the weary faces of those forced to fight on their behalf. They are oblivious to the fatigue of those who serve, those who fight and those who grieve. I can no longer sit still, pretending all is fine. I refuse to sit idle, complicit in this mockery of our suffering. The priestess and the princess within me war against such folly.

How could I excuse myself without embarrassing myself or my husband? I didn't want to upset Hektor, but I had already lived this once-celebrating while the wolves circled the door, blind to the true cost it would bring. I offered deep curtsies to King Priam, Queen Hekuba and Hektor, before granting the happy couple a shallower gesture-too engrossed in their joy to notice my quiet departure. I slipped from the room with practiced grace.

Still unfamiliar to the direct route between the Megaron and my chamber, I wandered, searching for something recognisable in the dim glow of scattered lamps. The rarely used halls, long abandoned to neglect, remained draped in cobwebs. Intrigued by the tapestries lining one wall, I paused-just long enough for a hand to lunge from the darkness. Fingers closed around my upper arm, yanking me into an even darker space concealed from view. The grip was iron, unyielding, bruising and merciless. A dull thud-a tapestry collapsing against stone-suggested more than mere neglect. This was a concealed chamber, veiled in secrecy, untouched by the light of those who walked the palace halls. Lost in the memory of time.

'What game are you playing, Selene?' Hektor's voice was rough, filled with frustration. Seeing the slight wince at the biting pain, he dropped my arm, watching as I cradled it carefully.

'None.' I would not cower before the man who claimed to protect me. 'I could not continue to sit there and listen to their pretty delusions while the real world turns around them. I could not eat such a feast knowing there are those who go without while defending our walls.' Smudges of color bloomed where his grip had been rough.

'You think starving yourself makes you one of them? Is that what you're trying to prove?' He was angry at me for cutting our time together short.

Mindful of my words, knowing that the palace walls had ears and many thrived on the misfortunes of others, I spoke gently, 'The gods and goddesses may play games with all our lives, but I refuse to play them with yours. Less than a day ago, you stood against the Greek army on the beach. The dragons of Thera are coming. They thirst for blood more than the Greeks ever could. You chose me -not for love, but to honor tradition. To fulfil expectation. You care for me as one of your own, yet at times you do not care enough to truly see me. I have obeyed every command without hesitation-unless it would tarnish your name. I will not apologize for rejecting the illusion they readily embrace.'

I had his attention. Now, I had to tread carefully-to protect both my position and his pride. I lowered my voice and softened my tone, 'Better to slip away feigning a headache than to name her highness's folly for what it truly is. We squander our time, raising toasts to Alexander and Helena as if war is but a distant thought.'

A sudden wave of dizziness slammed into me. Hektor's face blurred-my balance wavered, my world tilting beneath me. His muscular arms catch me, holding me safely against the armour he wears. Armour that offers no protection from what is happening.

'Selene! Speak to me-what's wrong?' His voice is raw, frantic, as if sheer willpower could keep me from slipping away. Our bond flared-bright, undeniable-snapping into place, tethering me to his life as I teetered on the brink between consciousness and oblivion.

'Poison.' The word barely escaped my lips before darkness swallowed me whole.

I could hear Thea's voice-sharp with anger-cut through the haze nearby, but my vision blurred, betraying me.

'She's fitting again.' My body seized-muscles twisting into unnatural forms, each convulsion a brutal demand for change.

'I've got you.' Theron anchors me steady and unyielding, *'You will not change before the humans. You will not die this day, little moon.'*

Bile surged up my throat as something tore deep inside-searing, relentless pain. Heart racing like the wild winged horses of Emberis-racing-then faltering-barely fluttering. Body shuddering in effort not to bow to the poison within.

In the dining hall, Crinos slipped into the shadows, her eyes darting to Helena, who was still riding the lingering triumph of her wedding. She had ensured Selene would be out of the way, clearing the path for her chance with Hektor. Helena and Alexander's continued oblivious chatter about love and escape masked the true danger that lurked within the palace walls. Crinos' treachery was only the beginning.

Her plans would unfold gradually, a web of deceit and manipulation that would ensnare even the most vigilant. Remembering Selene's new circlet glinting in the candlelight, she thought with a cold, calculating smile, soon enough that pretty little circlet will be mine. Her braids clacked softly as she settled into the darkest corner of the room, observing everything. Her thoughts were a whirlwind of schemes and plots, each more intricate than the last. She revelled in the chaos, seeing it as a perfect backdrop for her rise to power. When the poison reached its crescendo, Hektor would need a second wife-and Crinos had already chosen herself for the role.

As Helena and Alexander prattled on in conversation, oblivious to the impending peril, Crinos allowed herself a small, satisfied smile.

Her eyes, cold and calculating, settled on the pair as she mentally mapped out her next steps. The palace was a labyrinth of secrets-twisting, treacherous, riddled with forgotten corridors and whispered betrayals. Crinos intended to wield them all to her advantage. She had gathered them like jewels-glittering, deadly, dangerous. Beautiful in their allure, waiting to be placed into the hands of the perfect enemy.

In the recesses of her mind, she cataloged each player in this deadly game. Selene, adorned with her new circlet, was merely just another piece on the board. But Crinos understood a fundamental truth-sometimes, the smallest piece was the one that shifted the game. She would watch. She would wait. And when the moment arrived, she would strike with precision. For now she wove her web drawing everyone closer to their downfall.

Seconds felt like hours and when I finally resurfaced from oblivion, I was back in my chambers, the familiar surroundings comforting on my battered body. The scent of fresh herbs and incense fills the air along with the desperate whispers of my sisters praying. Every breath was a battle, my throat still raw with the remnants of poison.

Thea's worried face hovered over me, relief flooding her features as my eyes finally opened. 'Selene, thank the Goddess,' Thea whispers, her voice trembling with exhaustion. 'You were poisoned...and lost your unborn child.'

'Hektor.' I croaked wincing in pain. 'He isn't allowed to see you right now,' she reassures me.' You've been fighting for your life for two days, Selene. He will return as soon as he can.' Brushing my hair off my forehead she whispers quietly, 'Neither of you knew, did you?' Her voice is quiet, hesitant as if speaking about the child will make the loss harder to bear. Even the smallest movement sends pain through me, but I manage a weak shake of my head. 'A star dust child that lived only in my heart, only in memory.' I force the words out, 'Hektor cannot know.-it would shatter him. He longs for a son. Troy demands that he continue the legacy.'

Her eyes shimmer, heavy with unshed tears as she replies softly, 'Your body will heal, Selene, though it will take time. And when the goddess is ready for you to be a mother, another child will come. I have seen one born of fate, not loss.'

Her prophetic words gave me something to hold onto during the long hours until Hektor's worried face hovered over me. Dried mud clings to his tunic, proof that he hadn't stopped to change-had come straight from his horse to my side. 'Selene-thank the gods.' His voice is raw, unsteady. 'I thought I had lost you.' My sisters move quietly from my side-Raya to deal with Hektor's dirty armour and Thea brings him a wet cloth to wipe his face with. His lips brush my brow murmuring, 'I could not let you slip away believing what you do. Not like this.'

'What do you mean?' My voice, still rasping, barely rises above a whisper. 'You left the wedding feast and we had a fight. I was angry, but you...you were right. We forget, too easily, that you were raised to rule. You think like a Queen, though you have rejected your crown. You pointed out plainly that the Greeks have brought the dragons of Thera and that we are not ready for them. Nor do I believe we ever will be-if they take flight against us. You and Andromache must survive this war. Without either of you, I-' he falters, a tear splashes on my cheek and he swipes at it roughly with his thumb. 'Gods. I almost lost you, and without you, I would have lost half of myself.'

'Who?' The word barely had to form on my lips before his face changed into pure fury. 'We don't know yet. When we do their choice of weapon will be their death.' His words are kept short as Thea reminds him gently that I need my rest. He stays by my side, his presence a small comfort in the midst of the pain. Andromache had an army of hands to guard her, to protect her unborn child. We had just lost ours. A child I could never speak of. A child lost before I ever knew to hope. Her child would survive the odds against him. Hektor would have his son.

Hektor's grip tightened around my hand as he curled in around my body behind me. We were safe in this moment and that is all that mattered to us.

Shadows of Treachery

Shadows of Treachery

Weeks passed before I was allowed to spend small amounts of time in the courtyard below my balcony. My balcony had become a place of solace, a perch from which I observed the daily rhythms of the courtiers below. Some entertained me with their frivolous games, while others-more cunning, more dangerous-left a shadow of unease in their wake. *Why did Helena's gaze linger, her eyes tracing each window as if searching for my chamber? Had she heard whispers of my defiance under the guise of serving the goddess? Or was she simply curious—another player in a game I hadn't yet learned the rules of?* Before I knew it, the flowers had burst into bloom, and I was led to sit beneath the ancient oak, its branches stretching like protective arms overhead. Guarding me from dangers lurking in the greenery.

Andromache, was the first to visit, finding me leaning against the ancient oak. Her loose, flowing garments draped over her growing belly as she sank onto the bench beside me, relief softening her features. 'I am so glad to see you still with us, sister.' Her uncertainty sends shards through my heart. Hektor has been spending more time with me.

'You shouldn't have come, Andromache-your time is near, isn't it?' I studied her face-the fine lines of worry, the exhaustion clinging to her eyes. Palace life was wearing her thin. 'You must keep your strength, for the son that waits to meet you.' 'I am neither an invalid nor am I an idiot.' she states with some asperity before adding quietly, 'I was worried for you and needed to see for myself you are healing.'

We subsided into companionable silence for a while before she asked, 'Hektor-he spends his nights with you?' 'Yes.' I answered, steering the conversation. 'You'd be welcome to join us in the evenings so that you could see him as well. Maybe we can find a location that will suit us all?' 'Really?' The disbelief in her voice was clear, as if the idea had never truly been an option before.

'I am here because you chose this path for me.' I worked through my thought process more patiently for her remembering when Mother had needed such help. 'I am here and willing for you to spend time with our husband and myself in a neutral location so that we become the family we need to be. This war will end-perhaps not too soon, but it will. And when it does, there will be more battles to come. But marriage to Hektor is not just a duty; it is a life entwined with his, for both of us. Children will come. They ask a lot of questions about these sorts of things so do we let this divide us, leaving Hektor to navigate two households? Or do we stand together, ensuring he finds strength in the family he already has?'

Raya, stands watch over us from a slight distance. Ever vigilant, her eyes sweep the shrubbery, as if expecting an assassin to burst through the greenery and shatter our peace. The dark circles under her eyes reveal the strain she bears-from the weight of her brilliant designs to the burden of my health. She hardly slept these days and with my poisoning her hyper vigilance might be her undoing. A grim, unyielding determination hardened her features, barely concealing the guilt she bore-for letting the unseen threat slip past her guard, for allowing the poison to reach me. Appointing herself my chief cup bearer she would not let any food near me without first tasting it herself.

Andromache's soft snort of disbelief draws me back to our conversation. 'You would truly allow this? A place where we can both stand beside him-not divided?' her brow furrowed, doubt flickering across her face. Without missing a beat I reiterate the central idea. 'A neutral space...for both of us. Would the palace even permit us to change our living arrangements? This will not be taken well.' Her fingers find mine, a tentative plea for something familiar, 'I have missed him more than I expected. I do not begrudge you your time, but I cannot remember the last time I saw him beyond fleeting moments. I feel forgotten. This child takes more from me than I ever imagined. I am tired, Selene-tired of waiting, tired of carrying this weight, tired of feeling like all I do is endure.'

Thea dressed neatly in the robes of a royal healer asks Andromache, 'May I examine the health of your child, your highness? I will not linger, I swear it.' Conditioned to obey, Andromache nods despite the uncertainty flickering in her eyes. Closing her eyes, Thea raised her hand slightly off Andromache's belly and moved it over the baby in a circular motion. Her healing patterns weave through the air, restoring vitality to mother and child alike-an echo of the goddess's favour. As Andromache's gaze followed the fluttering of birds beyond the courtyard, she remained unaware of the golden glow flickering beneath Thea's palm. 'He's strong and he's healthy.' she announces after a few minutes. Relief softened Andromache's features as she exhaled a breath she hadn't realised she'd been holding.

A quiet bubble of laughter escapes from her lips as Thea and Raya abandon their serious roles to play a game of tag. 'I don't know who upset you Andromache but you are part of our family.' The tension between us had been more than I could bear and in that quiet moment I hoped she could feel the truth of my words deep inside her bones. A yawn escapes from my lips. Thea, ever attentive, helped me adjust my position on the bench, her touch gentle and reassuring. 'You must take it slow,' she admonished softly. 'Your recovery is not something to be rushed.'

Our fragile peace shattered as the assailant I had mocked in my thoughts emerges from the shadows, gripping my arm with brutal force. Blade poised at my throat they crouch behind me waiting. I didn't know who they were. Not yet. But the blade was real, and the intent behind it was clear. Heavy breathing filled my ears as the world paused. What was the assassin waiting for? I had eluded death twice already, then with a motion so smooth Raya was pure action. She drew our guard's sword from its sheath and drove it deep into the assailant's side. The guards rushed Andromache, putting her behind them in case there were more assailants to come. Raya plucked the sword out from the dead man with Grecian features and kept it ready in a loose grip helping Thea to raise me to my feet before backing us into the recess of the tree out of the sight of everyone and planting herself in front of us.

'What now?' she demands controlling her breathing, eyes scanning the area in front of us rapidly. 'I've stolen a sword to protect two Princesses of Troy.' 'We'll deal with it later.' I reassure her trying to peek past Thea to check on Andromache. 'Andromache?' I question still not able to see past my sisters. 'Is protected as are you.' Raya remains firm. Hearing Hektor's voice in the distance, she flips the sword around in her grip before silently offering back to the guard she stole it from. 'Keep it. You have need of it. I do not.' He tries to reassure her but the grimace is a too terrifying reminder that danger surrounds us even when we least expect it.

Striding with precise footsteps, Hektor emerged from beyond the courtyard wall. His eyes swept over Andromache, then me, searching for injury. The air sizzled with electrical undercurrents as he prowled the small space—serenity long gone—listening to the explanations of our guard.

His fingers tightened slightly as they brushed the shallow cut on my neck. He held up two fingers, red with my blood.

'Are you hurt elsewhere, Selene?' His voice carried no warmth, only urgency—like a man who'd come from one battlefield and stepped into another.

'I'm fine,' I said, though my voice trembled. The adrenaline was wearing off faster than I'd hoped.

'Let's go.' He glances over Raya's perfect stance-her hand still touching the sword and then lingered on my face before gathering Andromache under one arm. She leans into him as he tightens his hand on her arm. 'Can you walk?' *Of course I could walk.* The guards surround us flanking us from every side and we move together as a group with Andromache, Hektor and I at its centre.

He swept us inside the walls of the palace. A building that was beginning to feel more like a prison with each passing moment. With no relief indoors or out from the ever present threat of danger I opened the barrier in my mind in a moment of exhaustion.

Between one heartbeat and the next I feel Theron fill the spaces of my mind where he has never been.

I feel him recognise the danger surrounding me yet again.

'I am coming for you.' His voice pours through my entire being, stamping the finality of his words on the connective tissue between my cells. Hektor would kill to save me but Theron would burn the entire world and not look back.

The silence after his words was worse than the roar I knew was coming. It seemed the dragon shifters of Thera were no longer content to wait and nature held her breath bracing for what it knew would arrive. Theron was coming.

Part Three

Theron's fury and devotion

(Theron)

She had been moved to an isolated tower at the back of the palace complex. Easier to guard from the inside but easy access from the outside walls. She was no safer. An ancient oak with spreading boughs had grown against the wall, making an easy ladder for any who wished to infiltrate the city. Its branches splayed tight against the pitted stone. The wall had weakened with its weight over time. It would be a perfect breach point. She was still in danger-fools!

Hektor did not consider that the danger could come from below. His focus remains above the ground. He is searching for the would be assassins in the faces he knows. There is danger where he does not look. Beneath Wilusa, spread a tunnel network. The network was complex in nature, a labyrinth twisting beneath the city. Tunnels that led from the caves on the beach into the heart of the city.

She had opened her mind to me in a moment of weakness and my world had detonated with colour. Colours I had never known existed. Her flame nestled against my inferno. I could feel her heart beginning to beat in sync with mine. The pull to transform into my dragon form had been immense. I hesitated-just barely-before disbelief curled through my mind. A thought unconsciously shared-a half vision of a sword at her throat. Two fingers coated in her precious blood. What had I just seen? Was it a memory, a premonition or something happening right now?

Someone dared spill the blood of my little mate. My iron grip on my control over my temper slipped. A shadow stretched from me, flickering erratically as my body partially shifted, transitioning faster than I could contain, claws burst through my skin. Pain flickered at the edge of my awareness as I struggled to hold onto my humanity. The temperature rose as the inferno inside me threatened to explode. My rage tasted of ice-the kind that lingers, biting unforgiving. The edge of the cleanest snow drifts turned sharp and cruel. My hands curled into fists by my side. The time for patience had long since passed. I would not wait another moment. Forcing my shifter side to subside beneath the skin of my human half I wait until I am in control before throwing the hood of my cloak over my head and striding towards the dark entrance to the tunnels. I pressed against her mind, allowing her to feel the force of my fury- bound in chains of judgement and retribution.

'I am coming.'

The tunnels to the surface had long since been mapped and used daily by my companions. I had spies throughout the city working meaningless low paid jobs-watching, waiting for my signal that we would remove the last of phoenix kind from the Trojans. They are ghosts silently observing and blending into the city's fabric. Three female shifters. The three of the prophecy. As the last of their kind, this much was certain. I would wager my last scale on it. But were they ready to step into their destiny? Navigating the tunnels with ease, I emerged into the shadows between the wall and the tower-deep enough to conceal me. I leaned against the wall waiting for my chance. The lingering impact of repeated transformations flickered beneath my skin, forcing me to slow down. I did not want to scare my little mate. It had been years since we last met. The boy she once knew was gone. In his place stood a male, forged by fire, by battle, by time. My breathing slows as my muscles stop jumping under my skin. Every thought, every instinct narrows to one singular truth: her.

'I know you are nearby. My sister is coming out-do not harm her.' Selene's words are cautious-timid, as if she fears for the safety of her loved one in my claws. *'Your loved ones have nothing to fear from me or my kind, Selene.'* Weariness colours my psychic voice, resonating like a whisper in her mind, mirroring the deep exhaustion settling in my muscles.

'Theron, follow me.' Bending shadows to her will, Raya is leaning on the stone wall beside me with practiced ease. Not a strand of her dark red hair visible, yet I sensed the air beside me shift. I stilled my mind, focusing-just before blocking a punch to my chest. Flipping her hand over I clasp her wrist lightly. I knew what this was-a test and a warning wrapped in sisterly love delivered silently. 'Your reputation still precedes you, Princess Nuraya.' A hint of a smirk-friendly white teeth flashing briefly in the darkness. I had met Nuraya before as she had travelled with her father that last time during the Conclave. Her skills as a warrior of Phoenix kind were well known amongst my people, respected and tried against some of our younger warriors.

The tower is too quiet. Too still. A place meant for safety and yet it brims with vulnerability. Stone walls are the only barriers keeping her from me. Inadequate and old at best. Cracks in the stonework create a way for scaling up to the second level. No real barriers to one such as I, but they are the barriers Nuraya leads me through, guiding me into the warmth of a roaring fire. The cold of the night air claws at my back, lingering even as I step over the threshold, deliberately slowing my steps as my gaze sweeps the room, seeking the one I have come to shield-Selene of Emberis.

She meets my gaze, silver eyes brimming with unspoken questions. Standing tall beside the fireplace, firelight flickers-casting shifting shadows across the folds of her dress. She holds herself in place despite leaning imperceptibly toward me. *'I felt your presence'* she whispers, her voice threading through the telepathic link that has bound us for years. *'Are you real? Are you here?'* A bond that weaves us together in the most beautiful of ways-our soul mate connection. The glowing tendrils pulse in sync with our heartbeats, stretch out between us and weave tighter together like gravity until all I can do is breathe in her presence. The crackling of the fire fills the room as she waits for me to speak.

'Selene.' I breathe her name like a prayer. My gaze roaming her appearance-lingering on the bandage at her neck, still spotted with her precious blood. 'I'm here little moon.' 'You're here too late.' Her voice cracks slightly, her face awash in anguish, 'You swore to my father-to protect us after Emberis. Yet my marriage took place the day before you landed. My father fell when the Myrmidons took the Temple of Poseidon. Where was your protection then, Theron of Thera?' Her crushing words are too heavy for her to bear. She sinks into the nearest seat, weary, waving me toward the other. Her grief pulses through our bond unspoken, raw and cutting.

'I failed him, Selene. I know that.' I slump into the other chair the weight of my broken oath pressing down on my shoulders, 'If I could fly back through time to prevent that moment I would so that you could have your father with you now. But I also swore to protect you and your two sisters to the last breath left in my body and nothing-nothing will stop me from protecting you now.' My breath comes slower as I straighten my posture before kneeling at her feet and bowing my head as was customary for such words to a Queen. She exhales a singular staccato breath in astonishment. 'I make my oath to you, Selene of Troy & of Emberis. I, Theron of Thera, Tiarna Draíochta of the United Dragon Clans, do solemnly swear that you will never be left unprotected again. I will always come for you-to be your sword. I will stand beside you, shield your back for you for the rest of eternity. May my magic surround you-even if it costs me everything.' My words echo through the bond, snapping another glowing line between us-not golden like the others, but crimson, throbbing with the weight of the oath just spoken.

The weight of her small hand on my head is unexpected, as are the words that follows. 'I, Selene Amethyria of Troy and of Emberis, accept the protection of Theron of Thera, Tiarna Draiochta of the United Dragon Clans. But know this, Theron-I do not accept it as a helpless queen, nor as one bound by duty alone. Yet let it be known-I do not accept this vow as one who seeks shelter, but as one who carries her own duty. My path lies in service to the displaced, the forgotten, the ones who must find new beginnings. Where danger seeks me out, I will not deny your shield. Nor will I reject your presence. I will trust in the strength of your oath as I honor my own. This bond between us is not fleeting, we are long lived creatures and I swear to you our time will come. May my magic support you-even if it costs me everything.' She speaks the ritual words as they well from deep within her.

'Service to the displaced. The forgotten. The ones who must find new beginnings.' her words struck a chord deep inside of me. The trauma of her flight from Emberis must affect her still. 'You speak of new beginnings. But who will lead them into that unknown Selene?'

Hesitating slightly she nods her head to Raya who slips from the room. Speaking into the lingering silence that follows Selene twirls the end of her braid around her finger, an ingrained habit that calmed her as she thought, much like she did the day I met her.

'I cannot help but wonder what will happen to the innocent of Troy when the Greeks invade. Our supplies are already beginning to dwindle. We ration our own food, ensuring others do not starve-but it is not enough..' she paused continuing to gather her thoughts to present to me logically. 'I do not hold hope that Wilusa will stand forever. Not against them. Not when you already know the secrets of the tunnels. I have thought of reaching out to the Temples across the country asking if they could take groups of ten, perhaps twenty women and children seeking refuge. But I do not have the resources to get them there.'

Years ago, during one of Evander's visits to the Dragon clan of Thera, a young Selene wandered through the lush forests surrounding the clan's stronghold. She loved exploring, her adventurous spirit often leading her to places she probably shouldn't have been. It was on one such exploration that she stumbled upon me fishing in a serene lake, enjoying some time out from important negotiations.

She never told me whether she too had felt an immediate, inexplicable connection, but for the rest of their visit, she was never far from my presence. We spent hours talking, playing, and simply enjoying the presence of one another.

The warmth of the fire at our backs reminds me of that day and I look past the image of the girl I once knew-the child who laughed in sun-dappled forests, untouched by war-to see the woman before me now. Blooded. Tried. Weighed down by duty, yet still fighting for what she believed in.

She has been chased from her home amidst bloodshed, lost her father, poisoned and put to sword point. Yet she worries not for herself but for those everyone else has forgotten. She clasps her hands loosely together in her lap steeling herself for my reaction to her unspoken request.

'We will lead immediate rescue operations as soon as the temple network is set up as safe havens. I have my people hiding in plain sight throughout this city. They work as merchants, slaves, shop vendors and palace staff. They are part of your guard detail and vet your food before it leaves the kitchens. The Greeks think to keep us chained by ancient oath. To use us as their weapon of mass destruction.'

A deadly calm sweeps through me, as I assess the resources we will need to complete these missions. Her plan-it is audacious, impossible even. And yet...

By the god, if she succeeds, she will do more than protect the innocent. She will galvanise the city. She will rally the army-make them fight not just for Troy, but for their families, knowing their loved ones are no longer in danger.

Soft shuffling on the staircase alerts us to the fact that we are no longer alone. 'Raya is bringing our sister to meet you.' She explains with a small smile of relief. 'Raya and Thea will be instrumental in setting up the network,' she continues, her voice steady, assured. 'Vital for sending messages, for keeping us connected. Thea is a palace healer and a priestess with the Temple of Eileithyia. Raya knows weaponry. She is skilled at evading the enemy and masking her presence. If there is anyone I trust, it is my sisters.' My little moon had good survival instincts-for which I thanked all the gods in existence. But there was more to it than that. She bore the weight of countless others, shielding them in ways they would never see. She had no idea that our lives, though lived separate, were tied together. One day, she would count me among her inner circle. Even a queen needed allies she could trust.

'You have put a larger target on my sister's back by being here this evening.' Thea's green eyes narrow with suspicion. Her seemingly innocent mask cracks-a shift in her posture, the weight of forced maturity slipping beneath the healer's calm facade. Each word spoken with a forced detachment, as if this child has seen far too much and begs for my help. 'I have not found a wall in this city without an ear glued to it. And yet, you sit here drinking with my sister, unbothered. Unconcerned. Do you even realise the danger you've brought upon her? Last night one of the sisters overheard whispers in the marketplace-whispers about us. She reports that the merchant is a new face. A spy, perhaps. As if we are not already hunted. This hiding place you have chosen? It is a mistake. The cost of that mistake will not be yours to bear. It will fall upon her. Upon us.'

'Hektor has put the target upon your backs little healer.' She should be braiding flowers in a field somewhere, learning the duties of her royal role. Not here. Not like this. But she is not just a child. She is a priestess, a healer. And though I do not want to see the weight on her shoulders, I must admit-she carries it well. 'This area is too easily infiltrated. The wall is old, the tree a perfect ladder, its branches tight against the stone. Someone is playing a game with your lives in the shadows, and yet your sister's husband places you more firmly within it.' Keeping to the facts, I hope to defuse her ire. Turning to her sister I ask, 'Is this also your assessment, Princess Nuraya?'

'Raya, please. Our kingdom is dead. And yet I remain-a priestess, a weapons architect, my sister's personal guard. That is all I can be now.' She pauses, considering the facts that I have laid out, 'I agree with your assessment however the implications reach deep-too deep. Entwined with the royal family in ways I dare not name. I have my suspicions. But I cannot act. Not yet. Prince Hektor demands it be thus. And he is her rightful husband.'

Selene leans forward as I rise instinctively. Raya is right, Hektor is her husband-not me. Not yet. Selene has promised that our time will come. And gods help me, I will hold her to that oath. Her lips part, a fleeting breath caught in hesitation. Then a foot falls outside the tower. Light. Controlled. My eyes meet Raya's. Her fingers brush over a pommel at her waist. Someone who does not wish to be heard. Someone who does not wish to leave the tower alive.

Hektor's calculated command

Hektor's calculated command

(Hektor)

Wilusa stands tonight, ancient and unwavering. We breathe a collective sigh of relief that the Greeks have stood down for now. They are re-examining their strategy, regrouping and rearming. Preparing weapons that may soon rival those of Raya of Emberis-and when they return, they will not come empty-handed. This short reprieve will not last. It never does. Wars do not pause; they shift and evolve.

And I must keep two steps ahead of each evolution. Our people's lives depend upon it. Troy's survival demands it. I have seen the Greeks' champion—Achilles. His reputation is not exaggerated. But what is one legend, no matter how fierce, against the might of the Trojan Army? I do not yet know the full extent of his power. I've seen him strike—but not yet in open battle

Troy demands my strength, my strategy. It always has. And I have never wavered. But tonight, war does not fill my thoughts alone. Tonight, I think of the women who hold my heart-and the battles I cannot fight for them. Andromache is heavily pregnant and surrounded by my best soldiers to guard her and our child yet to be born. Selene-since becoming my second wife—has endured slander, poison and the edge of a blade. She is my greatest weakness. And yet, perhaps, she is also my greatest strength. I would cut down any man who sought to harm her-but a blade only protects what stands before it. My protection is more than steel. It is foresight. Calculation. Restraint. And it must be-because I cannot fight what I cannot see. The moment I falter in this plan-Selene will pay the price. There is no room for hesitation. Not in war. Not in love. If I am to be the shield between her and the world, I must ensure there are no cracks.

I could not fight a war and have her back at all hours. And that is the curse of kings: there is always something left unguarded. The war room lies in eerie stillness. Maps lay scattered, their parchment edges curling under the weight of choices I must soon make-choices that will decide the fate of Troy. I sink into my chair in the chamber, the leather worn beneath my grip. For a moment I close my eyes-not to sleep, but to think. The silence I crave does not last. A subtle shift in the air. A draft where no draft should be. I open my eyes just as a shadow moves, as the tapestry at the far end of the room parts with deliberate slowness just enough to reveal the silhouette beyond. A figure steps forward, unhurried. I straighten shaking off the weight of exhaustion. The clasp at his throat bore the sigil of the dragons of Thera-a dragon coiled around a flame. With a crown floating above. No mistaking it. The flame in his eyes flaring with emotion not seen stamped on his features. Theron of Thera had not come to merely visit my war chamber.

'You have entered my home uninvited Theron of Thera.' I could not afford to make an enemy of the leader of the dragons of Thera. Not tonight. Not ever. 'An old friend called out to me for help.' He smirks, 'And I do not leave my own behind. You, of all people, should understand that.' 'This old friend of yours-should I consider them a threat to my city, Theron? Or just a danger to me? Because I have no patience for either.' 'Selene is your wife, is she not?' His blue eyes flicker in the candlelight, glowing like embers barely contained. Theron's voice is deceptively smooth, but there is steel beneath it. 'Do you truly believe locking her away has kept her safe? Because from where I stand, it looks more like an invitation.'

Theron has seen her. Spoken with her. She warned me about his kind, yet she opened the door.

Did she ever belong to him—not in body, but in heart?

I don't know. I don't want to know.

She let him in. That means something.

And I'm not sure I'm ready to understand what.

'You have seen my wife, then?'

I keep my voice level, though the words land heavily.

'I trust she made herself clear-that she doesn't need your interference.'

Glancing at his granite expression I can tell he isn't willing to rise to the bait.

'Unless you believe otherwise.'

'She was my betrothed before she became your wife. I led the rescue party to retrieve her family from your beach. I respect your marriage. We share a bond—one forged before Troy claimed her. A soul bond. She is mine as much as she is yours. I protect what is mine just as you will protect her. I do not seek to challenge your place beside her. Only to honor the oaths I have made to protect her.'

Soul mates. He speaks the word like law. One etched into foundation of his kind. The gods of Troy had spoken and yet if Thera recognises soul bonds as law, then I could be trespassing on something that could lead to another war we cannot win.

The dragons were already on our beaches-they would obliterate us from the earth if we disregard their sacred traditions.

She is my wife. *But what was she to him?*

'I am already fighting an unwinnable war with Greece. Tell me Theron of Thera are we to be at war with you as well? Should I move my people underground, fearing fire from the skies?'

I do not raise this question lightly.

The dragons are already on our beaches.

Our historians have warned us of what their kind once did.

Of our great city turned to ash, of skies that burned for days.

That is why we banned dragons from our shores.

I will not see Troy become another legend of ruin.

I nod toward the empty chair beside me. I am ready to hear what the shifter has come to say. He sits as if the world is pressing itself down on his shoulders. Maybe it is. I know little of the dragons' politics. And that ignorance could cost me. His eyes hold many secrets. He holds his hands out and places them palm up on his knees. A gesture of truce perhaps. Or is this how they conduct their war discussions? His calm posture speaks of peace. But it is not Troy he seeks to protect—it is her.

'Selene is vulnerable in that tower. My people flood your city guarding her from the shadows. I have people everywhere from your throne room to your kitchens and from your markets to your temples. Four more attempts were made. Unreported. In just three nights. She is not safe. Not behind stone. Not behind steel. She will not take kindly to being sequestered where her sisters may not reach her. Their shadows are watching. But so are we.'

No one remained to protect her the way she deserved. As my second wife, Selene held the title but not the priority. Raya was her sole fierce protector and I had seen what she could do with a sword.

We took untried male children from the kitchens. Trained them in the ways of war. Preparing for the inevitable which I could only pray would end in our favour. I had given her my name, but not my shield...not yet. Andromache had the guards. Selene had my heart. Theron owned a piece of her soul. The part that never answered to me.

''You say she is precious to you. Then prove it. Keep her alive from the shadows you seem to love so much. But if you fail, Theron, I will not forgive you.'

I rub a hand over my face, trying to stay awake.

'It seems I must tolerate your presence. But make no mistake-Selene's fate is hers alone. Not yours. Not mine.'

I would need to make time to visit Selene. It seemed I had delayed long enough. She had waited long enough. And I had no more excuses.

Before I could rise to seek her out, Theron's voice cut through the silence. His tone low and laced with something more than warning.

'There is something else you should know. Selene has made use of her network and is planning to evacuate the innocent from your city and spread the refugees throughout all the temples in Troy.'

Theron's voice belays his own weariness as he continues, 'she has asked me if my army will help with the evacuation so that yours may remain to defend the city. I will not move until the passage routes are established and the logistics are all in place.'

Selene had been moving as if she carried the future of Troy in her hands. Perhaps she does. Now, she was safeguarding the very future I had failed to see through the haze of war.

My little love was taking precautions I had not even begun to consider. If the temples could shield the people, then the plan held merit. And if Theron was willing to wait for the routes to be secured, then perhaps he was not here to challenge me but to save what I could not.

I had underestimated her. I could not afford to again.

'She does not do this to undermine your authority Prince Hektor of Troy. She does this because she must do something to protect those who cannot protect themselves. Others move lives around as pieces on a chess board. She sees them as individuals-friends that she visits with at the Temple who have lost loved ones in this war. She would protect all that she holds dear.'

She would protect all that she holds dear. And perhaps, in doing so, she has safeguarded something I had not yet considered-hope. A future beyond the walls of Wilusa. Beyond my war.

He speaks again, voice soft with suggestion, 'Perhaps you will send Thea to the temples under the guise of learning a new birthing technique for your princess. Raya has agreed to be our messenger. Send her to me when you are ready to begin. But work quickly-because if the war creeps any closer, hesitation will cost lives.'

'You have your messenger. You have your strategy. But tell me-do you have the certainty that this will work?' I could not keep the skepticism from my voice

'The alternative is too horrific to bear thinking about.' Theron's blue eyes bore into my own. 'Selene prays for the souls of her dead family daily along with her entire people. She has already walked this path once. I trust her judgement-the question is do you?'

I have trusted her with my home. With my name. But have I trusted her with my people? Andromache had the trust of my people. I had expected this moment to be hers, the future Queen of Troy. But Selene does not wait for a crown-she moves as one already crowned.

'If she has seen this path before-then I would be a fool to ignore her. And I am no fool. You trust her without question. I have never had that luxury, Theron. We have been at war with the Greeks almost as long as I have known Selene. But perhaps this is the moment I learn it.'

King Agamemnon waits-biding his time, preparing to strike in the name of Helena. Soon, he will be knocking at our gates once more. But tonight, it is not war that commands my focus. It is Selene-the woman who sees my people more clearly than I ever have. And if I cannot trust her now, then I have already lost.

A glimpse of the truth

A glimpse of the truth

(Selene)

Hektor's visits drift through the darkness-whispers of presence, shadowed apparitions that only arrive when sleep take hold. They blur the line between reality and exhaustion, leaving me to wonder if he is flesh and blood or merely a spector conjured by my weary mind. Recovery stretches endlessly, broken only by my sisters' fleeting visits-their concerned faces a stark contrast to the spectral echoes of Hektor's presence.

Below me, the palace sprawls-vast, alive with movement, its people scurrying through their daily duties. And yet, I remain above it all, caught in silence. Thea is away visiting the temples in the north and west. Hektor sent her to study new birthing techniques. I sent her to secure sanctuaries for those who have nowhere else to go. Two missions, one journey-each carrying the weight of futures yet to be decided.

I hear him arrive late one night after my eyes are too heavy to open properly. Frustration bleeds into my dreams, where countless Hektors stand like specters-watchful, silent, always near but never close enough. Why does he keep coming if we cannot talk to each other? Dawn's first fragile gleam barely touches the horizon when I jolt awake-to find him there, leaning against cold stone, sword in hand, a silent guardian against unseen dangers.

Sliding through the thick shadows to his side, I attempt to maneuver his solid frame toward the bed. A hand quicker than lightning grabs my wrist, bending my arm behind me. The blade grazes my throat, its cool edge a whispered threat-not deep enough to draw blood, but sharp enough to remind me how close danger truly is. My pulse stammers in my throat as realisation dawns-he's not fully awake, trapped between instinct and exhaustion. Time stretches unbearably as his grip remains unyielding, the steel pressing firmly against my skin-a silent promise of pain should I make the wrong move.

At last, his body sags, the tension draining from his muscles as recognition flickers in his eyes-slow at first, then undeniable. The sword is put away, and he releases me, his breathing heavy. He takes a measured step back, widening the space between us-not for caution, but for control. He needs the distance. Needs to shake off the lingering pulse of danger.

'Selene.' His voice is hoarse, frayed at the edges. 'You shouldn't try to wake me, little love. My reflexes are too sharp-too dangerous.' He exhales, rough with exhaustion, regret laced between each breath.

'Why do you come when we cannot speak?' The words slip from my lips, a fragile plea laced with confusion and longing, my mind still reeling from what just happened. Silence hangs between us, thick and suffocating, as the dim light carves long, distorted shadows across our faces-shadows as fractured as the distance between us.

He exhales slowly, dragging a hand down his face as if wiping away more than just sleep-weariness clings to him, heavy, unshaken. This conversation is inevitable-silence has stretched between us too long, pulling taut like a bowstring on the edge of snapping. 'You let Theron in. That means something.' His voice is measured-controlled, yet tight enough to strain at the edges. 'Tell me Selene-do you still belong to me?' His tone lowers, deliberate, nearly aching. 'I do not need illusions of peace, Selene. I need certainty.'

'Ask me what you truly wish to know Hektor. I would have no se-crets between us.'

'You say there are no secrets between us. Fine. Then tell me-does his presence mean nothing to you?' His tone is even, deliberate but there is weight behind every word.

'I am yours, Hektor. My heart is yours. Theron knows this, and he does not challenge it. But my soul was bound to his long before you and I became what we are. That cannot be undone-but it does not change who I have chosen. I let him in to honor the oath he made to my father. I let him in because he is my sworn protector and shield just as Raya is.'

'A sworn protector. A shield.'' Hektor exhales, gaze sharp. 'Then tell me this-if I fall, does he inherit you?'

'I will not be bartered between men like relics scavenged from a grave.' I level him with a stare, cold tendrils tightening around my heart, my voice edged in steel as I bite out. 'I had half a mind to help you to bed, to offer you comfort in what's left of the night-but now? Now, I think I need a cup of tea instead.' His accusations have wounded me and I prefer the view from the window to the visage of my husband.

'I thought I understood you.' the whisper tears the words from my soul. 'But tonight, I am not sure I do. You asked me for certainty. And yet, you speak as if I am something that can be taken, lost or given away.'

I slip down the stairs, moving quickly but not hurried-drawn to-ward the quiet glow of the fire where I left my pot of tea. Curling into my chair, I let the warmth press against me as tears slide free-silent, unchecked, unguarded. What kind of woman was I, that my own husband could wound me like this-with words sharp enough to carve doubt into my bones?

A heavy footfall echoes on the stairs. He lingers in the doorway, his silhouette carved by the flickering light, waiting-watching. I do not rush. I finish my cup, letting the warmth settle me, forcing myself to breathe. Only then do I speak. 'I do not need a sentinel standing watch outside my door, Hektor. I need my husband. Tell me-are you still that man?'

He does not move for a long time. The fire crackles softly, its warmth mocking the cold silence between us-the only sound in a room filled with unspoken words. 'I have wounded you.' He does not soften it, does not justify it-only speaks the truth for what it is. I will not meet his gaze-not out of weakness, but because I refuse to find pity in his eyes. I will not beg for his comfort. I will not beg at all. His steps are slow, deliberate, closing the distance between us.

'I will not do it again.' A vow spoken like a battle oath-one he means to keep, no matter the cost. 'You are my wife. Not a possession. Not a prize. Not a woman to be bartered. I see that now.' He kneels, forearms braced against his thighs, unmoving-waiting for me to look at him, waiting for me to see something worth believing. He waits until my gaze flits over his face searching for the truth. 'You asked me if I am still your husband.' he exhales gaze locked onto mine, 'The answer is yes. And I will prove it-not just once, not just with words, but as many times as it takes for you to believe in me...in us again.'

My fingers tighten around the delicate porcelain of my cup. Once, I had no say in the choices made for me. Once, I was placed in a room I never intended to enter, a pawn moved by hands more powerful than my own. I had chosen him that day under a cloud of fear of repercussions to my family. He was freely choosing me without the weight of royal duty pressing against him. 'You chose me then-I choose you now.' The words barely escape before his warmth crashes into mine-his kiss searing through me, branding me in a way fate never could.

His muscles are set like stone beneath my hands. Does he ever truly rest? Has he ever let anyone do this for him before? 'You're still in pain.' I murmur brushing a tentative finger along the side of his face, 'You never ask for rest. You never ask for anything. But I will not let you suffer in silence.' My fingers sweep lower, tracing the hard lines of his collarbone, slipping over the tense curve of his shoulder. Beneath my touch, warmth unfurls-not sudden, not jarring, but a slow healing pulse sinking deep, coaxing him toward relief. I do not care that I have forbidden my sisters from using their gifts with the humans. Hektor is injured and in pain.

Closing my eyes I stretch out with my senses following another pulse through his body. Twisting and turning through the veins, arteries, joint connections and muscular attachments. There. My eyes fly open and I concentrate on sending my healing to the strained ligaments he had been hiding.

At first, his body fights it-a reflex against something unknown. I know the moment his resistance crumbles, his weight pressing against my legs as the warmth thickens, wrapping around him like the heavy embrace of a summer's heat. His breath stutters-brief, sharp-before settling into something slower, deeper, as if his body finally understands it is allowed to rest.

'What-' His voice is rough, uncertain. He tests the shoulder I have just mended for him rolling it both ways.

'I am your Selene.' I whisper, voice steady-because tonight, there is no doubt left between us. If they knew-if anyone knew-this would not be mercy, but command. Expectation. Obligation. A chain bound to my sisters and me for eternity, forged not from duty, but from need. Slowly, deliberately, I pull my hand back, folding it into my lap as if keeping the truth pressed against my skin will keep it from escaping. I watch him, breath held, waiting. Will he push? Will he demand more? Have I already shattered the fragile peace between us, without ever meaning to?

Hektor does not speak. Instead, his breath steadies-slow, measured, a silent declaration written into the rhythm of his lungs. This time, he does not ask for certainty. He does not need to. He has already chosen to believe. His silence is not empty-it is steady, solid, a foundation laid between us without need for explanation. And that, I realise, is enough.

Echoes of Hope

Echoes of Hope

(Thea)

Hektor's endorsement had done little to pave the way into opening negotiations with the temples to the north and east of Wilusa. Their hesitation stretched the days thin, stealing time I could not afford to lose-each moment spent waiting was a step further from securing the safety we needed. The heavy scent of incense clinging to stale air turns my stomach. The murmured prayers may be real but their words feel false to my ears.

Zeleia felt different the moment we crossed its borders-the uncertainty still hummed in the air, but this time, it did not bring rejection. When the temple doors opened, it was not with hesitation, nor with caution, but with quiet, unmistakable welcome. Yet the spectacle facing us as we enter into the inner sanctum has my stomach tightening into knots.

Warrior priests clad in armour stood like statues against the walls, arms crossed, unreadable-an unspoken challenge mirrored in the presence of my shifter guards. Their postures, rigid hands hovering near their weapons, with me firmly in the centre for my protection. The air between them crackled with restrained power as they scrutinise each other for weaknesses. 'If Wilusa falls, the Greeks will not spare those hiding within your walls. But if you act now, you can save them-and yourselves.' Countering their reluctance with logic had made some headway in our previous locations. My heart hammering against my ribs as my guard still have not released the pommels of their swords. They are on high alert and so am I.

For a moment, the only sound filling the cavernous space is the rustling of fabric as a priest prays facing away from us for guidance. He turns to face us. Face serene speaking with conviction. 'We will take any who need refuge and cannot find it at other temples. You have proven your point Lady Althea.' He lifted a hand, wordless command passing through his warriors like a silent war drum. In one fluid movement they come to attention the sound echoing throughout the temple. 'We will send men to Wilusa-not just to defend, but to reclaim. The gods demand retribution for this insult, and we will answer.'

The urgency in their actions demands an answer. I sink into a grateful curtsey. 'We travel onwards to Thrace on behalf of Princess Selene of Troy and Emberis. I will send word ahead of your warriors to alert Prince Hektor of your offer of support.' The tension between his warriors and mine dissipate gradually as their muscles loosen and hands move away from their weapons. Seraphinus gives a slow nod to the warrior priests-an unspoken acknowledgment, neither dominance nor submission. They part so that the priests and I might have a personal conversation. I expect reciprocal demands almost immediately, however I am pleasantly surprised by the offer of a chamber for the night and lodgings for my companions. For the first time in weeks, I do not need to beg. I do not need to fight for scraps of mercy. It has been given freely, without cost, without hesitation. And that alone feels strange.

Luxuriating in the sensation of warm water running through my scalp, I work my fingers through tangled strands, easing the knots free. What a sight I must have presented to the priests-for them to quietly offer me a herbal oil, fragrant with lavender, thyme, tea tree and mint.

The rinse and repeat of the action keeps my thoughts from spiraling, grounding me in the rhythm of movement, in the simple certainty of clean skin and water.

Soft laughter drifts in from the next room, a reminder that I am safe, that I can release the weight of setting up the refugee network-because it is done. Now I can concentrate on the second part of my mission. This part, I do not for Wilusa, nor for the people we serve but for myself and my sisters. Selene thinks only of our people; Raya, of our security. Yet, during my shifts-deep in the quiet of the night, when all my patients sleep-I think of something different. A place to run should Wilusa fall. Somewhere safe, known only to us. A sanctuary where our enemies will never find us. Last time we fled, we followed our father blindly, with no destination in mind. We ran on instinct, desperate, lost. This time will be different. This time, I will ensure we have a direction, a place of refuge-a safe space we choose, not one that was chosen by another.

I sit by the fire, the map Hektor kindly provided spread before me. Its parchment curling at the edges in the flickering heat. The night air is cool against my skin, the thin fabric of my night dress offers little protection. With slow, deliberate movements, I run my fingers through my damp hair, letting the fire's warmth coax the lingering moisture from the strands. Tracing the river's course with the tip of my finger, I follow its winding path toward the Propontis. Each bend, each tributary, a choice, a possible escape. We would have to find a way to cross, to press forward into Thrace. But from there-where would be most unexpected? Where would a princess of Troy flee to, if not into the arms of those who sought to destroy her? Not the familiar routes. Not the sanctuaries our enemies would anticipate. There, they would find refugees from Wilusa-but they would not find us. No, I would find a place where they'd never think to look.

Five days later after a grueling trek off the route Hektor had carefully marked out for us to follow. Seraphinus and Alexios had questioned my sanity. Their questions kept me warm through the unknown and now the perfect safe house was up on the rise ahead of us. The villa stood in slight disrepair when I first found it, nestled on the border between Thrace and Macedonia. Its walls, weathered by time, bore the weight of forgotten stories, but its foundation was strong-solid enough to shape into something of our own. Sliding off my horse, I thrust the reins into Alexios's waiting hand leaving him and ignoring Seraphinus's warning rumbles before striding across the courtyard. Hope bubbling up inside my chest. Then, I see it-embedded in the dust-laden tile mosaic at my feet. Our symbol. A phoenix. It was meant to be. A quiet omen, a whispered decree from the gods themselves. The goddess had spoken. This would be our safe house.

'Lady Althea. What is this place?' Alexios's voice is quiet but firm, his golden eyes scanning the shadows, searching for the dangers hidden in the dim light. He has followed me inside, his presence a silent challenge. Always watchful, always assessing. Waiting-for what, exactly? I meet his gaze, my tone steady. 'This-this is something I wish to keep secret.' I level him with a stern look. 'From my sisters. From Theron. If you cannot keep this between us, I suggest you wait with the horses.' The sharp edge in my voice unsettles me. I don't like the harshness, don't like the weight of command that has woven itself into my words. But survival has already come with too many costs. If the time comes when my sisters need this place, I want it to be an answer-not another uncertainty. Alexios exhales, his expression unreadable as he leans against the wall beside the doors leading into the atrium. Folding his arms across his chest, he watches me carefully. 'Don't be long,' he murmurs. 'Seraphinus will become suspicious and leave the horses to tend to themselves. Maybe, one day, I'll be able to earn your trust, my lady.'

'I see you like my house.'

Alexios draws his sword and sweeps me behind him in one motion.

She steps into the light. Hands raised in the universal gesture for peace. 'I was loading the last of my belongings on the cart out the back with my sons. Put that sword away sonny. I am no threat to your Lady.'

Alexios sheathes his sword watching as I begin bargaining for a sound price. This is the place the goddess has meant for us to hide. I can feel it deep in my bones. Gold exchanges hands as I purchase the safe house just as Seraphinus turns his attention back to us. A muscle ticks along his jawline, his stormy blue eyes locking onto mine-a silent warning that I may have some explaining to do. For now, he remains silent. I do not want to be untruthful with the ones that Theron has assigned as my protectors. I do not want to hold this secret close to my chest. But secrets have a way of escaping when you least expect them to.

'What will you use this place for?' The wife of the previous owner asks, her eyes brimming with memories-of raising her children, weaving cloth, of long winter nights by the fire in silent companionship with her husband, now passed. I clutch the deed to my chest, my voice soft but certain. 'We will turn it into a place of learning, perhaps for young ladies, so that they might know letters and numbers as well as wifely duties.' Relief washes over me, overwhelming in its quiet intensity. My knees threaten to buckle, but Alexios presses close, steadying me, holding me upright as he sees the woman off with polite words. 'You did well.' He reassures me, his voice low and warm. Then, with a hint of amusement, he entreats, 'Come and sit down, my lady, before I am forced to carry you.'

Seraphinus holds out a flask, his grip tight, his expression brooding. He is angry-even if he does not voice it. 'If I explain, 'I begin tentatively, untangling the web of thoughts in my mind, 'you must keep this to yourselves. It is so sensitive that even telepathic conversation about it is dangerous.' Seraphinus remains silent, patient. Waiting. I inhale deeply. 'Wilusa will not hold forever. We need a place to retreat to, should the worst happen-somewhere where our enemies will never think to find us.' I wave a hand vaguely in the direction of the villa. 'We may set up a school as our cover, but the House of the Phoenix's true purpose will be as a safe haven for us.'

Alexios steps closer, his golden eyes locking on to mine. The concern in his gaze remains, but there's something else-an intensity I can't decipher. 'We should stay the night.' he states firmly. It is not a suggestion, not a simple agreement. It feels like something more. Why does his voice sound heavier than before? Why does my stomach twist at the certainty in his tone? Seraphinus, lounging against the low stone wall, smirks-but there's a flicker beneath the humour. He sees something too. Not the weight of negotiations, but...something else. 'A night's rest won't kill us.' he remarks, voice easy, teasing. Then his gaze flicks toward Alexios. 'Besides, he looks ready to put you to bed himself. 'His words hang between them-between us-charged with something I do not understand. They exchange another glance, unreadable to me but thick with meaning. What am I missing? My brain spins, cycling through possibilities, searching for answers that will not reveal themselves. It's not just exhaustion, the weight of the negotiations have certainly taken their toll on me. There is something else clawing deep inside of me, something I cannot name. Alexios interrupts my thoughts before they spiral too far.

'Come, little dove. 'His voice is steady, but his expression-his expression-

It is full of something I cannot quite grasp

'Show me this villa that you have just bought.'

The Lesson of Steel

(Thea)

We had camped in the foothills of Mount Ida. Wilusa lay two days' ride ahead, and I was looking forward to getting back to my patients. In the soft, golden hush of dawn, Alexios approached, holding out the dun-coloured robe they had insisted I wear when we left Wilusa. 'Wrap this around yourself, make sure your hair is covered, little dove.' I reached for the robe without question and swirled it around my shoulders. Alexios adjusted the hood over my hair, fingers lingering for half a second too long, his golden gaze carrying a restless urgency he had not been exhibiting over breakfast. Seraphinus sat by the fire, his posture deceptively relaxed. The flickering flames casting restless shadows across his robe-the same dun shade as mine. His gaze swept across the horizon-searching. A sudden glint caught the corner of my eye-steel flashing in the morning light. I met his gaze, my silent question unspoken but urgent. Breaking the calm was the twang of a bow string and a low curse word. Alexios joins us pressing in on my other side. Without hesitation, he placed a firm hand on my arm. 'We're about to have company. Stay calm. *Stay closed.*'

The arrow hissed through the air, its path unyielding, a streak of death cutting toward me. At the last moment, Alexios caught me-his grip firm, his movements swift-and spun me out of danger. The arrow buried itself in the dirt, trembling in the spot where I had sat just seconds earlier. The message was clear. We were under attack.

'Dragons of Thera. We know you travel with a priestess from Wilusa.'

'Should we count you as traitors to the cause?' a second voice shouted.

'I know that voice,' Seraphinus muttered, wincing at Alexios's raised eyebrow, 'A drinking buddy of mine-one of Menelaus's men. He goes by Isandros.' Alexios didn't react immediately. His gaze slid my way, a silent check-reassuring himself that I was safe, at least for now. 'There are two of us.' Seraphinus state quietly. 'Two of us are enough.' Alexios agreed before turning to me, 'When we tell you to run, little dove, you do not hesitate. You do not stop. You do not look back. We will find you when it's over.' A quiet promise that no harm would reach me if he could help it. And goddess help me-I believed him.

Something rippled beneath the skin on his forearm. A shimmer of green scales catches my eye-just enough for me to grasp what is happening. 'Do not be afraid, little dove.' he reminds me. 'You must be brave now.' *Run.* The word explodes through my mind, obliterating my thoughts, shattering every barrier I have built, triggering my own transformation for self protection. No. Selene's command shackled my innate desire for safety. We were never to reveal our other form in the presence of humans. Her words had been more than a command-they were an oath, whispered to the goddess in prayer. It was too late. Oh goddess-I was trapped between forms, caught in a transformation that my Queen had expressly forbidden. I was grateful for the robe Alexios had insisted I wear, as it covered most of my transformation. Feathers swept across my face, forming an elaborate half-mask from the bridge of my nose into my hairline. There was no hiding my face-no concealing the fact that one eye glowed far brighter than the other.

'Monster!' Seraphinus bares his teeth-elongating, sharpening into something no longer human.

'Abomination!' Alexios sheds his robe, caught in the inescapable space between man and beast.

'Kill the beast!' Voices rose sharp in anger and immediate judgement. Using my sensitive hearing, I realise we are completely surrounded. Completely surrounded.

They creep on their bellies-these humans...these monsters claiming that one species is preferable to another. I cannot move. One foot and one claw. Neither half moves in harmony, each part resisting each other. The attack unfolds before me, its patterns rising like spectral threads in the air shifting into swirling hues, dipping and dancing in a chaotic battle hymn. Steel-a silver streak in slow motion. Until the electricity of the battlefield hums a silent symphony meant for my ears alone.

An emerald-scaled arm snakes around my middle, pulling me close. Tucking me under his belly, Alexios crouches over me. He stands his ground, holding true to his oath of protection.

'I told you to run.'

His mind voice rumbles, raw and unrestrained.

'I find you half in flight, little dove. Are you trying to give me a heart attack?'

I do not understand why I can hear him inside my mind. No matter how hard I try, I cannot send words back to him. If words will not suffice, perhaps I can send him snapshots-fragments of what I saw. 'You saw it coming,' he murmurs. His breath washes over me, hot and close. 'You saw their movements. *But you didn't move.*'

A snap of teeth, a tremor shaking the earth-a thunderous roar that leaves my ears ringing. I curl into myself, as small as possible, pressing against the earth. A flash of red and gold scales-then blood. A severed leg dangles from Seraphinus's lips. A wail of disbelief tears through the clearing-agonizing and raw. 'You monstrous bastard!' Isandros tears at his hair. 'You just ate my brother!'

'You are nothing....no you are less than nothing!' Isandros screams.

'I have never been nothing.' Seraphinus's dragons voice is chilling. 'I am blood of the dragons. We are of clan Thera, and we protect those that cannot protect themselves.'

'You have no creed-no conscience and fight for the highest payer. You pretend to be respectable but you are nothing but a sell sword.' Alexios added. 'Run away, little sell-sword, before I eat you to break my fast.'

Sitting up as gracefully as possible underneath Alexios, I peer around his forelegs, regarding their target with wide eyes. He has collapsed to his knees, trembling in terror. He looks ready to tattle to any who will listen. He looks like he needs a few harsh truths knocked into him.

Finally finding my voice, I say, 'Do try to tell your kings about what you have seen. They willingly made a binding oath with the ancestors of the Dragons of Thera. They already knew who was sharing the beach with you. This world is much larger than your mind perceives, perhaps you should open your eyes and really see what is around you.'

The sensation of feathers rubbing beneath my skin is beyond irritating. Pinprick beads of blood form along my exposed arm and muscles strain for dominance over my avian half. Trying to calm my breathing I know I cannot stay like this. Alexios's golden eyes regard me thoughtfully as realisation dawns. He shifts slightly, leaving me exposed. We have no time for Isandros and his theatrics now. 'You need to transition back before you lose yourself between your halves.' Seraphinus steps in front of me, his blood-soaked robe clinging to him, irritation melting into concern. Still covered in scales, Alexios kneels, pressing a steady hand against my shoulder, grounding me. 'Breathe slowly,' he instructs. 'You're not trapped-you just need to find the balance. Focus only on your desire to return to your human form. Picture your body as it should be-whole, steady, unchanged. Hold that image. Breathe deeply.'

The phoenix half of me dissolves, retreating, until only my human form remains. The feathers vanish and the glow dims. I am human again, but the ache of failure lingers. Raya always worried that this would happen and I am left shaken, raw-betrayed by my own mind when I needed it most. Where my shifter guards saw danger, I saw beauty in the colours and symmetry in the patterns in the attack formations used by the Greeks-leaving me helpless with no way to protect myself. Shame sweeps over me, my cheeks flush as I sit up in the silence that descends upon the three of us. Alexios unsheathes a knife that he wears on his belt and hands it to me. 'You don't have to be a fighter,' he says. 'But you need to know how to live through a battle.'

I have held blades to heal and I do not like how this blade fits my hand. My fingers adjust as if I were holding one of my instruments, not a weapon. The blade shifts awkwardly in my grasp, its weight steeped in violent emotion-a force I can feel but do not understand. It's too heavy. Too cold. I shiver as the lingering embrace of Alexios, anger envelops me. This isn't right-this isn't who I am. I know how to cut-with precision, with control, with purpose. I save lives. This is not my blade. It was never meant to be held by someone like me. I don't like this at all. My eyes sweep the space where Isandros soiled himself. He was gone. I did not like that he was out there. Grief had a way of twisting up a person's perspective and cowards like him planned carefully.

Seraphinus has gone to break camp, while Alexios lingers, his gaze steady as I struggle to find my place with the knife. He does not intervene-does not offer correction, as he would with a soldier under his command. Instead, he waits-watching. He lets me struggle-not just with the knife, but with its purpose, its meaning. He lets the truth settle, gives me space to understand what survival will one day demand. Could I carry the weight of it-the blood, the consequence, the irreversible mark it would leave on my soul?

'I have never met someone so brilliant and so unprepared at the same time.' His expression is a blend of fascination and exasperation. 'I prefer my battles to be won before swords are drawn. Less work for me that way.' The knife remains foreign in my grasp, an intruder rather than an extension of my arm. He nods, recognising that I have a healer's mindset. A mindset that could not be easily broken in a single knife lesson. 'At least let me show you how to hold this knife correctly.' He steps behind me, close-closer than my own shadow. His fingers adjust my grip, shifting it from healer's precision to warrior's necessity. But a scalpel can also be a weapon when used in the wrong hands. The way I now hold the blade feels more natural. He moves with me guiding my hand through a sequence of fluid motions-each one deliberate, precise. He repeats the movements until I understand their purpose, until they become natural-until I no longer hesitate. I refine each motion, shaping them into something real, something undeniable. They become instinct-etched into muscle, woven into a new mindset.

Alexios still watches me practice, his gaze weighted with something I cannot name. He does not see me as fragile, as incapable. But he knows-I am no killer. Yet, I am not helpless. A silent understanding passes between us-one that may never be spoken aloud.

I don't need to be a warrior. *But I must be something more than what I have been.*

But am I his to protect?

Tucking the knife into my belt. I know that steel will never be my first choice. It would be my last resort. Alexios exhales, his voice quieter this time. 'You will not always be shielded,' he tells me a truth I have learned the hard way, 'But you will not be alone, either.'

'You cannot be with me at all times.' I wonder what he is trying to say to me. We are not bonded soul mates-not yet. If we were, I would hear him beyond words, feel him as if he were a part of me. But the connection remains out of reach, lingering on the edges of something greater. He doesn't argue. Doesn't tell me I'm wrong. He only watches, as if waiting-waiting for something neither of us can touch, something neither of us can name.

'No, I cannot be with you at all times.' His tone is measured, reassuring in a way that I do not understand. 'But that does not mean you will ever stand alone.' I cannot sense his emotions-not the way I wish I could, not the way I should be able to. But that does not matter. Not yet. Alexios stands before me, a silent guardian, unwavering. But the distance lingers between us-not something that is able to be measured but something far greater, something not yet fully formed.

I almost believe him-almost. But belief is not protection. Not when kingdoms conspire in shadowed hallways.

Collusion

Collusion

(Helena)

The shadows of the palace flickered in the torchlight as I moved silently through the corridors. Overlooked. Forgotten. But no longer-I would change the course of fate itself. Selene's rising influence grated on me-I needed an ally to execute my scheme. Crinos, simmering with jealousy and discontent, was the perfect pawn-just waiting to be moulded into something useful.

Earlier that morning, I had carefully extricated myself from Alexander's embrace. Alexander was a devoted lover, too perceptive for carelessness. It took every ounce of my cunning to slip away unnoticed. I glanced at our sleeping child, nestled in the arms of a trusted nursemaid, before slipping silently from the room. Though I cared for my family, my ambition would not be silenced. My duty to the crown could no longer be ignored.

I found Crinos in the stables, tending to her favorite horse. The scent of hay and damp earth filled the air-a stark contrast to the perfumed corridors of the palace. Her small braids, adorned with delicate, brightly coloured feathers, swayed as she moved-a silent testament of her Amazonian heritage. Her fearlessness unsettled me-the confidence, the freedom Queen Hekuba indulged in her was nothing short of scandalous. At her age, I had already married and borne two children. Freedom was never given to women like me-it was carefully measured, controlled. But she? She was Amazonian born, shaped by a world that did not bow to men.

I wrinkled my nose, displeasure curling through me as I approached. My dress-delicate, embroidered, weighted with beads-stood in stark contrast to Crinos's riding attire: leather trousers and a corset that left far too much of her exposed for all to see. She wore her freedom like armour. We each carried our own weapons-shaped by the hand the gods had dealt us.

'Crinos,' I called softly, my voice honeyed with false sincerity, soft but deliberate. 'I've been thinking... about our place in this palace.'

Crinos glanced up from brushing her horse, eyes narrowing with suspicion. 'What do you mean, Helena?'

'Selene's influence is growing,' I continued, I stepped closer, ignoring the stench of the stables. 'And where does that leave us? Drowning in her shadow. But it doesn't have to be that way. We could change things. Together.'

Curiousity warred with resentment in Crinos's gaze. 'What are you suggesting?'

I smiled, sharp and knowing, calculation flickering behind my gaze. 'If Selene were to be... removed, we would no longer be forced to the sidelines. We could claim power-the influence-we deserve.'

Crinos hesitated, doubt and desire taking root beneath her composure. 'How would we even do that?'

'Leave that to me,' I murmured, letting the weight of my certainty settle between us. 'We tried once before-the poison failed. This time we take no chances. At the next truce, we meet with someone who can make this happen. Someone who has just as much to gain from Selene's downfall.'

I leaned in closer to Crinos. 'Alexander let it slip that Hektor suspects Selene is pregnant.' Whether this was true or not didn't matter.

Palace gossip such as this tidbit would only drive Crinos further into my machinations.

Crinos's stilled. Then, slowly, her grip on the reins tightened, jealousy flaring in the sharpness of her indrawn breath. 'Then we have no time to waste.'

Despite her words, hesitation flickered in her eyes. Crinos had been brought up with the code of the Amazons, valuing honor and bravery. She was beginning to tire of my manipulations-a reluctance I needed to quash before it took root.

Beneath the fragile shield of peace, Crinos and I slipped toward the grove of Thymbraean Apollo. The grove was neutral ground-Greek and Trojan soldiers milled together, exchanging wary glances, forced smiles, and unspoken grievances.

I led Crinos into the darkened grove, where shadows curled and a figure waited-patient, expectant, dangerous. "Isandros," I murmured, letting my voice dip low-conspiratorial, deliberate. 'Thank you for meeting us.'

Isandros emerged from the shadows, his expression unreadable, yet undeniably intrigued. 'What do you want, my queen?' Curious. He usually had his brother with him. Perhaps he had died on the battlefield. No matter. He had never had a part to play in my plans.

I smiled, satisfaction curling at the edges of my lips. I knew Isandros from Sparta and was well aware of his disdain for the shifters of Thera. 'We have a proposition,' I said smoothly. 'Selene of Emberis is a threat to both of us. We need her... gone. If you help us, Troy will be destabilized from within, making it easier for you to conquer.'

Isandros's eyes gleamed with interest. 'And what do you gain from this?'

I cast a glance at Crinos, then back to Isandros. 'Power. Influence. Selene is the obstacle between us and what we are owed. Help us eliminate her, and Troy will be yours for the taking.'

Isandros weighed the offer, his gaze sharp, calculating. Then, slowly, he nodded. 'Very well. I'll provide the means to carry out the assassination. But make no mistake, my queen-failure will cost you more than you can afford.' There was something he was hiding from us. Something that might have a bearing on this conversation should we fail. We weren't going to fail.

I smiled, my eyes glinting with cold determination. 'We won't fail. But Isandros-have you considered seeking the gods' blessing as a way to level the field? Perhaps they could grant you the same gifts as the shifters. Imagine-your own power, matching theirs. That would certainly make things...interesting.'

Isandros's eyes narrowed thoughtfully. 'A compelling notion, my queen. I shall seek the gods' favour. With their blessing, our victory will be assured.' He paused, a smirk playing on his lips. 'And my Queen-one more thing. By blood, Lady Selene is the eldest surviving royal of the coup in Emberis. You should call her Queen, whether you like it or not.'

The mere thought of Selene-a nobody-being spoken of in the same breath as a high born sent fury rippling through me. 'Thank you for the information, Isandros. Rest assured, we'll give her the respect she deserves.'

Crinos was silent as we walked, but her silence spoke volumes. 'Helena,' her voice was low, hesitant. 'This goes against everything I was taught as an Amazon. I don't like sinking so low to see the results we desire.'

I turned to her, my eyes hard. 'Crinos, power and influence demands sacrifice. If you hesitate now, you'll never rise beyond what you are. When Selene falls, the throne will not longer be hers to claim-only ours.'

'What of Andromache?' Crinos ventures, her tone careful, measured. 'What of Andromache?' I echo, my tone dry, almost amused. 'Surely you've seen it-how Hektor's eyes stray, how his attention shifts. His second wife holds him far more than his first wife ever will. Maybe his loyalty is fracturing-only time will tell.'

Crinos sighed nodding reluctantly. Doubt lingered in her eyes, but for now, she remained by my side.

I couldn't help but recall how just a few days ago, I had watched Selene's priestesses handing out grain in the square. The square had brimmed with movement, with voices lifted in praise for Selene. They treated her priestesses as saviours, their hands outstretched for grain that should have come from me. I watched them, fury curling beneath my skin-their eager hands, their grateful murmurs, their loyalty wasted on her. Not me. Never me. How could they favour a nobody like Selene over me?'

Selene would fall, and Andromache soon after-her squalling newborn nothing more than an obstacle. With them gone, my child would take his rightful place as King of Troy. Crinos would take the fall, and with her gone, I would finally stand at the centre of the court's gaze-where I was always meant to be. My mind raced, electric with the possibilities-the sheer thrill of power so close I could taste it.

My conspirators melted into the shadows, our plans already in motion, leaving whispers of treachery in their wake. Selene's fall would clear the path. With her gone, Crinos and I would rewrite Troy's future, shaping it in our own image.

Greece would grow bored with a war she could not win. Allies were already sending missives to the Palace promising to send warriors to fight alongside the trojan army. Either way-I would survive.

Anticipation coiled in my chest as I stepped through the palace doors, the air thick with the scent of victory. I would play my part to absolute perfection, weaving the court in my hands, bending them to my will. Selene's fall would mark the rise of something greater-me.

First Blood

First Blood

(Nuraya)

My sister had been given the title of the Moon of Troy in the Megaron by King Priam. He saw her dark, radiant beauty as the direct opposite of Lady Helena's golden glow. She was not untouchable but her presence cast long shadows, and I had learned to move within them, unseen but never idle.

The message she entrusted me with for Theron tucked inside my robes rustled, reminding me of my mission.

We knew that the shifters camp was hidden within the outer caves of the tunnel system that riddled the subterranean level beneath Wilusa. No one simply wandered into a dragon shifter's domain unannounced. To do so was to invite disaster. That was more than reckless - it was a violation of an unspoken law.

The moon provided a guiding light as I made my way toward the cave entrance.

Silence stretched between the flickering Greek campfires and the restless whisper of wind through brittle leaves. My heart pounded with a mix of fear and determination; failure was unthinkable. Heavens, the cold was relentless tonight. The cold clawed through my thin cloak, its bite merciless.

I hurried onward, vanishing into the hush of the night. I couldn't be caught outside the walls after first light, or Selene would be in danger from every warrior within a thousand schoinos. As if the dangers within Wilusa weren't already enough.

I hadn't figured out which high-born harlot had conspired against her - not once, but twice. But I would. Sooner or later, a breadcrumb of truth would land in my grasp. And when it did, I would not miss it.

'It is not safe for you to travel the killing fields without an escort.' A voice, edged with amusement, rumbled behind me. The air shifted, warming my frozen body, it carried a faint scent of scorched earth on the breeze. Only the blood of the dragons carried that kind of heat.

I did not turn. I did not need to. I knew who walked beside me.

'Who told you I required one?'

I kept my gaze forward, steps steady.

'Tonight you will walk beside me, dragon kin of Thera. Whether you wish to or not. I must reach the cave encampment and speak with the Tiarna Draíochta. Ravens cannot be relied upon to reach him unharmed. It takes but one Greek soldier to intercept our feathered friend to expose our alliance to ears that do not need to hear of it. I must return before the sun's first light touches the sands.'

I chanced a glance behind me and a blond dragon shifter stood there. Seraphinus. A flicker of confusion crossed his rugged features, barely disrupting the mask of discipline. He hadn't expected me. Good.

He was Theron's second in command - I knew that much. I didn't need introductions. Thea's report had been thorough, and my memory was sharper than most.

I knew who he was. And I knew what I needed from him. The deadline I'd set wasn't ceremonial. It was survival.

Seraphinus had made himself part of that equation.

'How do you know you can trust me?' he challenged, sweeping back my hood to reveal the face a woman with the sharp lines of a warrior's resolve.

'Red hair,' he flung the words into the night like a casual barter - no hesitation, no thought. 'Fiery nature, most likely.'

I endured his scrutiny, allowing him to circle me - my senses sharp, my stance unwavering. The night air was crisp, carrying the distant crackle of Greek campfires, the restless whisper of leaves stirring in the wind. I pinned him with a steely glare. 'You're the one who keeps company with Phoenix kind, aren't you?'

I let him play his game. His slow circling that moved in tight arcs around me testing my boundaries. My senses roared their warning. I did not indulge lightly. I allowed his dominance - but only just.

My words struck their mark - his rapid movements stilled, hesitation flickering in his stance. My opening had arrived. With a swift, low kick, I took his feet from beneath him. Between one breath and the next, my blade pressed against his throat. Dragon kind or not, I was not so easily swayed by misplaced faith-not like my sisters.

I watched warily, scanning for any further challenge from every direction. Five more beats passed before I allowed him to rise. His eyes flickered - surprise laced with a hint of respect-as he stood. I did not falter.

Raising my hood, I melted into the night but not completely. The moon caught the edge of my cloak, just enough for him to follow. Just enough to remind him that I was still in control.

I knew he had followed me through pitch black tunnels on Thera as I walked under the mountains. We had been children. We had been playing at war. He knew the way I moved. He would find me if I was walking into danger. *He would eventually remember who it was who he had been challenging.*

He blocked my path across the sand yet again before murmuring softly, 'Not that way, my Lady-you tread a path that leads straight to the Spartans.' The teasing flicker in his expression hardened, replaced by something colder-something unyielding, etched in certainty. His steel blue eyes flicked toward me, measuring the weight of my words before he added, 'Your sister's game is a perilous one, sending you into the lion's den. If your mate is near, he won't let you carry the Tiarna Draíochta's answer back to her.'

His words struck a long forgotten yearning in my heart. Deeply buried under layers of duty to the crown.

If my mate was near, then this mission had just become far more dangerous. I did not have time to contend with a mate who came with expectations. My loyalty lay with my sisters. While I longed for love - dragon kind were fiercely protective of their mates. No female served in their armies. It was unheard of for one to risk their life the way I was prepared to risk mine.

'I must.' The intensity in his gaze chipped away at my resolve-just slightly. 'I have no need for recognition before the gods of man, nor to be remembered for my role in this tragedy. If my mate finds me, I will be protected. But my sisters-they need the certainty this night will bring a safeguard for the days ahead.'

With deliberate precision, I slid my dagger into its scabbard, the weight of steel grounding me.

'Ask Theron of Thera why he chose me as his emissary-why he placed me between Princess Selene and himself.'

He exhales sharply, shaking his head-but there's no real frustration in the movement. Instead, there's something else-something unsettled.

I hear him in my mind with crystal clear clarity, *'Your mate will protect you? You mean me.'* The words slip out, deliberate but heavy with unspoken meaning.

He studies me for a moment, something shifting behind his gaze-realisation, hesitation, inevitability. *'And tell me, little flame-what happens when I'm not there?'*

Not a challenge. Not a taunt. A genuine question. One he's not sure he wants answered. 'You are either very brave,' he concedes aloud, 'or very foolish. I haven't decided which yet.' His eyes search mine, looking for confirmation of what we both already know. I won't give up my mission. He won't push me to stay.

'You will find me close to the part of the wall near the tower your sisters sleep in when you need escort to our encampment.' A promise. Not forced, not demanded-but spoken as if were always meant to be.

'I will personally see you safe back to your sister.' And whether it's duty or instinct, it no longer matters. Because it is already decided.

'You will stand watch over us personally?'

It felt like too much. Too soon. I could not let my new mate side track me and yet I did not want to be separated from him now that I had just found him.

He doesn't react immediately. His jaw tightens as his gaze moves across my face, weighing my words as if trying to understand exactly what it is I am asking, trying to divine my feelings through my words.

'I will stand watch.'

His words are firm but quiet-final, as if the decision has already been made. He lets out a slow breath, breaking the tension just slightly. 'Tend to your mission. I will see you safe back to your sister-Nuraya of Emberis.' I feel the weight of his command wrapped in his casual use of my name. A part of me wanted to trust him, but another part screamed that I was losing control of the situation. Control I couldn't afford to surrender-not yet.

'Nuraya of Emberis... and of Thera'

His mental voice wraps itself around my soul filling the empty spaces inside of me. Warming in a way that I never thought I'd ever feel.

'Raya.' I murmured softly, the name slipping from my lips-the first fragile surrender to the bond.

'Finn, 'he answered, his voice carrying the weight of something unspoken. 'Only you may call me this. Only when we're alone, little flame.'

His warmth seeps into my skin, a quiet claim.

His breath ghosts over my ear, voice dropping half an octave in quiet reverence, 'Do not fear the bond, Raya. Do not fear me. Do not fear what we could become.'

War raged around us, but it wasn't the bond I feared. I feared losing him before we even had a chance to begin.

Under Finn's guidance, we reached the entrance to the cave system, hidden within an illusion woven with the threads of ancient draconian magic. The rock face loomed, unyielding. Its surface untouched by time-yet Finn strode forward, as if sensing a hidden path woven into its core, passing through the illusion as though it were mere mist. Finn beckoned me forward, his gaze steady, unwavering. I inhaled sharply, bracing myself, and stepped through, feeling a brief, tingling sensation-a whisper of magic-skating across my skin as I crossed the threshold.

I shook off an involuntary shiver as the brief iciness of the magic washed over me. Inside, the cave shimmered with the ethereal glow of embedded crystals, their charge humming softly as they illuminated the path ahead. As we ventured deeper into the cave, the air grew warmer, the oppressive chill of the night fading away. Intricate carvings and ancient runes sprawled across the walls-testaments to the dragons' long history and their sacred bond to these caves. The gods had once walked these paths. The priestess in me longed to pause, to unravel the mysteries-to pay my obeisance before stepping deeper into a place weighted with power and an enigma that seemed to resonate with the very earth itself. Faint, ghostly remnants of an ancient language linger at the fringes of my hearing. A shiver runs through me as I wonder-had we awakened something that should have remained undisturbed?

Seraphinus guided me into a vast chamber, where a group of shifters stood waiting. Their gazes flicker toward him, registering the quiet challenge in his stance-the hand resting on his sword hilt. Some hesitated, smirking at him-eyes flicking over me with cool dismissal. Without a word, they step aside, parting to grant passage to the secondary chamber. This chamber resonates with the distant hum of shifting magic. I sink into a deep ceremonial curtsey, head bowed, watching from beneath my eyelashes-silent, waiting. With a single, weighted glance, Finn steps away, leaving me with Theron. Their silent exchange crackles with meaning, heavy with something unspoken. A King in a cave is still King. The rules do not bend for circumstance. One must always obey the niceties. I could still hear my mother's voice instructing me in courtly ways even now. I would not rise until Theron gave me leave to.

'Rise, Lady Raya. What tidings do you bring from Wilusa?' Theron's voice rings out, commanding-formal. Then, his tone softens, a quiet thread of something more urgent slipping through, 'What news of Selene?'

'Selene is well,' I begin carefully. 'She is with child again - and she begs that you spare the father's life.' I weigh my words against the storm in his expression before adding, softer now. 'She is married to another,' I remind him gently. 'You swore you would not intervene-not yet, Theron.' His expression remains unreadable, offering me no anchor-so I shift to the message from Wilusa. 'Prince Hektor assures me that the network is now in place and the first group of refugees are ready to smuggle from the city. They travel light-one bundle of survival wrapped in cloth, the weight of their flight resting in trembling hands. You have Hektor's permission to infiltrate the city for the next 24 hours to move previous inhabitants of lower town to the temple at Alexandria Troas.'

'We have located the second ancient relic-an artifact binding us to our oath with the Greek kings. It would be wise to delay the first mission until it is retrieved, preventing any further misunderstanding between Prince Hektor and myself.' His mask fractures, fatigue seeping through the edges-a man worn thin by too many impossible choices. For a fleeting moment, the weight of command cracks, revealing the toll it has taken. 'A private message to your sister-do not fear for the life of your child's father. His fate is beyond my power to decide.'

Hesitating for a moment, the words stick in my throat-I feel the need to thank him for Thea's safe return. His head remains bent over his rough-hewn table, his mind already occupied with the next problem. The lines around his eyes have deepened, shadows forming beneath them. Still his voice remains steady as he asks, 'Is there something else you wish to discuss, my lady?' 'My sister, Althea, credits her survival to the guards you assigned her. She asks that you thank Alexios for the blade lesson and assure him she practices daily.' I force the words out, steadying myself before adding, 'Forgive my intrusion, but Selene will ask-are you quite well Theron?'

Surprise flickers across his face-eyes widening, like a man caught off guard by an unexpected kindness. He hadn't expected me to notice. His features harden, then ease into something unreadable. His usual stoicism wavers, only for a breath. Details are my business, and so is the welfare of my family. Technically, he was family too. His voice is measured, but laced with quiet defiance: 'We are planning to sever ties with the Greek kings. They guard their ancient relic with religious zeal, never grasping its true value. Its twin is buried behind layers of deception and deadly entrapments. The risks are high-physically, politically-but not insurmountable.' The edge in his voice softens, but his words remain sharp. This isn't sentiment. This is strategy. 'I cannot afford to appear weak before the shifters in the next cave. Their trust is fragile and I cannot let them believe they hold power over me.' A beat of silence. Then, something quieter slips through the cracks. 'But...thank you for asking about my welfare.'

A deep curtsy, measured and deliberate. He waves me off, his attention already shifting to the next battle ahead. Seraphinus steps forward, his presence a silent promise of safe passage. No words pass between us-only the weight of duty. Finn pulls my hood securely over my fiery hair, his grip firm, protective. A final gesture before we step into the night. 'We do not stop until we are inside the walls of Wilusa.' His voice is low, edged with urgency. A pause-then a warning: 'The Greek army is preparing to take the field for the day.' The weight of his words settles over us like a coming storm. The journey back is swift. We move like ghosts, silent, unseen. The landscape a shifting maze of danger and refuge. Every step is calculated, every breath measured.

The wall looms before us, silent and steady-a familiar boundary between war and refuge. Finn halts, turning to face me, his presence like a stone, unyielding. There is something ancient in his stance, something that has endured far beyond battles and time. His voice is low, firm-more vow than request: 'I will watch this wall for you should you need a guide in the future.'

His expression darkens, stoic, save for the quiet promise woven between his words, 'I will be displeased if you do not call for me, little flame.' The weight of his next words settles into my bones-meant for me alone: 'I have waited a lifetime for you and would see you safe.' The air between us hums with something unspoken, something inevitable. And then, just like that, the moment passes.

A slow nod, deliberate, unwavering. I expect nothing less than his complete attention-his devotion is a certainty, not a question. A soul bound to the right person is a rare and beautiful sight. And he is bound-to me, to this moment, to something neither of us can name. His touch is barely there, a whisper of warmth against my forehead. A fleeting promise, a silent vow. Then, like mist dissolving into the night, he fades. The shadows swallow him whole, but I know he is watching. I turn toward the palace complex. His presence lingers, unseen but undeniable.

Prince Hektor's voice is sharp, cutting through the air like a blade. Lady Helena stands rigid beneath his fury, caught between two worlds, neither fully hers. Troy burns because of a woman who cannot decide where her heart belongs. The weight of war rests on fickle shoulders, and the city pays the price. Watching from inside the forge where my weapons are being made, mostly hidden by tools larger than me, I catch snatches of the conversation where he pleads with her not to do what he thinks she's about to. Troy is committed to the fight with Greece and if Helena returns to Menelaus - Greece will still wipe Wilusa off the map. He reminds her that Alexander goes to fight for her that same day and tells her to go back to the palace where she belongs.

The sun hangs high, scorching the sand as Prince Alexander steps forward. The sword of Troy gleams in his grip, but his hands tremble-too young, too untested. King Menelaus stands opposite him a warrior carved from war itself. His stance is steady, his gaze unwavering. He has seen too many battles to fear this one. Alexander falters, his courage slipping like sand through his fingers. The weight of love, of duty, of expectation presses down, suffocating. Menelaus does not hesitate. He moves with the precision of a man who has already won, Alexander-poor fool, hopelessly ensnared by a woman who was never truly his-stands no chance.

Retrieving the Amulet

Retrieving the Amulet

(Theron)

I had chosen two teams for two different missions. One goal-retrieve the relics. Newly bonded, Seraphinus would stand watch over the phoenix sisters while we went to ground. He was balancing his naturally protective nature against a female who had been raised to protect others. I did not envy my brother.

For all my oaths I had made to Selene and Hektor, I yearned for the other half of my soul. Her absence was an enduring dull ache that never seemed to ease. His mind was struggling with his decision to let Lady Nuraya go back to Wilusa. Tradition and necessity were the opposite sides of a conundrum we shared together. He stood within the shadows against the cave wall, arms crossed, his gaze sharp and assessing-silent, but ever watchful. Always poised to act, should I give the word.

The team to the left preparing to go into the midday sun was highly skilled in infiltration camouflage. The team to my right was graceful on their feet, quick thinking and could fight in the darkest cavern with no light. Each team chosen for what the mission demanded based on skill not clan allegiance.

'Do not-under any circumstances-touch the relics with your bare claws. If you are not soul-bonded to the one who holds the other half, your mind will tear free of your body-untethered, lost, and beyond salvation. Without a tether, madness will consume you. A fate worse than death-one from which no soul returns. I will not put a shifter down for carelessness-but I will not watch one unravel either. Should this fate claim you, you will answer to Seraphinus.' I meet each set of eyes in turn, 'We move swiftly and silently. Tunnel team-the ancients were wily creatures; we must be prepared for anything. Beach team-the Greek kings rarely leave the relic unattended. Your window is brief-take the relic and vanish before our advantage is lost.'

'My mate is in the tower, along with yours-and I suspect Alexios's.' Seraphinus spoke gently, knowing what I wish to say. 'I will protect the heart of our existence with my life.' mind focused on the relics I answer his vow with a silent chin lift, then turn to lead the tunnel team from the room toward the sinkhole in a distant passage.

The temperature plummets until we can see our breath as clouds of white mist hanging in the air in front of us. The tunnels are wide enough for our animal forms to trek comfortably in single file. I suspect the ancient ones designed them this way. Funnelling us toward fate. Toward destiny. Toward the edge of the abyss-forcing us to shift forms to descend into the obsidian unknown. We found purchase on the rock face using our claws and tails. This climb is fraught with danger, each movement a battle against treacherous footing. Patches of damp moss, slippery with ice, catch us all and through the thick shadows I can hear the strong flapping of wings flaring out occasionally to steady someone's descent. A weak stone outcrop crumbles -a roar of frustration echoes as claws scramble for the next hold. One by one, we land at the bottom, surrounded by the same glowing runes humming with the ancient magic that fills the air, illuminating the carvings on the walls topside. This was a well designed trap for any not born of dragonkind.

As we moved deeper into the labyrinth, an unsettling sense of anticipation settled over me. My chest tightened at the fear of the thought of encountering ancient guardians or mythical beasts, like a Cerberus from the depths of legend. It gnawed at the edges of my mind. I had the uncanny sensation that we were being watched. The runes pulse and shift, their colours deepening as we pass, forming a picture. Translated into Drakkon, it depicting the legend of the relics- how they were only to be wielded by the soul-bound pair leading the nation and the gifts it would bestow upon their people.

Suddenly, a sharp metallic click echoed through the tunnel-a sharp unnatural sound that lingers in the air on a frequency barely audible to our ears. Almost as if it were a mosquito buzzing just out of range.

A blade whistled through the air-then struck. The shifter crumpled, twitching momentarily and then lifeless. A grim reminder of what awaited us. The metallic tang in the scent of his blood fills the air forcing me to breath through my mouth.

"Keep moving!" I commanded, urgency driving us forward. We navigated narrow passages, leapt over chasms, and dodged falling rocks. Water dripped in eerie rhythm, each drop sharpening the sense of impending danger. Darkness pressed in, every shadow thick with unseen threats. A living entity-a nightmare wrapped in light and shade.

We reached a chamber filled with ancient mechanisms. Walls shifted in slow, deliberate movements, the puzzle revealing itself in fragments. "We need to find the right path," one of the shifters said, his eyes scanning the intricate puzzle before us. With quick, precise movements, we worked together to solve the riddle, each second that stretched, was weighted with urgency. The thought of what might be hiding in the shadows pushed us to move faster, our nerves on edge.

Just as we thought we were in the clear, a low growl resonated from the darkness. My heart raced as a massive, three-headed guardian- Cereberus incarnate-emerged, its eyes glowing with an otherworldly light. 'Steady,' I whispered, drawing my weapon. Inside my mind I was weighing the probability of survival. The battle was fierce, blades clashed, claws scraped stone, each movement a battle between survival and oblivion. The fear of unseen horrors sharpened my resolve.

Then, a thought struck me-why destroy something simply because we don't understand it? Especially when we ourselves are creatures of myth. 'Wait!' I called out to my companions. 'Is there anyone here who can sing?'

There was a moment of confusion before Gwydion stepped forward. The hulking and deadly shifter-renowned for his fierce combat skills and ruthless nature-was the last person I expected to answer. His mere presence was enough to intimidate even seasoned warriors, and the idea of him singing seemed almost absurd. Yet, determination flickered in his eyes, a quiet resolve defying expectations.

Gwydion's deep, resonant voice, usually reserved for commands and battle cries, began to produce a low, melodic hum. His voice weaving an ancient Drakkon lullaby meant to soothe not only the beast but the echoes of spirits bound to the relic. The sound was both unexpected and eerily beautiful, echoing through the grove. The guardian's growls faltered, its heads tilting curiously as the eerie, unexpected melody filled the grove. The spell of tranquility woven through Gwydion's song softened the creature's eyes, its fierce stance unraveling into cautious serenity.

The guardian plopped backward onto its haunches, listening quietly as soft growls faded. Then, it dropped its heads onto its massive paws. As Gwydion completed the final notes of the lullaby, deep, rhythmic snoring filled the air, vibrating through the ground. We edged past the sleeping beast cautiously, moving deeper into the labyrinth's heart. 'I thought we would have to fight our way through.' Knowing Gwydion was one of the shifters I did not trust fully I added, 'Thanks to Gwydion, we avoided further bloodshed.'

A fleeting flicker of pride softened his otherwise stern expression, an emotion rarely visible on his hardened features. 'Strength isn't always measured in steel,' Gwydion murmured, his voice rough yet strangely lingering with the echoes of his song. 'Sometimes, it's the power within us that truly shapes the battle. Something I learned at my mother's knee.' Before anyone could make belittled remarks about his mother, I murmured, 'Mothers are powerful warriors in their own right. I wouldn't want to take on an enraged female who felt they had been disrespected.'

Suspended in an intricate web of shifting light, thrumming with power, its siren call luring me close. My hand reaches out, fingers passing through the light beams, activating the large rune carved into the wall behind the pedestal. Before our eyes, the rune shifts, revealing ancient words etched in glowing script 'The amulet and coin were forged by the gods-but cursed by men, ' the inscription warns. 'Once torn apart, their essence fractured, casting our great nation into turmoil, scattering its clans across the world. Only those born of the royal line, bound by true soul resonance may wield them with consequence.'

I wrap my fingers around the amulet, then carefully place it in the box where it pulsed once. A searing pain pierced my forearm as if I had been struck by a sword. My scales rippled under my skin as ink appeared in the shape of a fractured sigil. The lines shimmered, incomplete. Waiting-for her touch, her presence, her fire to strengthen our bond. 'What's wrong with him?' one of Gwydion's clan asked reaching a hand out toward my shoulder. Gwydion smacked his hand away, planting himself firmly behind me. 'He is absorbing the knowledge bound to the amulet. You must stay back from the Tiarna Draíochta.' I expected such loyalty from Seraphinus and Alexios but to hear it in Gwydion's voice while I suffered earned him a spot beside me on the council. Not out of obligation, but out of respect for the strength he showed when I needed it most.

When the other team arrived back in camp they were ushered straight through to my private chamber where the amulet rested in the box, its power thrumming faintly-waiting for its lost twin. 'You said not to touch it.' Alexios produced a cloth bound item from the pocket of his cloak and placed it on the table between us, 'The coin was locked within an obsidian container, its surface carved with human glyphs-ineffective wards that did nothing to mask its true power.' 'The entire team made it back safely?' The death of Lukas weighed heavily on my mind. 'There was a near miss with the patrols, but all shifters made it back safely.' Alexios assured me swiftly.

I could feel the deep, resonant hum in the air as tendrils of power stretched across the space between the relics on the table like hands reaching for something lost. A shiver runs down my spine as the resonance intensified, the relics calling to each other with urgent, harmonic pulses. The amulet thrummed in its box, answering the coin's song with a frequency I could feel rather than hear. Would they fuse if placed together? 'Alexios look,' I murmured, my voice barely more than breath, reverent in the presence of their awakening. 'The coin-it's reacting to the amulet.'

'In the cave where the amulet rested, it told the story of the origins of the relics. I was born of the original royal blood line. Selene is my soul mate.' The weight of the revelation settled over me-I knew we needed to act swiftly. 'Send a runner to Seraphinus. They must leave immediately-Selene needs to hear this now. Have her meet me at the grove of Thymbraean Apollo. Our fates depend upon it.' The relics pulsed with something ancient and restless, their connection shifting the very fabric of our struggle against the Greek Alliance. The amulet's power whispered of untold depths-I would unearth its secrets, no matter the cost.

The twin relics

The twin relics

(Theron)

Just before dawn's first light, I moved as if summoned to the grove of Thymbraean Apollo, my pulse erratic beneath my skin. My body drawn to this ancient sacred place, nestled between the Greek and Trojan lands. This neutral sanctuary, offered warriors solace and counsel, untouched by war's hostilities. Ancient cypress and olive trees towered over the landscape, their branches whispering secrets to the dawn breeze. Secrets that I could almost understand. Knowledge flickering at the edge of my fractured mind. I had been cursed by the amulet of this I was sure and she was the only one to heal what had broken within.

It was common knowledge that this temple was where Princess Kassandra received the prophetic power that consumed her. Her madness from a god's touch now a life long affliction for her family to bear. I would not be like Kassandra. Our bond would restore my sanity as soon as I placed the coin around Selene's neck. Hidden in the shadows, watching as attendees from both camps trickled in, ready for the day's revelry and worship. The rising murmur of voices as booths were being set up around the edges of the area, a fragile gesture toward peace between our two nations.

Masks concealed identities, royalty walked amongst commoners unnoticed. The hum of conversation rose above the melodies of the musicians hired for the day. Incense thickens the air, curling in fragrant plumes. Its scent mingling with the sweat and perfume of those pressed close in celebration. Selene wove through the crowd, a sister on either side, their faces hidden beneath hoods and intricately feathered masks. The masks shimmered under the rays of light piercing the grove. One moment, she is nearly before me. The next, the crowd presses in-bodies shifting, laughter ringing as it surges forward.

As the crowd parted once more, I caught her wrist and pulled her gently forward, steadying her with careful hands. 'Come with me, ' I murmur into her ear, leading her away from the chaos. '*My sisters will worry.*' she sends across our bond. 'Alexios and Seraphinus have them safe.' I turn her, letting her witness it-her sisters slipping free of the swirling revelry. Her gaze darts back to her sisters, relief flickering in her eyes, though the weight of uncertainty still lingers between us.

The noise of the festival fades into the rustling of ancient trees as I lead her to the ruins of a temple chosen for privacy. She lowers her hood, allowing her feathers to retreat, melting into her features. 'In the tunnels, I uncovered something-the origin story of the relics. You need to hear this.' She leans against a stone column, one hand resting lightly on her belly, watching as I make short work of spreading my cloak over the dusty temple stairs. I help her sit, waiting patiently until she is ready before I begin. 'Forged by gods, tainted by man-the relics carry both divinity and curse. They can only be worn by a male dragon shifter of the original royal line and his bonded soul mate. If any but the chosen were to wear them, madness would consume them.'

'My father told me the royal line of dragon kind was all but extinct. The great nation of Dragon kind was divided into clans, each with leaders of their own.' she ventured, sharing the fragments of our lore that she had been taught. 'Your father was right.' I assure her, then add, 'but not completely. The royal line still exists-in me. A secret so well kept that only two other shifters remain who know.' Her eyes widen at my revelation, the pieces falling into place in silence before she draws in a sharp breath. 'Our bond is strong-strong enough to carry the weight of the relics.' *She was mine-bound to me through the dance of time-an unbreakable tether woven by fate itself. Yet the sigil on my forearm shimmered with fractured lines, incomplete. A bond half-formed waiting for her fire to seal it whole. Her husband lived... I could only pray the histories were right and placing the coin on her would be enough. It must be enough.*

Searching Selene's face for a long moment I asked, 'Do you trust our bond enough for me to place this coin around your neck? I believe the power of the relics will protect you until I can do so myself.' She tilts her head, examining the coin as it spins freely at the end of the chain in my hands. 'How does the coin work exactly?' she asks, her voice edged with unspoken fear. 'It's simple, yet powerful.' I began, my voice steady. 'My father told me that should I ever place the coin around the neck of my soul mate and don the amulet we would be connected by dragon magic. The relics feed off our energies, creating a protective barrier.' 'Like a parasite-draining my magic?' she interjects, trying to mask the horror in her voice. 'No little moon. Not parasitical-more symbiotic. The relics do not steal our power for themselves. They enhance our gifts. They allow us to communicate across great distances, shielding us from those who seek harm-which, in turn, safeguards our people.' The chain glints between my fingers, its weight far heavier than mere metal. This was more than a gift. It was a bond, a covenant sealed in dragon magic.

I watched as Selene's expression softened, her understanding deepening. The dawn light framed her silhouette, and in that moment, I felt a surge of protectiveness and determination. This coin was more than a relic—it was a promise of protection, a tangible connection between us. 'Selene, for this to work, you must trust implicitly in our bond. Do you believe that we have a future together?' I search her softly glowing silver eyes then I see it. The moment she finally accepts our bond. A breathtaking surrender-a quiet, beautiful acceptance of what was always meant to be.

'Let me show you,' I said, and gently placed the coin around her neck. She did not resist me. As the coin settled against her skin, the glow deepened, wrapping us in golden radiance-warm, pulsing, alive. Her hair lifts, weightless, as I slip the amulet over my head letting it fall against my chest. 'By the goddess-what sorcery is this?' Selene exclaimed, her breath caught, fingers hovering over the coin, as if testing whether the warmth was truly real. 'Not sorcery, little moon—dragon magic,' I chuckled softly, amusement flickering in my gaze. I watched the sigil on my forearm complete itself. Clarity slipped over me like a cool breeze gently blowing the fog of the last few hours away. Our bodies would remain in place but our minds would be transported elsewhere to another plane of existence.

One blink-that's all it takes. A gentle tug between heartbeats, and suddenly, I'm standing just inside the cave entry on the beach below Lower Town. I spot Selene approaching from the far end of the beach, her curls a riotous cascade of silk, caught in the restless breeze. The waves drag across the sand-rhythmic, cyclic, moving in harmony with the moon's pull. Before either of us utters a word, a luminous phoenix, streaked in azure and purple, and an ebony dragon tinged with violet soar across the sky, descending gracefully before us.

'I've never seen my other half before-unless reflected in water.' Her voice trembles with reverence, as if daring to disturb the sacred presence before us. 'Selene, I have heard of this phenomenon-we call it the Convergence of Souls.' My voice is hushed as I turn to my other self and ask, 'Great one, why have you come?'

'We are here to warn of trials ahead. Alliances will crumble-beware the danger lurking within the palace. Beware the unseen alliance, hidden in the shadows.' He growls his warning before the Phoenix adds, 'We are here to acknowledge the future. A child born of Phoenix kind.' The dragon lowered his head, inhaling deeply drawing Selene's scent deep into his lungs. 'This child is of fire and shadow. He carries the strength of both parents-and the weight of your choices.' The dragon's growl vibrates through the earth, a warning etched in the ancient tones of prophecy. The dragon nudges Selene, holding her steady as she struggles to stay upright.

Between them, a flickering ember-purple and brown-materializes, fragile and shifting in the space between worlds. The ember pulses weakly, shifting like a dying star, its glow wavering between existence and oblivion. One hand stretches toward the ember, the other tightening instinctively across her stomach. The phoenix trills mournfully, 'Not all flames endure. Some are meant to burn brightly, then fade.' Our spirit guides flicker and dissolve-nothing more than whispers in the night-taking with them the soul we were never meant to carry with us across planes of existence. The phoenix's final note lingers-heavy with the weight of things left undone.

Her hand brushes the air where the soul of her unborn child was. Hissing, she lifts her hand, revealing red marks on her finger tips. A small smile tugs at her lips, defiant yet tender. 'This child still fights for his future.' Her eyes bright with unshed tears. She would fight to keep her child despite being told he would not live. I wrap her in my arms, cradling her for the first time-holding her like she was always meant to be there. Knowing that, on the other side, I must let her go-back to her husband.

A moment between sisters

A moment between sisters

(Selene)

I stepped onto the rough bark of the lowest branch of the old oak tree, my bare feet pressing into its textured surface. Perched comfortably against the tree trunk I watched as my sisters climbed higher, their movements fluid and determined seeking the sky while chained to the earth. In the distance, festival fires flickered, sending trails of glowing embers spiraling into the night sky. Here, in this sacred tree, we were no longer guards, princesses, healers, or queens-we were simply sisters, reveling in a fleeting escape-a brief return to the girls we had once been, before fate's relentless loom wove us into the ever-unfolding tapestry of life.

'I met someone.' Raya hesitated, choosing her words with deliberate care. 'He escorted me to Theron and then back to the tower afterwards.' Thea shifts on the branch, her silent plea unmistakable-she wants her hair done. 'Why wasn't this in your report?' I ask in a mildly reproving tone. 'Hektor was in the room.' she explains carefully before huffing, 'He's golden-haired, green-eyed and carries a presence that could fill the temple itself.' 'What is his name?' Thea asks tipping her head back shamelessly begging still. 'Seraphinus.' Raya's voice softens, her head tilting as she meets my gaze, 'He all but ordered me to call him before travelling outside of the city on my own again. He respects me enough to stay unseen-but his protection goes beyond mere safety. He guards his heart, shielding us from the moment I step into danger, long before I even realise it's there.'

'*Fire waits.*' The whisper rose from within me confirming my thoughts. Raya had found her soul mate and he had allowed her to remain with us for now. Raya unwinds a silver-threaded bracelet from her wrist-its one Mother wove in quiet dreams of her daughter's future. She weaves the silver strands into Thea's hair, threading Mother's dreams into each braid-a silent promise of protections passed from one sister to another. 'We have lost too much.' I murmur aloud realising that Thea probably wouldn't even know the significance of such an act. 'But we still have each other.' 'For those who shine the fire before us.' Thea whispers-an Emberisean prayer I never knew she carried 'For Mother, for Father and for our little brother.' Raya adds reverently and I conclude, 'For our nation burning bright among the stars-we will remember you.' Sensing the sorrow heavy in my chest, my child whispers, barely more than a breath, '*Still here.*'

I meet each of my sisters' eyes in turn, grounding my words with quiet certainty. 'You are both loved-deeply. Never forget that. We have survived our upheaval to be thrown into further turmoil and now it seems we are finding our significant others before finding peace together.' Raya takes a deep breath before sharing her battle knowledge. Small but invaluable tricks-ways to slip past seasoned warriors unnoticed, and the locations of hidden escape routes scattered throughout the city, should we ever need them. Thea shares the latest healing techniques she has mastered-methods that could save our lives, should we find ourselves wounded in flight once more. 'One of these methods...it might have saved Father from his long recovery.' she murmurs, a quiet ache threading through her voice. 'We are not just Princesses or priestesses, or warriors or even healers. We are the last of our family-the last of our kind.' Raya's voice is unwavering, forged in resolve. 'We must be everything for each other.'

'I think I met someone too.' Thea's' uncertain tone tightens the space between Raya and me. We exchange a long, measured look-one heavy with silent promise: if this shifter had harmed her, there would be consequences. 'Go on,' I say evenly, resisting the urge to push too hard-knowing full well she might keep this locked inside, rather than speak at all. 'His name is Alexios. He was protective. More than any guard I have had before. I felt something...I see glimpses of him, fragments of something real-but is that fate, or merely connection?' We wait for her to gather her thoughts. 'With him, I could not share my voice. Only fleeting images-scattered glimpses of what I saw, slipping between us like half-formed thoughts. Selene, you speak of sharing full conversations with Theron mind to mind. Raya you speak of this bond you feel deep inside. Why do I not experience any of this with Alexios?'

'*Heart knows.*' my child's whisper rises through me, curling around my ribs-a quiet confirmation, as steady as breath. Thea had indeed met her soul mate but neither of them had acknowledged it yet. At last, she asks the question that has lingered unspoken, 'You love Hektor, but You are bound to Theron. What is the difference?' I hesitated, searching for words that wouldn't make it sound cruel. Hektor was a choice; Theron was destiny-an inevitability etched into the fabric of my very being, written in every hydrogen atom of my DNA. I craved him more than breath itself. There was never a choice-only the pull of something ancient, something absolute. Something that I had refused to admit to myself but there was no choice. '*No choice.*' my little echo murmurs in between my heart beats.

A memory surfaces-*my parents, whispering their guidance from beyond the stars.* 'Father and Mother were soul mates before they were ever chosen for each other. They were private beings both in peace time and war. Father would never have spoken of his shattered bond before he passed-and I would never have asked him to. Watching them together was like witnessing two planets locked in perfect orbit-revolving in a timeless celestial dance in harmony. Mother once told me that soul mates are not chosen-they are found. And sometimes, they find you before you are ready to see them. You asked me the difference between Hektor and Theron. Hektor was a choice but Theron is...Theron is my life. I have a husband who I love. I have a soul mate who will wait-beyond time, beyond mortal constraints-for me. If you find yourself standing at the crossroads of soul mate and chosen, then the fates have not yet revealed their truth to you.'

Resting a hand against my stomach, my child shifts, pressing against me-'*Still here.*' a quiet reassurance curling through my chest. A gentle heat blossoms as the words fade, wrapping around me-chasing away the night's lingering chill. Thea's green eyes catch mine, her expression unreadable as she silently absorbs my words. Raya finishes securing her hair before dropping onto my branch-her silent solidarity a steady force beside me. The quiet certainty of her gaze tells me-I had spoken the right words.

She steadies me as I descend from the wall, then shifts-once more the ever-watchful personal guard. Thea straightens with one last giggle, lighthearted and fleeting, before the dignified healer settles into her place. The weight of duty presses down on my shoulders once more-I know our brief respite has passed. I place a hand against the old oak-our silent witness to a world that now exists only within us.

'Princess Andromache is in danger of losing the child.' Shouting from the lower level of the tower has Thea racing for her medicine satchel her braid flying in the wind. One last look in my direction before she disappears with Queen Hekuba's personal slave. Determination shone in her eyes. Andromache's child would live.

Dragon Knowledge

Dragon Knowledge

(Selene)

The child within me was growing more aware as time passes. He had progressed to two word sentences communicating from beneath my heart as he grew. Thea did not have the knowledge I needed to understand what was happening. Why this child? Why was he able to reach out to me before his birth? Theron was the only person who could tell me what I was experiencing. There were things only he could understand and our bond was crucial now more than ever.

'Find him.'

Find him I would but first I would remain discreet and unseen. Not even my sisters could know that I had left the tower for the night. Shrouding myself in the shadows I slipped out my window and down the tree where our dragon guard stood watch. I did not look back. The answers I sought were before me in the great lair of the Dragons of Thera.

Dropping to my feet lightly out of the tree behind him, Seraphinus moved instinctively forcing me to hug the wall lest his steel blade end my life and that of the unborn child. His blade halted a breath from my throat, the steel shimmering faintly in the moonlight before he drops his sword arm and bows his head in recognition. 'Lady Selene of

Troy, Queen of the great nest of Thera and of Emberis.' He sheaths his sword, eyes sharp as he assesses me, 'Where are you going my Lady?'

'I need to see Theron.' Drawing myself to my full height I add quietly, 'I have heard that you do not approve of me putting your mate at risk. Here I am. Will you guide me to him?' He studies me for a long moment, the silence between us thick with unspoken truths. Then with a nod he pulls the hood of my cloak further forward before turning toward the tunnel mouth. I was afraid that we would be separated in the maze beneath the earth but determination steeled my resolve as I slipped through the hidden entrance behind some debris. It had been strategically placed to conceal the entrance from prying eyes.

The passage was narrow and dimly lit, the air heavy with secrecy and anticipation. I felt the weight of my fears pressing in on me as he warned me to remain quiet and follow his footsteps exactly. The tunnels twisted and turned, a labyrinthine network that the dragons had marked by a series of straight lines on the walls where the tunnels connected with the next one they needed. Each step echoed softly, my breaths measured and steady. The flickering torchlight cast eerie shadows on the walls, adding to the atmosphere of suspense. The scent of damp earth and faint traces of sulfur filled the air, creating a sense of foreboding. The whispers of distant water and the occasional skitter of unseen creatures heightened my awareness of the dangers lurking in the depths.

'State your business shifter.' one of the two shifters guarding a door, growled hands shifting to their sword hilts. 'Do you require further demotion for insolence Linus?' Serarphinus roared his displeasure smoke curling from his nostrils. 'You will show respect to our guest. Apologise. Now.' He bit the words out in short sharp sentences.

'Show no fear.'

He'd graduated to three words. 'He's right to be suspicious. The line between friend and foe is growing very fine.' Removing my hood I allow the cloak to fall open showing the coin hanging from my neck.

'I am Lady Selene of Troy, displaced Queen of Emberis. I have urgent business with the Tiarna Draíochta. Theron. He's not expecting me.'

The coin glinted in the torchlight forcing their attention to it. They straightened further before exchanging glances. 'Wait here. We need to confirm that he is available to receive you.' The unnamed shifter spoke up before bowing slightly and disappearing beyond the door. I stood in the dim light, my heart pounding with anticipation. I knew the importance of their duty and respected their caution. After a tense moment, he returned with a nod.

'Follow me, my lady,' he said, his voice less guarded now. I turned to Seraphinus. 'You will guide me back?' question not a demand. He was my sister's mate. Family. I would not jeapordise the newest thread in our tapestry.

The guard led me through the cave system, the rough-hewn walls and flickering torchlight creating an otherworldly atmosphere. The whispers and glances from the dragons conveyed a mix of caution, intrigue, and irritation. The air was thick with the scent of burning wood and the faint tang of dragon fire. I felt the tension but remained composed.

As we moved deeper into the caves, a larger group of dragons gathered, their expressions showing their displeasure. One of them, a particularly imposing figure, stepped forward, his eyes narrowing at me. The air seemed to grow hotter as he approached, and smoke rings curled from his nostrils in an attempt to intimidate me.

'And what is this little human doing here, invading our nest?' he growled.

I stood my ground, my eyes meeting his defiantly. Without a word, I shifted enough to unfurl my wings, revealing the azure and purple feathers of my heritage, my silver eyes glowing eerily in the low light from the fires. The sight was enough to silence the murmurs and draw respectful nods from those around me.

'I am here to see the Tiarna Draíochta, Theron,' I said, my voice steady and unwavering.

The imposing dragon's eyes flashed with anger, but before he could retort, a powerful roar echoed from across the cave. 'Gwydion, stand down!' The voice was commanding and filled with authority.

Alexios, Thea's possible mate, stepped forward from the shadows. His eyes flicked down to check that I was unharmed before the light glinted off the green and gold scales covering his arms, his talons extended, ready to fight on my behalf if needed.

Gwydion, now clearly identified, immediately lowered his head in deference.

'Hunger is no excuse for bad manners.' Alexios chided. Hunger. I looked closely at them with bird sight rather than human eyes and saw what no one had told me. 'When was the last time you had full bellies?' I asked them. These shifters had been moving our refugees from Wilusa running on near to empty. Imposing males shifted their postures waiting for Alexios to answer. 'We have had no food for a week maybe two.' Folding my wings against my back I noticed Theron, his scales black and purple, preparing to back his friend up. His presence added to the tension, ready to rescue me from the teeth of one of the most feared dragons of the united clans.

'Supply chain issues.' he spoke out aloud, making his way through the crowd gathered around us. *'You're here.'* he speaks telepathically, keeping eye contact with me. *'Are you alright?'*

'We should speak privately about why I have come.' turning from him I address the shifters gathered around. 'I cannot give you much. I already share my grain portions with the hungry in Wilusa. But I know the locations where the Greeks have taken our cattle that they have stolen. Will that be enough to tide you over temporarily?'

'Why are you helping us?' a voice calls from the back. 'Why wouldn't I?' countering his words lightly seemed to help break the tension, 'You are all aiding with the evacuation of Wilusa because of me. I will do what I can to make sure you have enough to eat.' Theron reaches out for my hand leading me through the silent shifters each offering a respectful nod as we passed.

He leads me to his personal cave, a spacious chamber with natural stone formations and a small fire burning in the center. The air was cool and carried the scent of earth and embers.

Without hesitation, Theron stepped forward and checked me over for any signs of injury, knowing the dangers I must have faced coming through the cave system.

'Selene, what are you doing here? Are you alright?' he asked, his eyes scanning me for any harm.

'I'm fine, Theron,' I reassured him, touched by his concern. 'But there's something we need to discuss. When the convergence of souls took place it awoke the child I'm carrying. He speaks to me in three word sentences. We have no experience with this and no one to ask. Do you know if this has happened before?'

His expression filled with awe and tinged with sadness both beautiful and terrible to behold. 'I do not.' he admits, adding, 'You should cherish this connection to your son. The bond that has formed between you is undeniable. Does Hektor know his son is strong?'

'Hektor does not know what I am-only that I am his. How do I explain that his child is half shifter? That he might be a hatchling instead of a baby human. That my seclusion is shorter than that of Princess Andromache but comes with feathers.' Tears form in my eyes at the thought of the deception I would need to play in order to conceal our child's differences.

'Do not cry little moon.' rough finger pads wipe the tears from my cheeks. I had not realised that they had spilled. Pulling me close he holds me against himself. 'You came seeking assurance and found hunger. You have solved our hunger but I cannot give you the assurance you seek.'

Tipping my face back he brushes a kiss on my brow. 'No more wandering the tunnels. Use the coin. You must think of your unborn child. Promise me.' How could I not.

Moments of Grace

(Selene)

As the sun began its descent, casting a warm golden light over the city of Troy, I made my way through the palace halls with Raya at my side. She insisted on accompanying me, her protective nature evident in every step. She had been waiting for me when I returned from my excursion through the tunnels. Upset that I had chosen to exclude her from my plans. Yet wise enough to realise it was something that I had to do alone. The war had cast a long shadow over Troy, and the threat to my life was ever-present. She was hyper vigilant about my safety. The palace, once a place of joy and celebration, now felt like a fortress, each corner holding whispered fears and unspoken anxieties.

Inside, Andromache sat by the window, cradling little Astyanax in her arms. Her face lit up as she saw us, her eyes reflecting the fading sunlight. 'Sister, you've come! We were just sharing a quiet moment,' she said, her voice soft yet filled with warmth.

I smiled, feeling a sense of peace wash over me, a rare reprieve from the constant tension. 'I thought I'd join you. It's been too long since we've all been together like this,' I replied, my voice laced with a mixture of nostalgia and longing.

Raya gave a nod of acknowledgment before stepping back to stand watch by the door, her eyes ever watchful. Hektor, who had been sharpening his sword with deliberate care, looked up and grinned, a rare sight that momentarily lifted the heaviness in the room. 'It's good to see you, Selene. Come, sit with us.'

Grateful for a chance to sit down, I settled beside Andromache, reaching out to gently touch Astyanax's tiny hand. The baby cooed and grabbed my finger, his blue eyes wide with curiosity, innocence untouched by the horrors outside these walls. His dark, wavy hair framed his face, a perfect blend of his parents' features. 'He's grown so much,' I said softly, my heart swelling with a mixture of joy and sorrow. 'He's a light in these dark times.'

Andromache nodded, her gaze tender as she watched her son. 'He gives us hope, doesn't he? A reminder of what we're fighting for,' she murmured, her voice carrying a quiet strength.

Hektor's expression grew serious as he sheathed his sword and placed it next to his gleaming armor on the stand, the metal reflecting the dimming light. 'And he will grow up in a free Troy, if I have anything to say about it. But it's more than just fighting, Selene. It's about finding moments like these, where we remember why we endure,' he said, his voice filled with conviction and a hint of melancholy.

I felt a pang of guilt for the secrets I was keeping, but I pushed it aside, focusing on the present moment. 'You're right, Hektor. These moments are precious. We must hold onto them,' I agreed, my voice steady despite the turmoil inside.

The evening passed in quiet conversation, punctuated by Astyanax's playful giggles and the soft, loving exchanges between Hektor and Andromache. I cherished these moments, feeling the warmth of family and the strength of our bonds. I couldn't help but think of the future and the possibility that I might one day be the one to raise Astyanax. The thought was both daunting and comforting, knowing I had a role to play in his life.

As night fell, Hektor stood and offered his hand to me. 'Let me escort you back to your chambers. We still don't know if another threat to your life is out there,' he said, his voice a mix of protectiveness and concern.

I nodded, grateful for his protective presence. We walked through the palace halls, our footsteps echoing softly in the dim light. The night sky was clear, a canopy of stars twinkling above, casting a gentle glow. A cool breeze drifted through the corridors, causing me to shiver slightly. Hektor noticed and frowned. 'You should have brought a cloak, Selene. The nights are getting colder.'

I offered him a reassuring smile. 'I'll be fine, Hektor. Your presence is enough to keep me warm.'

As we reached my door, two of Hektor's friends stood guard, their expressions stern and resolute. Hektor chuckled and addressed them, 'Try not to look so grim, you two. You're scaring away all the pleasant dreams.'

One of the guards, a burly man with a thick beard, cracked a smile. 'Just doing our job, Your Highness. Someone has to keep an eye on your lady.'

Hektor grinned back, the tension easing slightly. 'Fair enough. But try to remember, we're not just here to fight. We're here to protect what we love.'

The other guard, his tone slightly bitter, countered, 'We're here to protect the lady you love and her family. What we love, who we love, doesn't matter in the larger scheme.'

Hektor's smile faded as he stepped closer to the guard, placing a hand on his shoulder. 'It matters, my friend. It matters more than you know. Every face we protect, every life we save, it all adds up. Your loved ones may not be here, but they are part of what we fight for. Your courage, your sacrifices—they make a difference.' 'I am grateful that you are here.' I add softly. 'There are still plots surrounding me and I do not know where the next attack will come from. Your sacrifice with your family is appreciated.'

The guard looked down, his bitterness softening into a semblance of understanding. 'I never thought of it that way, Your Highness.'

Hektor nodded, giving his shoulder a reassuring squeeze. 'We're in this together. Never forget that.'

Hektor turned back to me, his eyes softening with a mix of concern and affection. 'Selene, you mean the world to me. Your safety is my highest priority. Please, take care of yourself and the unborn child. The days ahead will be challenging, and I need you to stay strong.'

I nodded, touched by his words. 'Then you also must be strong, not only for us but for the men you lead on the battlefield. They all depend on you.'

With a final squeeze of his hand, I stepped inside, finding solace in the knowledge that, despite the dangers that lurked in the shadows, I was not alone. The love and protection of my family and the bond we shared with our loyal protectors were my greatest strengths, and I would need every bit of it in the days to come.

Hektor's Resolve

(Hektor)

The torchlight flickered against the stone walls of Troy's war chamber as I paced back and forth, my mind racing with plans and contingencies. The war had taken its toll on the city, and I knew that our current strategies were barely holding the Greeks at bay. We needed a new plan—something decisive and bold to ensure the survival of Troy.

'The King hears what he wants to hear—tell me what he won't.' Alexander demanded striding swiftly to my side. 'Truly? You would be willing to listen after all this time?' Pointing to one of the seats drawn near to my table, I wait until he is comfortable. 'This mess started with the failed trade mission to Sparta.' I look him in the eyes. Direct. He was old enough to understand the mess we were in because of his actions. 'Instead of securing peace you stole the King's wife. Then you proclaimed her yours without clearing her prior entanglements. You gave Greece a reason to unite against Troy and an armada landed on our beach the morning after I was married. Your precious Helena has caused the deaths of many and instead of taking responsibility she tried to defect back to Greece in the early hours of the morning. Your wife is not truly innocent and I wonder what game she is playing.'

Alexander's jaw tightened but he didn't look away. 'She hampers the evacuation mission by following my sisters through the city.' Selene appeared from the shadows at the other end of the room, feathers woven through the crown of her hair. 'She wanders into places she should not go.' Raya added half a pace behind her sister. 'I have caught her copying battle plans in Prince Hektor's private chambers.'

'I have intercepted a coded message referencing the feathered queen.' Theron's words ended with a snap of his teeth. 'Hektor, Selene. Raya.' He acknowledges us sending Alexander a menacing look. "Your female is not to be trusted. We found her lingering two corridors from the one that leads to the tunnels. There is no point in defending the walls if the enemy knows how to enter from below.'

Alexander's fists clenched at his sides, but he didn't speak. The silence was louder than denial. His eyes flicked up at Theron as his scales rippled under his skin, disbelief written across his face. 'I thought the dragons of Thera were myth.'

'I am no myth boy.' Theron growled. 'My people go hungry while evacuating your innocent. Your woman jeopardises everything Lady Selene, Lady Raya, Prince Hektor and I have been working towards.'

Alexander's jaw flexed, but he held Theron's gaze. 'She's not a traitor.' The words were quiet. Uncertain.

My gaze sharpened, the warlord in me rising. "If she's mapping the tunnels, she's not just wandering. She's preparing." My eyes flicked over to my wife. She met my gaze serenely. One hand rested lightly on her growing belly. She refused to remain passive while intrigue swirled around her.

'She bears watching.' Raya agreed in measured tones adding, 'I would like to believe that she is innocent but we are at war and she is of Sparta. Her behaviour is completely suspicious.' She had stationed herself behind her sister's chair at her back to shield her from danger and ready to step in front of her to protect her from harm.

Alexander finally spoke, voice low and strained. 'She's mine and she's also pregnant. Doesn't my child deserve our protection?'

I didn't flinch. "Then prove she's loyal. Or step aside while we protect what matters." I needed to trust my brother fully and I could only pray that he would not hand our rescue mission over to the Greek armies unwittingly.

I paused at the large wooden table, cluttered with maps and scrolls detailing the city's defenses and enemy positions. My eyes traced the lines and markings, calculating every possibility. The Greeks had grown more aggressive, their relentless assaults chipping away at Troy's strength and morale. We needed more than just strength and courage—we needed a plan that could outsmart our foes.

Could I trust Alexander? My eyes met Theron's across the war chamber. He nodded almost imperceptibly. The support from one who was supposedly an enemy filled me with an emotion I dare not name. I could not afford to be too friendly with someone who had a half claim on my wife.

Under the heat of his gaze I wondered whether I suffered misplaced guilt for keeping a soul bond separated or was it gratitude for his patience with our situation? Either way my brother was waiting for a response. 'She's your wife brother. The information we entrust to you tonight is because we need another of Priam's children to know what is happening right under his nose without his royal decree.' My gaze flicked over Selene again and this time she shifted in her chair.

It was long past time for her to be comfortable in her bed. I wished I had a cup of her favourite tea to offer her. All I had to hand was a goblet of wine-bad wine at that. 'We have been smuggling our citizens out of Wilusa and sending them in small groups through out the temple network in greater Troy.' Selene spoke, up her voice firm, 'Helena cannot know this.' Her silver eyes glowed slightly in the firelight. I pass the goblet to her anyway, 'It's not what you need little love. But it's what I have. One sip should not affect the child surely.' Even comfort had become a rationed luxury in the palace.

'Better not.' Raya scooped it out of her hand shooting me an apologetic look. 'Thea would make our ears bleed with a lecture on the dangers of child birth.'

'Where do you fit in Theron of Thera?' Alexander's voice was weary as he felt the pieces coming together in his mind. 'My people guide yours through the wilderness to the temple that will take them for the duration of the war. Lady Selene and I are childhood friends. When she realised I was among those encamped in the caves she sent me a message with a request I could not deny.'

He shot me a look with a raised eyebrow daring me to challenge his statement. I would not. There were things about Selene that I would not share with anyone else in my family-their true connection included.

Anger and concern churned within me at the thought of Selene making secret alliances without my permission. As her husband and the leader of Troy's defense, I should have been consulted. The secrecy gnawed at my trust, but I couldn't afford to dwell on it now. I should have dealt with these emotions by now. And yet, they seemed to appear when I least expected them. These were mine to contend with and I would not let my wife suffer from my jealousy.

'Will you keep our secret Prince Alexander?' Selene asks softly. 'Will you take Hektor's place should he fall in battle? Will you work with Theron of Thera, Leader of the United Dragon Clans and keep the alliance we have made?' Her questions resemble an oath one that would tie Alexander to our unsanctioned rescue group.

Theron leaned forward in his chair pinning Alexander with a stare, 'Many lives are at risk if you talk out of turn. I am not adverse to making you disappear in the heat of battle.' His grin is both fierce and feral as his shifter half shifts the scales under the skin of his face.

Alexander joins me in front of my table, studying the charts and maps silently. Emotions flashed across his face as he worked through everything he had been presented with. The fact that he had been fostered out, evident in this moment. He had not yet learned to conceal his thoughts from the mask he wore on his face.

'I will join you.' He finally spoke meeting each of our eyes in turn. 'Helena will not learn of this. Not from me. I swear it upon my own life.'

'Let the walls remember.' I respond lightly patting him soundly on his back.

As the night deepened, I continued to refine my plans, my determination unwavering. I would fight with every ounce of strength I had, but I also understood the importance of retreating strategically. The tunnels would be our lifeline, and Selene's alliance with the dragon shifters would be our secret weapon.

Weary from carrying the burden of the entire nation on my shoulders, I took a moment to reflect on my own life. The weight of leadership was heavy, but I found solace in the love of my family. I was grateful that my wives, Andromache and Selene, got along well, their bond strengthening our collective resolve.

In the quiet moments before dawn, I stood on the balcony overlooking the city. The first light of day touched the horizon, a reminder of the new beginnings that lay ahead. I knew that my duty was not just to defend Troy, but to ensure that its people—my family—would find safety and hope beyond the city's walls.

With renewed resolve, I turned back to my maps. The battle was far from over, but I would face it with the knowledge that I had done everything in my power to protect those I loved.

The Mask of Deception

The Mask of Deception

(Crinos)

The weight of the Amazon code pressed on my mind as I participated in yet another day of false smiles and hidden intentions. Helena and I maintained a façade of loyalty to Andromache and Selene, participating in public events and showing support to avoid suspicion. Each encounter was a test of my ability to conceal my true feelings and the growing doubts that gnawed at my conscience.

We attended a recent festival celebrating the harvest, blending seamlessly into the crowd. Helena, resplendent in her embroidered, beaded dress of fragile fabric, played the part of a devoted noblewoman effortlessly. My own attire—a finely tailored gown suitable for my status in the court of Troy—ensured I did not embarrass Queen Hekuba. Despite my warrior upbringing, I understood the importance of appearances and decorum.

As the festival unfolded, we spun a complex web of deception, creating false leads that pointed towards external enemies. Whispers of Greek spies and Trojan traitors circulated through the court, ensuring that any suspicion fell on outsiders rather than ourselves. The layers of lies grew thicker with each passing day. A maze of deceit that even I sometimes struggled to navigate.

Helena's cunning guided us through this labyrinth. She was a master at diverting attention, subtly guiding conversations to sow seeds of doubt and mistrust. Yet, as much as her manipulations served our cause, they also stirred a deep unease within me. Each step further entangled us in a web of our own making, one that could easily ensnare us if we were not careful.

The night of the assassination attempt loomed closer. Helena and I meticulously planned our alibis, ensuring we would be seen in public or with trusted witnesses. I attended a public dinner with Andromache, my presence noted by many. Helena, ever the strategist and keen on maintaining her social standing, made sure to be highly visible in the court. She mingled with influential figures, her presence marked by her charm and sharp wit, making her participation both noticeable and undeniable.

Meanwhile, Isandros prepared for his crucial role. In the dead of night, he knelt before an altar, the flickering candlelight casting eerie shadows on his determined face. He prayed fervently to the gods for their blessing, seeking a fair playing field. The gods answered his prayers, granting him superhuman strength, tracking abilities, and the knowledge of how to kill paranormal beings. Armed with these gifts, he was ready to carry out the assassination.

As the night of the attempt approached, the tension in the palace was palpable. I maintained my mask of loyalty, my thoughts a whirlwind of anticipation and dread. Despite my internal conflict, I followed the plan, knowing that any hesitation could lead to our downfall.

The stage was set. Helena and I, with our alibis secure and our plan in motion, awaited the moment when Selene would fall. The mask of deception we wore was nearly perfect, but the weight of our actions bore heavily on my conscience. The warrior within me struggled against the duplicity, even as I played my part in this deadly game.

Isandros's Faith

Isandros's Faith

(Isandros)

As the sun dipped below the horizon, I made my way to the stone temple dedicated to Athena. The temple, located in neutral territory shared with the Trojans, stood as a testament to the shared reverence for the goddess of wisdom and warfare. Each step felt heavier than the last, as if the weight of Helena's orders pressed down on my shoulders, threatening to crush me. The path was worn and familiar, yet the turmoil in my heart was anything but.

The scent of blooming flowers and the distant sound of waves provided a stark contrast to the storm brewing inside me. I needed guidance. I craved divine intervention to navigate the treacherous path ahead. As a devoted member of the cult of Athena, I knew this temple was my sanctuary, a place where I could seek solace and wisdom from the goddess herself.

Kneeling before the statue of Athena, adorned with symbols of her power, I began my prayers, my voice trembling. The statue depicted her in full armor, embodying the warrior spirit and strategic warfare. An owl, representing wisdom and knowledge, perched on her shoulder, and an olive tree, symbolizing peace and prosperity, stood nearby.

'Athena, I need your help. My faith is strong, but I'm struggling. The orders I've been given... they don't sit right with me. Please, give me a sign, some guidance, so I know what to do.'

The scent of heavy incense filled the air. Around me, offerings to Athena were meticulously arranged: animal sacrifices of sheep and goats, libations of wine and oil, and votive offerings such as figurines and pottery. The presence of the priestesses, who maintained the temple and conducted the rituals, added to the sacred atmosphere.

My thoughts raced, a whirlwind of doubts and fears. I spoke of my devotion, my desperate need for divine intervention, and my plea for reassurance. 'Athena, I'm just a man trying to do the right thing. Help me find the balance between my duty and my conscience.' Thoughts of the creatures that had slaughtered the lives of my brother and friends crept in. Filling my mind with doubt. Bowing my head, I begged Athena to help me cleanse the earth of these abominations. I slipped from my knees to lie prostrate in front of her altar. I begged for balance and for peace of mind.

The immense power Athena had granted me coursed through my veins, a constant reminder of the responsibility I now bore. The abilities of the non-human shifters leveled the playing field, but they also terrified me. 'Athena, this power you gave me... it's overwhelming. I don't want to misuse it. Please, guide me to use it wisely, to honor you and protect those I love.'

As I finished speaking, the temple grew still. A soft, warm light enveloped the statue of Athena, and I felt a gentle, yet powerful presence fill the space. Athena's voice, calm and reassuring, resonated in my mind. 'Isandros, my faithful servant, I have heard your prayers.'

I looked up, awestruck, as the goddess materialized before me. She appeared resplendent, clad in gleaming armor that reflected the flickering candlelight. Her helmet, adorned with intricate designs, sat gracefully atop her head, and her eyes shone with a wisdom that seemed to pierce through my very soul. Flowing from beneath her helmet, her hair cascaded in waves, a rich shade of chestnut brown that added to her regal presence.

Athena's presence was both commanding and comforting, embodying the strength of a warrior and the grace of a wise ruler. Her voice, gentle yet firm, resonated with a divine authority. 'I granted you these powers to balance the scales and help you in your mission. Your fear is natural, but you must trust in your strength and wisdom. Use your abilities to protect and serve, and you will honour me.' A white hot flash of pain flares on my inner right wrist. I am marked with her sigil. I wear the sacred spear and helmet. A reminder to be strategic in my planning and to always be ready for my opportunity.

Tears welled in my eyes as I lowered my head back to the ground. 'Thank you, great Athena. I will do my best to honor you and protect those I love. Your guidance means everything to me.'

Athena's presence remained, a comforting force. 'Remember, Isandros, you are never alone. I will be with you, guiding you, as you face the challenges ahead. Trust in yourself and in my blessing.'

The warmth of her presence began to fade, but the resolve within me grew stronger. The fear of my new abilities lingered, but so did the determination to use them for good. With renewed purpose, I stood, knowing that my journey was far from over and that the strength Athena had granted me would be both my greatest gift and my greatest challenge.

Part Four

A Warrior's Regret

(Hektor)

The weight of my armor felt heavier than ever as I made my way through the dimly lit corridors of the palace. The memories of the night battle haunted me—thinking I had killed Achilles, only to discover I had slain Patroclus, a mere child. The realization had struck me like a thunderbolt, filling me with a profound sorrow that was almost unbearable. This was not the kind of man I was.

Achilles' demands for a one-on-one fight to settle the war, echoed through the dawn air, his voice filled with rage and grief. He had been screaming since first light, calling me out to face him like the worm he believed I was. I knew that without me, Troy would surely fall, and the lives of Andromache and Selene would be in grave danger.

As the time for our duel approached, I gathered my family in the tower for what I feared would be our final moments together. The flickering firelight mirrors the shadows in our hearts. I held Selene close, my eyes taking in every detail of her face, her scent, the feel of her skin. 'Selene,' I began, my voice heavy with emotion. 'You must keep living for our unborn child. The thought of your unwavering support and the solace you have given me has brought me strength. Your presence has been a beacon of hope during the darkest parts of this war. Though words cannot fully express it, our time together has been a source of comfort and light for me.'

Tears streamed down Selene's face as she listened, her hand resting on her belly. 'Promise me you will find a way to survive, for our child's sake,' I urged, my voice cracking with emotion.

'I promise,' Selene whispered, her voice trembling. She held onto me tightly, knowing this might be our last embrace.

I then turned to Andromache, my gaze shifting to our son, Astyanax. 'Andromache, if I fall, you must leave the palace. Ensure that Astyanax is safe. I cannot bear the thought of him being thrown from the walls. You must protect him, no matter what.'

Andromache's eyes widened with fear and determination. 'I will, Hektor. I promise you, I will do everything in my power to keep him safe.'

I nodded, my heart heavy with the weight of my responsibilities. I kissed Andromache's forehead and hugged my son tightly. The gravity of the situation was not lost on anyone in the room. The heartache on their faces seared into my memory, a snapshot of pain and love that I would carry with me to my grave.

These two women had given me such love and remained stoic in our final moments together, sharing whispered words of love and comfort. The tower, usually a place of refuge, now felt like a sanctuary of sorrow.

As I walked one last time to the great gates in the wall of Willusa, the scents of the city filled my senses. The familiar smell of baked bread, the fragrant herbs from the market, and the metallic tang of the forge. Each scent was a reminder of the life I was leaving behind.

Achilles' voice grew louder with each step I took towards the gates. His insults and threats rang out, each one a reminder of the fate that awaited me. But I kept moving forward, driven by the need to protect my family and my city.

Before reaching the gates, a figure approached me, his presence commanding yet familiar. Theron of Thera regarded me with a thoughtful expression before saying, 'I have come to bear witness then watch over your women and children this day. You are a good man Prince Hektor of Troy, one I am honoured to call Brother.'

I placed a hand on his shoulder, feeling the weight of his words. 'Theron, my friend, promise me you will look after Andromache, Selene, Astyanax, and our unborn child. They are my heart. Guard them well. My name will echo only if they live to speak it.'

Theron gripped my arm firmly, his gaze unwavering. 'I swear it, Hektor. They will be safe, and your legacy will live on through them.'

The great gates loomed ahead, a symbol of Troy's strength and resilience. As I stepped through them, I took one last look back at the city I loved. I knew that my death would not be in vain if it meant that Andromache, Astyanax, Selene, and our unborn child could survive.

With a final deep breath, I faced forward, ready to meet my destiny.

A night of loss

A night of loss

(Selene)

The pain hit me like a wave, doubling me over and stealing my breath. I clutched my abdomen, a scream tearing from my throat as the agony intensified. The world blurred around me, and all I could feel was the excruciating torment. Tears streamed down my face as I realized what was happening. This wasn't just a cramp or a fleeting pain—it was my worst fear coming to life.

I could hear the frantic footsteps and urgent voices of those rushing to my side, but their words were a distant murmur, overshadowed by the roar of my grief. Blood pooled beneath me, confirming the horrific truth. I was losing my baby, and there was nothing I could do to stop it. "Please," I whispered to myself, "please, let this end."

At that moment, I felt a sudden connection, a warmth that cut through the pain. It was Theron. Despite the schoinos between us, his presence was palpable through our bond. The coin we shared glowed with a faint, reassuring light. "*Selene, I'm here*," his voice echoed in my mind, raw with soul-deep grief. '*I feel him too. The tenuous thread that has held your child this long is breaking. You are not alone. Hold on, my heart.*'

His words were a lifeline, and I clung to them, drawing strength from the bond we shared. Knowing that he could feel my pain and was with me in spirit brought a small measure of comfort. *'I'm scared.'* admitting this cost me more energy then I cared to admit. *'Selene. Stay alert. You're bleeding, but you're breathing. I need you conscious. Hold on little moon. Help is coming.'* Theron's voice sharp with urgency forces me to remain focused. I was still needed in this realm below the stars.

But the night was heavy with sorrow. Just hours ago, Hektor had fallen in single combat, his body mutilated and stolen by the Spartans. The grief from his loss was a constant, crushing weight on my chest. Guards who once stood vigilant had disappeared, leaving the tower eerily silent except for the echoes of my cries. On the ground level, inside the main entrance, Raya stood guard, her presence a small solace amidst the chaos. The women's wailing was so loud, it penetrated the stone of the tower room I lay in, a heart-wrenching sound that mirrored my own sorrow. In the distance, the Greeks celebrated loudly, their victorious shouts a cruel contrast to my despair.

The door to the room where I lay burst open, and Thea's face came into view, her eyes calm and focused. She moved with the practiced ease of a healer, assessing the situation swiftly. "Selene," she said, her voice soothing, "we're going to get through this."

I couldn't find the words to respond, the pain and sorrow too overwhelming. I felt Thea's hands on me, her touch gentle but firm. She quickly applied pressure to my lower abdomen, doing whatever it took to stop the bleeding. 'We need to stop the bleeding,' she said with a calm authority. 'Selene, look at me. Breathe.' I drew a breath, shallow but mine.

As the initial crisis subsided, the room fell into a heavy silence. The immediate danger had passed, but the weight of what I'd lost pressed down on me, making it hard to breathe. Thea stayed by my side, her presence a blend of compassion and strength.

Grief overwhelmed me, a dark, suffocating cloud. Hektor was gone, and now I was losing our child. The thought of enduring this pain, of continuing without them, was unbearable. I felt a desperate longing to join them, to escape the agony that threatened to consume me.

Theron, sensing my fading life force, begged me through our bond. '*Selene, please stay. I need you. Your sisters need you. The Greeks will not give up now that Troy's hero is dead. If you die, you break your oath to the women and children of Troy. You break the unspoken oath between us.*'

His words echoed in my mind, a desperate plea that pulled me back from the brink. The thought of leaving him, of giving in to the darkness, felt like a betrayal to everything we had fought for. I took a shaky breath, trying to anchor myself in the present, in the love that still surrounded me. 'Theron,' I murmured, 'I'm terrified... stay with me.'

Theron's response resonated deeply within me. '*Always, Selene. I swore to Hektor, and I swore to you. I'm not leaving. We hold the line—together. Now fight for us. Our time awaits.*' I heard him again, faint but resolute. '*Our time awaits.*' And I knew—I wasn't done yet.

As I lay there, teetering on the edge between life and death, I found myself in a strange, ethereal place—a crossroads. There, standing before me, was Hektor, his presence as strong and commanding as ever. In his arms, he held a little boy with perfect wings of pure white and beside him stood another smaller child, barely formed, glowing faintly like starlight. My breath caught. They were both mine. Both his. Both gone. 'I...I want to stay.' The words emanate from somewhere deep within me. They feel right despite the promises I have made to Theron. Dimly I am aware of his roars of anguish, feeling me slip through his claws.

Hektor's eyes were filled with sorrow, but also with an unyielding love. 'Selene,' he whispered, his voice gentle and warm. 'It is not your time. You must go back. Troy needs you. Your sisters need you. Theron needs you.'

I felt the pull of his words, the undeniable truth in them. 'Hektor,' I cried, reaching out to him, 'I miss you so much. I don't know if I can do this without you.'

His spectral hand touched mine, a tender caress that bridged the gap between the living and the dead. 'Enough, Selene. You've grieved. You've bled. But you may not stay. The oath you made to protect the innocent holds. Theron's life force is tied to yours. Go back. Lead. Live.'

With that, the crossroads began to fade, and I felt myself being drawn back to the waking world. At that moment, wrapped in my sister's care and Theron's unwavering presence, I clung to the hope that somehow, we'd find a way through the darkness.

Hektor's Funeral

Hektor's Funeral

Three days have passed since that fateful night. Two nights I have sat vigil. I do not speak. I cannot. Theron anchors my soul firmly to his despite the fact that I am healing well. Someone washes me, dresses me and sits me in my chair. I feel nothing until Queen Hekuba pays us a visit.

'My daughter.' She does not hold to court ceremony and folds me in her arms rocking gently. 'Selene. Hektor's come home. He's waiting for you.'

Hektor. Silent tears slipped down my cheeks. Warm. Salty. The first sign of life that I feel. 'Hektor?' my throat hurts from disuse. Thea presses a cup into my shaking hands. Sending me an approving glance as I take a small sip. 'Yes.' She replies, 'Hektor is home...and so is Briseis. Tomorrow we will send him on his way as befits a Prince of Troy. He would want you there.'

'I will come.' I promise and ask, 'Andromache? How is she?'

'She will be relieved to hear you are responding now.' Hekuba kisses my brow bidding my sisters to have me in place on time.

The first light of dawn cast a pale glow over the ancient temple, its towering columns bathed in a soft, golden hue. The air was thick with the scent of incense, mingling with the quiet murmur of mourners who had gathered to pay their final respects to Hektor. The solemn atmosphere was punctuated by the steady chant of priests, their voices rising and falling in a haunting melody that echoed through the sacred space.

I stood not on the dais where the senior royals gathered. My place was behind Andromache, who shared my grief, her eyes vacant and unseeing. She clutched the skeletal bouquet that signified her transition from the mother period of her life to crone with the death of our husband. The weight of my own grief threatened to crush me but I remained by her side, offering silent support. She needed me. I squeezed her hand gently, hoping she could feel my presence through the haze of her sorrow.

Hektor left no feathers. And I would not braid human hair into grief. Newly formed white pin feathers streaked with blood adorned the ends of one thin braid. I would remember my embers even if I could not remember their father in the same fashion. Andromache's hand closed around mine, sharp and insistent. The present demanded me back even though I wished for a moment of peace and solitude in which to mourn in our traditional ways.

The community had gathered in full force, their wailing and lamentations filling the air with a cacophony of sorrow. I felt a surge of anger mixed with my sorrow, my eyes narrowing at the sight of those who had sent Hektor to fight in their stead, now shedding crocodile tears. The noise and chaos felt overwhelming, and I longed for the quiet solitude of my private mourning. Ritual sacrifices were made to Apollo, the god to whom Hektor had always been devoted. The priests moved with practiced precision, offering food, flowers, and weapons to honor Hektor's warrior spirit and seek Apollo's favor for his journey to the afterlife.

As the funeral progressed, the procession moved from the temple to the streets. Each step was a struggle; my body still weak from childbirth, and every movement felt like a monumental effort. Despite the pain and exhaustion, I was determined to walk the distance, to honor Hektor and our child. The streets were lined with mourners, their faces etched with sorrow, some genuine and others, I suspected, merely performative. The air was thick with the scent of incense and the sound of sobbing, creating a surreal, almost oppressive atmosphere.

The procession finally reached the square where the bodies were laid out on towering pyres of wood. Hektor and our child would be burnt together, their spirits united in the afterlife. Despite the public displays of grief, I retreated into my own world of sorrow. I found a quiet corner of the square, away from prying eyes. On the edge of the mourners, I noticed figures in cloaks moving stealthily, their presence known only to a few. They were dragon shifters. Infiltrated into the city to guard me this night. Among them, I recognized Theron, his form concealed by a deeply hooded cloak. His eyes met mine briefly, a silent promise of protection.

Phoenix kind had rituals and customs which also had to be tended to. Our custom was to place a piece of black obsidian in the right hand of those we loved so that we may draw upon the energy from loved ones past to give us strength in times of great need. With trembling hands, I placed the obsidian in Hektor's right hand and whispered a silent prayer. I hoped that somewhere, somehow, they could hear me and feel my love.

Queen Hekuba moved through the mourners, trying to comfort her family members. She stood with Kassandra, whispering soothing words to calm her daughter's never-ending prophecies, and then moved to console King Priam. Her presence was a pillar of strength for those around her, yet I couldn't help but feel the sting of solitude. In my grief, there seemed to be no one to console me publicly, and I felt the weight of my loss even more acutely.

As dusk turned to night, the ceremony reached its peak. King Priam held his hand up for silence, and the murmurs and wails slowly subsided. We were there to honor the dead, and he was there to guide his son to the fields of Elysium. Placing two gold drachma on Hektor's closed eyelids, he kissed his bandaged forehead before calling for a torch. The flame burned bright against the dark night as he thrust it into the pyre, lighting it for all to see. The fire roared to life, consuming the wood and bodies, sending sparks into the sky.

As the flames rose, the coin I wore hummed with contentment. Theron was nearby. His presence anchored me to the present amidst the chaos of the royal funeral. *'I'm right behind you.'* Leaning in close from behind me, his voice echoed in my mind, *'I know this pain feels insurmountable, but you are not alone. Not now. Not ever. The strength of our kind runs through your blood. Remember who you are not who you have forced yourself to become.'*

His words, though simple, carried a weight of sincerity that eased a fraction of my sorrow. I nodded, trying to muster a weak smile, grateful for his support. I turned my head, exchanging a long look with the shifter that guarded me in one of the darkest hours, and in that moment, I caught sight of a shadow that looked out of place. It peeled from the wall, silent and deliberate. The blade caught the torchlight—too fast, too close.

Theron moved before I could speak. The bond must have warned him. He pushed me behind him. His hand found mine, pressing the hilt into my palm. No words. Just readiness. The dagger was warm from his grip and I silently promised him that I would survive.

Crinos sprang into action, wrestling him to the ground without hesitation. They struggled fiercely before springing apart. The crowd scattered around them before weapons clashed in a deadly dance. Dragon shifters formed a protective ring around me, ready to intervene if required. I should have known that Theron would not have come alone. Crinos's determination to protect me was evident in every calculated strike, her bravery shining through despite the overwhelming odds.

She bared her teeth at the assailant before he winded her badly, escaping in the ensuing chaos, leaving Crinos to face her actions alone. Crinos, too, was grieving. Her face a mask of anguish as she stood before Alexander and the squadron of soldiers he was leading. His eyes burned with a mix of grief and anger, but we knew this was not the time for questions.

Betrayal Within

Betrayal Within

(Alexander)

The warm glow of the oil lamps did little to ease the chill that had settled over my heart. The simple tapestries on the walls of the palace room, usually a comforting sight, now seemed to close in around me. Hektor, my beloved big brother, had been my guide and my protector. Now, with him gone, the burden of his final wishes weighed heavily on my shoulders.

I glanced at Helena beside me, her expression as solemn as my own. Across the table, Andromache sat on a comfortable cushion, her face etched with sorrow. Selene, still recovering from her recent miscarriage, was seated beside Andromache, her posture weary but resolute. Behind Selene stood Nuraya, a fierce presence with weapons visibly strapped to her, ready to protect.

The absence of my parents, too consumed by grief to attend, left a void that deepened the somber mood. My heart ached for them, and for the loss we all shared. But now, we had to confront another betrayal.

Crinos entered the room, a shadow of her former self. Her hair, once styled with minute braids adorned with Amazonian feathers, was now disheveled and unkempt. Her clothing, previously finely tailored and symbolic of her status, was now plain and functional. She had been denied the luxuries and servants she was once accustomed to, and her weapons were conspicuously absent. A visual testament to the scrutiny she now faced.

We had kept her waiting deliberately, not out of cruelty, but caution. The palace had not yet been cleared of threats, and her actions during Hektor's funeral—though swift and brutal—had raised questions we could not afford to ignore. Her quarters had been searched. In her quiver, a miniscule parchment was hidden with a Greek insignia still attached to it. The message itself read 'The tide turns at dusk. The flame must be extinguished before the mourning ends.' *Was this code about the attack? Did she have a change of heart about her actions?*

A pang of sorrow struck me as I looked at her, but I couldn't let it cloud my judgment. Hektor had entrusted me with the care of his wives and son. Crinos stood alone. Whether she had acted out of instinct or jealousy, we needed clarity. We needed truth. *I needed to know if Helena was involved.*

I steeled myself, my voice stern as I addressed her.

"Crinos, you have been brought before us to explain your actions. Your violent display disrupted the funeral rites and endangered the lives of those under my protection. Correspondence was found in your rooms with those in our enemy's encampment. Explain yourself cousin. You have strayed far from the Amazonian code you claim to still hold close."

Crinos took a deep breath, her voice steady but laced with emotion.

'I've lived apart from Amazon customs, yes. But I have not forgotten how to fight, nor whom I fight for. You may question my methods but not my loyalty. When one of our own is threatened, I act. I do not wait for a man's permission to defend my sisters. I grieve for Hektor as fiercely as any of you. I honour him by standing guard over what he loved. Do not mistake grief for guilt. I don't know what message you speak of cousin.'

Andromache's eyes, red-rimmed and swollen from crying, flickered with a mixture of disappointment and sorrow. Her lips were pressed into a thin line, reflecting her inner turmoil. As Crinos spoke, Andromache's expression shifted from anger to a look of deep, pained understanding. She could relate to the fear and insecurity driving Crinos, but the betrayal cut deep. Andromache places the parchment on the table. 'It was found deep in the base of your quiver.'

Shock crosses her features. Colour drains from her face. 'I have never seen it before. Alexander, I am being framed.' Her reaction is genuine. Flicking my gaze over my companions, Helena's clenched jaw raised suspicion. Her silence louder then any denial, while Selene and Andromache blank expressions gave cause for further concern. How I wished I could send Crinos back to her Mother but I did not have that luxury. I might have had a chance to reconnect with Helena and understand her true motives for aligning herself with my cousin.

'I do not trust her.' Selene spoke bluntly. 'You showed no grief and seemed to know exactly where this assassin's weak points were-that points toward familiarity with the person. I have lost my child and my husband on the same night and you dishonour their memory by lying to my ears.' Her eyes glowed eerily in the torchlight as tears trickled down her face silently. Selene's words cut deeper than any blade, Crinos clasps her shaking hands together.

'You show no remorse for your actions. Blame must be attributed to you for the public disturbance you caused, whether you were part of a plot to murder Lady Selene or not is yet to be decided. Have you anything else to add in your defence before we make our decision?' I leaned forward in my chair. 'Choose your next words wisely cousin. They may be the difference between life in Wilusa and being sent back to your mother in disgrace.'

Crinos's gaze shifted to Helena, who nodded subtly, encouraging her to continue. Helena's usually perfectly styled self seemed slightly off today—her hair not as meticulously arranged, her expression tighter and more guarded. It was as if her usual confidence had been replaced with a hint of anxiety.

'I ask for a chance to make amends. Let my actions speak for me. I am willing to do whatever it takes to prove my loyalty and earn back your trust. Please, give me the opportunity to show you that I am sincere in my remorse and my desire to set things right.'

Selene leaned forward, her voice firm but compassionate.

'Crinos, we need to know the truth. Do you have any knowledge of the assassin?'

I watched as Crinos's heart raced, her mind in turmoil. She hesitated, and I couldn't help but wonder what inner conflict she was facing. I could sense her struggle, knowing that revealing the truth could cause even more chaos and pain, yet concealing it could jeopardize her chance at redemption.

'I... I don't know who the assassin is. But I promise, I will find out and do everything in my power to make things right.'

We exchanged concerned glances, sensing Crinos's inner conflict but choosing to give her a chance to prove herself.

"Very well, Crinos. You will have your chance to prove yourself. But know this: one misstep, and there will be no more second chances."

As I finished speaking, Lady Nuraya stepped forward from behind Selene, her presence commanding attention.

'My Lord,' she began, her voice steady and resolute. 'Crinos may have acted out of misguided loyalty, but she followed the Amazonian code of honor when it mattered most. She saved Selene's life when it really counted. This code is ingrained in her, and it guided her actions in that critical moment.'

I listened intently, considering her words.

'Her mother and the Amazons are on their way to join us in battle,' Nuraya continued. 'They will stand by our side, guided by the same code of honor. Crinos has the potential to redeem herself and prove her loyalty, not just through words, but through her actions. Give her the chance to show you that she can uphold the values we all hold dear.'

Nuraya paused, her gaze unwavering.

'When I was young, I made mistakes that nearly cost me everything. I had to earn back my honor and the trust of those I had wronged. It was a difficult journey, but it shaped me into the person I am today. Crinos deserves the same chance. She can find redemption, just as I did.'

She took a deep breath before continuing. 'I had been working on a strategy with Prince Hektor, and I still have use for Crinos's skills on horseback. There is a mission that could open up another supply route for Troy. It is dangerous and could cost Crinos her life, but it would be a chance for her to prove her loyalty and serve the community once more.'

Selene's expression softened slightly as she listened to Nuraya's testimony. Despite her skepticism, there was a clear bond between the sisters. Selene respected Nuraya's wisdom and looked surprised yet cautiously optimistic about Crinos's potential for redemption. She glanced at Crinos, searching for any sign of sincerity in her eyes.

A silence filled the room as Nuraya finished her testimony. I felt a tumult of emotions within me—anger, sorrow, relief, hope. Could Crinos truly find redemption? Could she prove her loyalty and make amends for her past actions?

I glanced at Crinos, seeing the resolve in her eyes, and then at Nuraya, who stood firm in her belief in Crinos's potential. Hektor had trusted me to protect his family, and now I had to trust in my own judgment.

'Very well,' I said finally, my voice steady. 'Crinos, you will have your chance to prove yourself. But remember, there will be no more second chances.'

As I watched Crinos stand alone, her resolve unwavering, I couldn't help but hope that Hektor's trust in me would guide my decisions in the difficult days ahead.

Secrets of the bloodline

(Alexander)

The palace was eerily quiet as I made my way to the private chambers. The weight of the day's events hung heavily on my shoulders. As I entered the room, Helena was already there, pacing back and forth, her face a mask of frustration and worry.

Our chamber was usually a haven of peace. During the day, the room was airy and light, with sunbeams streaming through large windows, casting a warm glow on the stone walls adorned with tapestries depicting scenes of Troy's victories and legendary heroes. One prominent tapestry depicted Mount Ida, the place where I spent my youth, a symbol of the simpler times before the shadow of war loomed over us. At night, the room turned cozy. The soft flicker of braziers casting dancing shadows, creating an atmosphere of comfort and intimacy.

In one corner, my hunting bow and quiver of arrows were given pride of place, a symbol of my skill and the many hunts that had shaped my youth. On the other side of the room, Helena's weaving loom stood near the window, where she would often work on her intricate designs. Threads of vibrant colors lay in neat rows, waiting to be woven into another masterpiece.

Our two sons were already tucked up for the night, cuddling together in the same bed in the corner of our room. Their innocent faces were peaceful in slumber, blissfully unaware of the turmoil unfolding around them. We kept them far from court-most unaware that they even existed. Helena had lost the child she had claimed to be carrying when I had defended her actions to Hektor.

'Helena, we need to talk,' I said, closing the door behind me, my voice a hushed whisper. 'Crinos's actions have put us all in jeopardy. What were you thinking, aligning yourself with her?'

Helena stopped pacing and faced me, her eyes blazing. 'Alexander, you have no idea what you're talking about. There's more to this than you know,' she replied in a low voice, careful not to wake the boys.

I felt my anger rising. I ran a hand through my hair, a gesture of frustration I hadn't done in years. 'Then enlighten me, Helena. Because right now, it looks like you've betrayed us all,' I said, my words barely above a whisper, yet laced with intensity.

Helena took a deep breath, her expression softening but still tense. 'You need to know the truth about Selene and her sisters. Their true identities,' she said, her voice calm but emphatic.

My heart skipped a beat. 'What do you mean? What are you talking about?'

'They are the last of the royal bloodline of Emberis,' she began, her voice low and steady. 'In fact, they are all that is left of Emberis. Their lineage traces back to the phoenix shifters, a people whose very tears had healing qualities. They've been in hiding, and for good reason. Their heritage is not just royal, but also carries powerful, magical qualities that many would seek to exploit.'

I stared at her, my mind racing. 'Why didn't you tell me this before? Why keep this a secret?'

Helena's eyes were filled with a mixture of guilt and determination. 'It was for their protection. If the wrong people found out, their lives would be in even greater danger. Crinos knew their secret, which is why she acted the way she did. She was trying to protect them, in her own misguided way,' she explained in a quiet, urgent tone.

The implications of Helena's revelation hit me like a tidal wave. The true identities of Selene and her sisters added a layer of complexity to the situation that I hadn't anticipated. It also explained the looks passing between Crinos and Helena earlier.

'But Crinos's correspondence with the Greek army nearly cost Selene her life. How else would an assassin have known the exact moment to strike at Hektor's funeral?' I said, my voice shaking but kept low. 'How can I trust you, Helena? How can I be sure you're not hiding anything else from me?'

Helena stepped closer, her eyes pleading. 'Alexander, I would never betray you or our family. Everything I did was to protect them, to protect us. We need to trust each other now more than ever,' she whispered, her voice full of emotion.

I took a deep breath, trying to process everything. The revelation about Selene and her sisters' true identities changed everything. It added a sense of urgency and danger to our already precarious situation. But Helena's words felt like a distraction from something deeper.

My mind was a whirlwind of anger, sorrow, and betrayal. I had put my whole country in jeopardy and lost my beloved big brother due to the manipulations of my wife. And she seemed to be playing a complicated game that I struggled to fully understand.

How could I truly trust her words when she had left her own family in Sparta for me? The memories of her departure from Sparta flickered through my mind, a painful reminder of her willingness to abandon those she once claimed to love.

I turned to look at our two sons, their faces peaceful in sleep, a stark contrast to the turmoil within me. I needed to protect them, to ensure their future was secure. But how could I do that with Helena's deceit lingering over us?

I turned back to Helena, frustration boiling over. 'We need to come up with a plan,' I said finally, my voice a quiet resolve. 'We need to come together if we are to survive the onslaught. The Greeks are planning to invade the city now that Hektor is no longer here to protect us. These children... our children would be slaughtered if Agamemnon allows it. Helena, you are playing a dangerous game with our lives.'

Helena nodded, her expression resolute. 'Together, we can do this. We have to,' she whispered back, her eyes sliding away from mine—a clear indication she was lying.

Unable to contain my frustration any longer, I grabbed her shoulders and gave her a sharp shake. 'Do you understand the gravity of the situation? Our children's lives are at stake!'

As we stood there, side by side, I felt a renewed sense of determination. The path ahead was fraught with danger and uncertainty, but with Helena by my side, I knew we could face whatever challenges lay ahead. Yet, deep down, the seeds of doubt continued to grow. I didn't trust Helena to stand by me through the challenges ahead. And though I didn't know it yet, she was not going to settle for me. She was already eyeing my brother Deiphobus.

Alexander's Deception

Alexander's Deception

(Alexander)

Years passed. We remained in a stalemate situation with the Greeks. They refused to leave without Helena. She couldn't be trusted not to pass our vulnerabilities to them to exploit the minute we handed her back.

Polyxena, my youngest sister, was a vision of beauty and grace. At 18, she was a doe-eyed virgin, tall with long black hair cascading down her back. Her pale, unblemished skin and large, expressive eyes gave her an almost ethereal presence. Unlike Deiphobus and me, seasoned warriors hardened by years of battle, Polyxena had a gentle heart and a compassionate nature. We adored and protected her fiercely, our bond unshakable despite the chaos around us.

Her betrothal to Achilles, the famed Greek warrior, had been a strategic move intended to forge peace between the warring factions. However, this betrothal was born out of tragedy. I still remember the day Polyxena and her twin brother, Troilus, were fetching water from a nearby fountain outside the city walls. Achilles attacked, and despite their noble intentions, the encounter ended with Troilus's death. Polyxena was covered in arterial blood from Troilus's wound, her eyes wide with shock and horror. Yet, amidst the chaos, she held her composure, her voice steady as she spoke words that seemed to pierce through Achilles' rage. Something she said entranced him, and he agreed to marry her, hoping to atone for his actions and secure her loyalty.

'I have news.' Nuraya met with us in a rarely used corridor. Her voice was filled with reluctance, 'Crinos intercepted a message for Helena from king Agamemnon himself. Achilles has betrothed himself to your sister Polyxena. She shared this as an effort to prove her loyalty to Troy.' Her face hardened as she asked, 'Why should Prince Hektor's killer walk free when my sister mourns for her husband? You could use this to your advantage by hiding in the Temple of Apollo when they next meet.' Raya was one of the secret alliance and one of Hektor's trusted advisors. I trusted his memory and respected her judgement as a warrior. 'You walk a dangerous path, ' she warned, eyes filled with sorrow knowing the gravity of her words, 'Where does the retaliation for death end? Hektor killed Patroclus, Achilles killed Hektor and now...' she dashed the tears from her face, 'Polyxena will be hurt in the name of vengeance and I fear you will damage your soul.'

'I do not have the luxury of peace, but I will not abandon my soul to a war I brought to our doorstep. Polyxena is very young she will get over this heart ache.' I was aware of how callous I sounded in that moment as Deiphobus and I exchanged glances. Deiphobus was my younger brother and it was he who had stepped forward to help me defend Troy. He possessed the same dark, brooding eyes as Hektor. His hair, however, was a shade lighter, more like my own. Yet none cast aspersions on his parentage. His skin was golden from years of battle training under the scorching sun, his build muscular and imposing yet he did not have the warrior spirit that had seemed to fill Hektor. Each of Priam's children had their differences and one could not mistake Deiphobus for Hektor incarnate. We could not replace him no matter how hard we tried to fill his shoes.

Briseis had shared stories from the time where she had been held against her will inside his tent as a slave stripped of rank and dignity.

The thought of Polyxena marrying the man responsible for so much suffering was infuriating, but we knew that rage could lead to mistakes. In this crucial moment, we needed to keep our heads. There was no room for error in what we were about to do. With heavy hearts and clear minds, we decided to take advantage of Helena's tactical error.

That night, while the temporary peace surrounding Hektor's funeral held, we suggested that Polyxena meet Achilles before the Greeks could draw us into war again. Under pretense of acting as her guards we traveled to the Temple of Thymbraean Apollo, located in a grove some way from Wilusa, to seek guidance. The journey was a solemn one, the weight of our mission heavy on our minds. Polyxena believed we were on high alert for the danger that surrounded us as at every turn as we evaded multiple Greek held locations. Her dark braid blending with the shadows we kept to, doe eyes frightened, her back strengthened with the iron rod she had inherited from our mother. She held limitless courage for one who did not deserve her innocence.

The temple, nestled within the sacred grove, was a place of great reverence. Inside, the room was dimly lit by flickering oil lamps. An altar stood at the center, adorned with offerings of fruits and incense. Hand-carved likenesses of Apollo decorated the stone walls, each depicting the god in various divine poses, a testament to his power and grace. Raised on Mt. Ida, my reverence for Apollo was deeply ingrained. Apollo, the god of prophecy and archery, seemed the right deity to seek counsel from in this dire situation.

Under the cover of night, we positioned Polyxena in a secluded grove, her figure bathed in the soft glow of the moonlight. She appeared vulnerable and alone, a perfect lure for Achilles. 'Wait here for your betrothed.' Deiphobus told her smiling as I added, 'We will watch from the temple. You will be safe little sister.'

As we knelt before the altar, a brilliant light filled the room, and time seemed to stand still. In that sacred moment, it felt as if we had stepped outside of time and space, the world around us fading away. Apollo himself appeared, his presence overwhelming. He was tall and radiant, his golden hair flowing like molten sunlight. His eyes, a deep, piercing blue, held a timeless wisdom. Draped in a chiton that shimmered with celestial patterns, he radiated both power and serenity.

'You seek justice for your brother,' Apollo said, his voice calm but firm. 'I'm here to help. Use this poisoned arrow, infused with my divine power. It will bring down Achilles when the time is right.'

I noticed the anger simmering in Apollo's eyes as he continued. 'Achilles has shown no respect for the gods, desecrating our temples. But what really angers me is how he killed Hector, a mortal I greatly admired. His brutal treatment of Hector's body is something I can't overlook. This isn't just your revenge, it's mine too.'

With reverence, we accepted the arrow from Apollo. 'This will be our weapon,' he said. 'Make your shot count, and Achilles will fall.'

Taking up position for the perfect angle to loose the arrow from my bow, I could see the tension in her posture and the way she anxiously glanced around. Even though she couldn't know we were there, she seemed to sense the weight of the moment. She hadn't seen us slip from the temple to blend into the shadows surrounding the grove.

Time seem to stretch as we waited, our breaths bated and our eyes trained on the path leading to the grove. The tension was palpable, each passing moment stretching our nerves taut.

Finally, the sound of approaching footsteps reached our ears. Achilles emerged from the darkness, his gaze locked onto Polyxena. As he approached her, we readied our bow, the poisoned arrow glinting ominously.

Achilles Death

Achilles death

(Polyxena)

Now, standing in the grove, I felt a sense of anticipation mixed with a dread that I couldn't shake. The moonlight bathed the clearing in a soft glow, casting long shadows that seemed to whisper of the fleeting peace we were experiencing. The air was still, every sound amplified in the silence of the night. My stomach churned with anxiety, a knot of tension twisting within me and making me feel slightly nauseous. A dull headache throbbed at my temples, each heartbeat pounding in my ears.

I was dressed in my finest garments, a flowing gown of rich blue fabric adorned with intricate embroidery that shimmered in the moonlight. A delicate cloak covered my shoulders, the hood partially obscuring my face. This meeting was meant to be secretive, our identities hidden from prying eyes.

Achilles arrived, drawn by his fascination with me. He moved with purpose, his eyes locked onto mine as if nothing else mattered. His presence was imposing, yet I could see the curiosity in his gaze when he looked at me. Standing a head taller than me, his stature made me feel both small and safe. As he approached, my heart pounded in my chest, a mix of excitement and nervousness that only intensified my discomfort. My hands felt clammy, sweat beading on my palms, and a slight tremor shook my legs.

'Polyxena,' Achilles murmured, his voice softening as he reached out to me. 'You came. I thought this to be a trap.'

I swallowed hard, my voice steady despite the turmoil within. 'Achilles,' I replied, genuinely grateful for this moment to spend time with him during a time of peace.

Achilles took my hand in his, his touch warm and reassuring. 'There's something about you that I can't quite understand,' he said softly, his eyes searching mine. 'I want to know what makes you different to the other women of your family.'

My heart ached at his words, the memory of our last encounter still fresh in my mind. Losing Troilus had left a deep scar, and the grief still gnawed at my soul. Now, as I stood with Achilles, I wished I could forget the pain, if only for a moment. 'I'm glad you're here,' I whispered, my voice trembling. 'I wish things were different. I am not interchangeable with my sisters. We are too different. Especially Kassandra.'

He gently brushed a strand of hair from my face, his fingers lingering on my cheek. "We'll find a way," he promised, his voice filled with determination. "I will find a way to make things right for the death of Troilus. His death plagues you still sweet dove."

From the shadows, we heard a distinct twang of a bow string. Achilles whirled around, placing me behind him in a protective gesture. Time seemed to slow, each heartbeat echoing in my ears. An unusual breeze stirred the air, and a sudden glint of light illuminated the arrow's path. The poisoned projectile struck Achilles in the heel, his legendary weak spot.

Achilles staggered, his eyes widening in shock and pain. He looked down at the wound, realizing the betrayal in his final moments. 'Polyxena...why?' he gasped, his strength ebbing away. The anguish in his voice tore at my soul.

My eyes filled with horror and grief as I saw the arrow lodged in his heel. I fell to my knees beside him, my hands trembling. 'I didn't know,' I whispered, my voice breaking. 'I didn't know they would...' Tears streamed down my face, mingling with the blood on my hands. Desperate to save him, I pressed my hands against the wound, trying to stem the flow of blood. The rich blue fabric of my gown soaked up the blood, the dark stain spreading and seeping into the fibers, a mark that would never be removed, adding to the stain on my soul. In my frantic efforts, I accidentally nicked my finger on the arrow's sharp edge, the poison seeping into my bloodstream.

Deiphobus and Alexander emerged from the shadows, their faces etched with horror and sorrow. They rushed to my side, their eyes filled with desperation. 'Polyxena,' Deiphobus whispered, his voice breaking. 'little sister we didn't mean for you to try to save him.'

I looked up at them, my vision blurring. 'Why...why did you do this?' I managed to ask, my voice a mixture of pain and heartbreak.

'We thought we were protecting you,' Alexander said, his tone laden with guilt. 'We never thought you would interfere. I thought you were his as part of a peace treaty with the myrmidons.' As he spoke, he suddenly remembered Helena's words about the sisters true natures. He screamed in frustration that he hadn't thought to bring one of them along under the guise of Polyxena's companion.

'I'm here Prince.' Raya emerged from the shadows her hair braided tightly against her skull woven with cord and interlaced with feathers. She gripped weapons of her own as she scanned the under brush for further danger. Panic and urgency filled his eyes. "Raya! Help her!" he shouted, his voice cracking with fear. I wished I could reassure them that I did not blame them for my fate. Confusion fogged my brain and my sight began to dim.

Raya rushed to my side, her hands glowing with a faint light as she prepared to heal me. But the poison had worked swiftly, and my strength was fading faster than she could act.

Our gazes locked, a silent exchange of heartbreak and love. They claimed to adore me, yet here I was, dying in front of them. The reality of their actions bore down heavily upon them, their contrition evident.

As the poison took hold, I felt my strength ebbing away. With a final, resolute look, I collapsed beside Achilles, my heart shattered by the betrayal and loss. Deiphobus and Alexander watched in stunned silence as my body fell lifeless beside Achilles. The impact of Achilles' death would soon ripple through the Trojan army and the wider war, but in that moment, the weight of their actions bore down heavily upon them.

Raya knelt beside me with my blood covering her hands. I watched for mere seconds as she bowed her head offering a prayer to the goddess on my behalf. Her gaze wandered over to my brothers frozen in their suffering. She offered them silent understanding. Sorrow and regret filled the air like a rotten stench unable to reverse the tragic events that had unfolded, orchestrated by two princes bent on revenge. Raya drew a rune on her forehead in my blood and muttered, 'I can still feel you surrounding us Princess...this existence holds nothing further for you. Go to those who are waiting for you.' Warmth engulfed me and I knew no more.

Grave Consequences

Grave Consequences

(Alexander)

My hands were stained with the sticky warmth of Polyxena's blood, and the air around us reeked of iron and death. Deiphobus and I, numbed by the weight of our actions and the loss of our sister, gathered Polyxena's lifeless body. We knew we couldn't be seen, not after the murder of Achilles. In hushed voices, we decided to take the hidden paths, known only to the royal family and trusted few, to return to the palace undetected.

The bow and poisoned arrow, instruments of our tragic mistake, were concealed in a hidden compartment within my cloak. Under the cover of darkness, we moved swiftly and silently, navigating through secret corridors and concealed tunnels. The weight of our guilt and sorrow grew heavier with each step. The night air was cold, and the silence was broken only by our muted footsteps and the distant cries of nocturnal creatures. The scent of earth and damp stone clung to our clothes, mingling with the acrid tang of sweat and blood.

Upon reaching the palace, we laid Polyxena in a private chamber, draping her gently with a shroud. Our hearts ached as we looked upon her peaceful face, marred only by the traces of blood on her gown. We knew we had to deliver the news to our parents, and the dread of this task gnawed at our souls.

Deiphobus and I stood in Father's chamber, our hearts heavy with the burden of the news we were about to deliver. The room, filled with a blend of regal authority and intimate family touches, seemed to close in around us. Mother sat nearby at a small table cluttered with colorful embroidery silks, a delicate tapestry half-finished under her nimble fingers. Father looked up from his ornately carved desk, covered with important scrolls and documents, his gaze piercing and expectant. In a corner, a beautifully crafted crib stood, adorned with carved toys for the grandchildren, a visible reminder of the life and love that still lingered in the palace despite the shadow of war.

'Father, Mother,' I began, my voice strained with sorrow. 'We have...we have lost Polyxena.' *We have lost Polyxena.* Such trite words to use for the betrayal that we had orchestrated. Yet I had none other to offer them. We stood there waiting for their response covered in our sister's blood and patches of dirt from where we had buried Achilles where no one would ever find him. We had had our revenge at such a high cost I had no wish for the retribution that would follow should the myrmidons find his corpse. The slaughter would be absolute.

Mother's breath caught in her throat, her hand flying to her mouth as tears welled up in her eyes. Father immediately crossed the room to her, wrapping his arms around her as she wept. 'What do you mean? How?' she whispered, her voice breaking.

Deiphobus stepped forward, his face pale and drawn. 'It was an accident. We had planned to bring Achilles down, to avenge our brother Troilus. Polyxena was supposed to meet him...we thought it would be safe.' His voice faltered as he struggled to continue.

I took a deep breath, my eyes fixed on the floor. 'We didn't anticipate the events that unfolded. When Achilles was struck by the poisoned arrow, Polyxena tried to save him. In her efforts, she accidentally nicked herself with the arrow and...the poison took hold too quickly.'

Father's face hardened, his grief mingling with anger. 'You used your own sister in a scheme of revenge? And now she is dead because of it?' His voice was low, trembling with suppressed rage. He made sure Mother could stand on her own before swiftly moving before us. He back handed me across my face. I made no move to defend myself. I deserved his rage with such an ill thought plan. Raya had warned us that it was risky. She had begged us to think about what we would be sacrificing and I had told her that I would not abandon my soul to a war I was responsible for. *And yet, I had traded in my sister's soul in place of my own.*

'We never intended for this to happen,' Deiphobus said, his voice filled with anguish. 'We thought we were protecting her, that this would bring some peace to our family.'

Father rushed to reach Mother before she crumpled to the floor in her pain. Even a queen had her limits, and it seemed that after so much death and violence, Mother had found hers.

Her sobs filled the room as she clung to Father, who held her tightly. 'First Hektor, then Troilus, and now Polyxena...gone,' she cried, her heart shattered by the news. 'Where is she now?' she demanded, her voice rising in desperation. 'Where have you left my youngest child?'

'We brought her back through the hidden paths to ensure no one saw us. She is at peace now, in the private chamber,' I said gently.

Father's eyes, once filled with strength and wisdom, now brimmed with unspeakable sorrow. 'Our children...all gone,' he murmured, his voice barely audible. 'How much more must we endure?'

Father, still holding Mother, continued to address us. 'You are not fighting for yourselves... Andromache's son, Helene's children, and even Selene and her sisters—they are our future. We are fighting for the future of our family in this city. We are fighting for the city itself. The Greeks will not forgive this action. It is a good thing that I have called in every favor. All our allies are coming to fight for Troy. We must prepare for the battles to come and protect what remains of our family and our city.'

Though filled with guilt and sorrow, Deiphobus and I nodded in understanding. The weight of Father's words settled heavily upon us, a reminder of the grave consequences of our actions and the strength we would need to face the coming storm.

Part Five

The weight of silence

(Selene)

I could not endure the inside of this tower for one more day. I felt trapped and while I knew where Thea was,-she was in the corridor grinding herbs into powders restocking her medicines, Raya was not outside my door. Her room was empty. The fireplace cold. The silence unnatural. She had abandoned her post, one that she had fought for... and yet she had disappeared from my side. Father would not have understood this. Neither did I. Hektor had pressed her oath from her to guard me well. *She wasn't here to guard me at all.*

This was the first time since we had arrived in Wilusa that I could remember Raya acting strangely. Her whole life revolved around the tenants of duty and honour. She had forsaken her duty but for what? Surely her mate had not convinced her to run away with him when he was as needed in Theron's encampment as much as I relied upon her.

I needed air. We could not leave the city easily now with the surrounding countryside crawling with the enemy soldiers all looking for a way to breach the walls. Theron's shifters nod in silent recognition and respect. They do not question my presence in the tree that had grown attached to the weakest part of the wall. I settled in the branches to wait, hiding amongst the thickest leaves. I could see out but none but the most astute would see me and she would find me when she was ready. I could only hope that I was ready to hear what she had to say for herself.

As dusk set in Raya finally found me reading high in the tree. Her nimble feet treading lightly along the thick tree branch wide enough for us both to sit upon. 'You were not there when I looked for you.' cool words paused her actions. She passed me a bracelet with dried blood caked into the etching of a dove. Polyxena's bracelet. I take a closer look at my sister's hands. Stained red. 'She is not mine to mourn.' The princess's bracelet should have been returned to Queen Hekuba. Another protocol broken. 'She was ours to protect.' Raya replies, voice low, eyes empty. My thoughts spiral: *What had she been part of?*

'What have you done sister?' I search for the details just as Father taught me to. Raya was visibly shaken. She was never this shaken. 'I sent them. I had good intel and warned them of the risks they were taking.' her voice monotone as she walks me through her day, 'I thought it would end the retaliatory bloodshed. Alexander and Deiphobus targeted Achilles when he met with Polyxena. I thought no one would get hurt but I didn't account for human compassion.'

'You thought. You acted. You left your post.' my voice was cold. There had been enough death in our family and she had deliberately abandoned her post to orchestrate an ill thought attack. Raya continues as pain floods her features, 'When I tried to heal her the light did not come. It wasn't the goddess—it was my oath to you. Your word prevented me from healing a dying human.'

'That oath was meant to protect us as phoenix shifters.' the words were delivered with icy precision, 'The world as we know it no longer exists. My husband is dead. My children are dead. Now my sister in law is also dead. You want me to be the Queen of the phoenix shifters then heed my word now. My word is the law. You broke it and you broke your oath to a dead man. A good man. Hektor believed in you but at the moment—I do not.' I examine her face white and stalwart. She is prepared for any judgement I wish to pass upon her—utterly lost in the consequences of her own actions. Her own behaviour was almost punishment enough, however, 'You are not banished from Troy. But you are not to enter my presence unless I call for you. Some solitude out here in the tree will do you good where you will answer to no one but the wind and your own mate.'

Clutching the soiled bracelet in my hands along with my book I give her one final sentence of hope, 'Forgiveness will come when I am ready—not before.' She bows her head before reaching up into her hair and yanking hard. She does not beg for mercy. Warrior born my sister instead offers me one of her own crimson and gold feathers to weave into my hair. She silently wishes for me to wear it until we might one day speak again.

Weaving her feather at the tip of one of my braids I nod my head in understanding. She will be close by if I call but until then I must remember her as I do the rest of our family-in my prayers.

Climbing further higher into the tree she leaves me to my fractured thoughts, the pain of the loss of another family member and the heaviness that comes with leadership. I needed clarity...I wanted to see Theron. He was waiting for me but a few steps from the tree.

'I felt your sorrow before I saw your face and knew you needed me.' He was wearing the amulet and I touched the coin at the base of my neck where it glowed faintly under my dress. 'I don't know how to do this anymore.' I admit softly. Somewhere in the distance an owl hoots before flapping wings startle me. Theron reaches out and draws me to his side, gently shackling one of my wrists with his hand. 'Then let me carry some of your worries for you little moon. Come sit by the fire with me.'

In the void where words usually flowed, the fire dances merrily. Theron keeps it banked low with barely a bright light to be seen beyond our immediate huddle. His armour is in disrepair. If only Raya hadn't...I catch my thoughts breathing out with an almost gasping breath. The betrayal of an oath broken still raw in my mind. 'How do you do it?' I ask him as I stare into the fire, 'Continue to lead knowing one of your closest advisors has broken an oath to someone very dear to you-someone they can no longer make amends with.'

'You don't.' he says taking his time poking at the fire with a stick to keep it going. 'Not at first. You learn to work past it. You don't forget either. One betrayal is the difference between life and death. Trust grows back over time but you don't forget.'

'Who broke your trust?' He asks softly as a tear rolls down my face letting me process my grief. 'Nuraya.' I reply absentmindedly, 'Who broke yours?'

'Seraphinus.'

I study his profile in the firelight. I really look at him. 'You're tired love.' the words tumble from my lips as easily as my next breath does and the words that follow, 'I'm not ready.

His blue eyes glow with happiness but he doesn't move any closer. 'I know, ' he replies, 'I'll wait. I promised him I'd wait until you were ready.'

His admission startles me and he slowly raises his hand to stroke my hair, fingering the feather at the tip of my braid at the opposite end of all the others. Its significance evident for all who understood.

'I can't stay.' Hektor's personal guards continued to take shifts at the tower and with the danger closing in they were taking no chances with us now. 'They'll be looking for me.'

Theron nods, already rising to his feet. He doesn't argue. I want to give him more than some day. He'd already waited nearly ten years on that beach. 'I will send Thea to Raya and have her mend your armor.' We may not be on speaking terms but I could make sure the best armorer I knew attended him.

'You don't need to do that.' He bends down to brush a kiss over my brow, 'But I will wear the armor she mends. Not for war. For you.'

The tiny spark in my heart warms a little more and into silence I disappear.

Allies arrive

Allies arrive

(Selene)

As the palace prepared for the arrival of allied forces to bolster our army, Andromache and Astyanax quietly moved into the tower with us. It was our refuge amidst the turmoil. With the palace now filled with strangers and the looming uncertainty, Thea insisted that we stay away from the main halls. Knowing Andromache was with us and the future of Troy was protected brought comfort to us all.

I recalled Raya from exile earlier than I wished but we had trained from a young age to trust when it was required and quarrel amongst ourselves when we were alone. I continued to wear her feather near the tip of my plait. Her shame evident for all to see. I would forgive her completely when she had earned it.

Word of allies arriving from Raya and Thea reached me as I stood by the tower's window, watching the horizon for signs of change. A mixture of hope and anxiety surged within me. Theron doubled the dragons on our guard detail in anticipation of trouble. Without Hektor's protection, I was vulnerable to anyone who might take a fancy to me.

Penthelesia and her Amazon warriors arrived first, their presence awe-inspiring and almost otherworldly. The Amazonian women were tall and muscular, exuding strength and confidence with every step. Their armor was a blend of functionality and elegance, featuring simplicity in their design. Built for training. For battle. Not for show. They moved with synchronized grace and discipline under the eagle eyes of their commander and the other Leaders watching their display.

Penthelesia, their queen, was particularly striking. She led her warriors with an undeniable presence. She wore a headdress adorned with vibrant feathers, which added an air of regality and fierceness to her appearance. The feathers fluttered with every movement, creating a dynamic and almost mesmerizing effect. Her armor was more ornate than that of her warriors, signifying her status and achievements. Her sharp, focused eyes betrayed a lifetime of battles and leadership. Even from a distance, I could see Crinos's face cloud with shame as Penthelesia spoke with her away from the palace, her fierce demeanor imposing.

Following them, Sarpedon of Lycia entered with his Lycian army. The Lycians were a sight to behold, clad in tunics and robes adorned with intricate patterns. They favored bright blue and red colors, reflecting their connection to the sea and their warrior spirit. Each warrior carried a spear, a short curved sword, and a bow with a quiver of arrows, their shields round and reinforced with metal. The sight of Sarpedon and his men bolstered Troy's spirits. Their camaraderie and strength were evident, and they added a formidable edge to our defenses. The Trojans received them warmly, their gratitude evident in every word and gesture. These alliances were lifelines, fraying but vital.

Then, amidst the swell of hope, arrived Memnon of Ethiopia. His warriors, clad in animal hides adorned with intricate patterns, carried spears, long straight swords, and bows. Their shields, made of leather-covered wood, were reinforced with metal. Memnon's grim expression, a testament to the weight of responsibility he bore, was especially poignant after losing half his army on the journey. Yet, his determination and resilience were undiminished. He quickly integrated with the other leaders. Their shared resolve echoing through the great halls as they prepared for the final confrontation.

Finally, the warrior priests of Zeleia arrived. Thea insisted that we be there to greet them. Theron insisted that we take Alexios and Seraphinus as part of our guards. He trusted they would not let anything happen to me or their mates. I thought that male shifters were intimidating. Thea greeted them politely before they took their place beside the Ethiopians.

On the evening that all allies had finally assembled, King Priam and Queen Hekuba hosted a dinner. One that all royals were required to attend. Grief was etched deeply into every line of our faces. We wore our personal loss like armour. Our people weary of the endless sacrifice—all in the name of love. A love that was fast waning.

Alexander stayed close to Helena, his hand resting possessively on her arm. He never allowed her to leave his side, a clear sign of the distrust that filled the air. Not even our allies trusted her. Although he had not spoken of it, I could see the flicker of suspicion in Alexander's eyes. Helena, aware of the precariousness of her situation, stayed silent, her eyes darting around the room, absorbing the conversations. She knew she would have to act soon, one way or another.

The food was scarce, a harsh reminder of our dire circumstances. The warmth of the company, however, provided some comfort. Toasts were raised often, each one a bittersweet tribute to endurance and hope. Grim faces surrounded us, a silent acknowledgment of the struggle that lay ahead.

Penthelesia approached me with a somber expression. 'Queen Selene of Emberis, Lady of Troy,' she began, her voice tinged with sorrow. 'I must apologize for my daughter breaking the Amazon code. I was heartbroken to learn of the loss of your mother, my dear friend.' Her words were sincere, her grief genuine.

She continued, her eyes hardening slightly. 'Crinos's behavior was disgraceful. I assure you that had I known about the plot against you, it would have been swiftly dealt with. I attribute some of this to my own failings; Crinos has lived with Hekuba since she was a small child. I regret that I did not oversee her upbringing myself. However, I will personally see to it that Crinos faces the consequences. We cannot afford treachery in our ranks, especially not now.'

'Crinos has been misled but remembered the Amazon code when it counted,' I replied, seeking to ease Penthelesia's burden. 'My sister Nuraya, leader of the royal guard of Emberis, has taken responsibility for Crinos and is impressed with how much she has shown remorse for her behavior. You mentioned knowing my mother? I was not aware that she corresponded with anyone from the Amazon nation.'

Penthelesia nodded, a flicker of relief in her eyes. 'Thank you, Lady Selene. Your understanding means a great deal. I wonder why you do not wear the crown of Emberis. I have heard from Crinos that you do not flaunt your rank or even intrude on family life here in Troy. Your mother would be proud of you.' Her voice dropped, 'We travelled in the same circles. Straddling two worlds can be exhausting and having someone who understands the burdens it can bring is invaluable.'

'The loss of my people was excruciating to endure. The royal jewels of Emberis was lost in one night. I came to Wilusa to serve the people, not the other way around,' I said, offering a gentle smile. 'Titles can create barriers; I find it more important to connect with people through our shared experiences and challenges. The loss of Hektor has left me feeling somewhat isolated, so I have been focusing on helping in quiet ways.' I dropped my voice as well, 'Those who understand the titles offer the respect they deserve. I would like a chance to talk with you further if you are open to meeting with my sisters and I.'

Penthelesia smiled back, a glimmer of admiration in her eyes. 'There is a time for humility and a time to lead. Your time to lead is soon. I suggest you get comfortable with the idea. Your quiet ways are having an impact on lives and the people are beginning to whisper your name. I have heard that the shifters here have been running rescue missions with the humans.' she said, her tone softening. 'I support this wholeheartedly. Men may obey the whims of the gods, but we women will always protect those more vulnerable than ourselves. I would be happy to meet you in a more private setting.' Her acknowledgment was a shared understanding, a silent pact among us.

As the evening wore on, the sense of impending change grew stronger. The alliances forged, the resolve strengthened, and the shared grief and hope among us all seemed to weave together into a final, epic stand.

The night faded, but our determination remained as solid as ever. Tomorrow, the final battle between Greece and Troy would unfold, a culmination of years of struggle and sacrifice. The fate of us all hung in the balance, but for now, we clung to the unity and strength we had found in one another.

The Temple above the Sea

The Temple above the Sea

(Selene)

They were still celebrating in the megaron as my guards escorted me back to the tower. They had watched as Helena's eyes followed me through each conversation. When Queen Hekuba had chosen to retire so did I. Instead of a meeting of allied leaders it was fast descending into a party for drunkards, full of jests and loud boasts. Laughter spilled as easily as the wine. Andromache and Astyanax had planned to spend the night in the palace and Thea was diligently tending her patients. I missed Hektor. The echo of his scent filled my head for a moment and before I left the sitting area I poured myself a cup of tea. Toasting his ghost I felt the warmth fill me. Climbing the tower's stairs to my chamber I allowed the fatigue of the evening to settle into my bones. I could throw off my mask in my solitude. Without request, Raya had retreated outside to spend the night in the tree or in Seraphinus's arms-of which I was not sure, but did not begrudge them their time together. There were freedoms in not wearing the crown and I was glad that she claimed them when she could. I longed for Theron to hold me.

Moving slowly around my chamber I placed the feathers I wore into a small casket and ran my fingers through my curls unbinding all the tiny braids. Closing the lid of the casket with reverence I laid my hand on the lid pausing a moment, offering a quiet prayer for the family I had loved and lost slipped from my lips. Readying myself for bed I slipped into the fine linen shift that had been laid out warming near the brazier. It swirled around me then clung to my legs as it settled over my form. The quiet mocked me, echoing with laughter that no longer belonged to this world. I did not want to be here. Not like this. Alone. I yearned for companionship, warmth and a love to hold me through the night.

The coin hung at the base of my throat. The lines glowed, mirroring the ones etched into his skin like a beacon beckoning me to press it. I breathed in, closed my eyes and exhaled. My world shifted from the lonely tower to the cliffs above the beach where we had met on this plane so long ago. The weight I carried dissolved and the grass beneath my feet felt impossibly soft no prickles in sight. This was where I had first watched Hektor while offering morning rites to the goddess. Taking a deep cleansing breath in, I felt a warm gentle breeze play with the ends of my hair as I noticed a new feature to the landscape. Something that did not exist in real life. Something I was not sure if I should treat as a threat.

A stone temple, clad in ivy, unweathered by time and the salt in the ocean breeze looked ancient but stood strong. It was not here last time I visited this space. Reaching out to touch it I hesitate only a moment drawing my hand back. Was this meant for me? I convince myself to lay my hand flat against the stone wall. It was warm to touch as if it had always been, and yet I was not sure whether I should enter. Who would be waiting? I wore only my nightdress. My hair unbound to the elements. Sea mist rolling in behind me forced my decision driving me to move inside. It would be unwise to remain high on the cliffs when I would not be able to see my hand in front of me.

Torches flared to life, one by one as I passed them in a tunnel like entry. Theron stood in the doorway to the next room waiting. He wore no armour only an open robe belted at his waist. Shame had no place between us in this moment. The linen clung to me, and I knew he could see the outline of my form beneath it. If he had words, they dried in his throat. I did not need them. 'Did you call me here?' I thought I had pressed the coin and yet he had been waiting for me. Theron cleared his throat replying. 'No. I built this for you. I think you called yourself alerting me to your arrival.' Catching a glimpse of the room beyond, our sigils were entwined etched into the wall. I had never seen them joined. Not like this. I had nothing to cover myself with, and no need to. He stood frozen and I did not wait for him to move. Entranced I brush past him. My body betrayed me with a blush, soft and unbidden. My emotions lay bare and I wore them like the jewels that they were.

This was unlike any temple I had been inside of before. The interior seemed to be a blend of shifter and human cultures with soft cushions lining the stone benches. Tapestries soften the walls. On a dais a bed with a canopy of ivy-thick in cover to hide the occupants from prying eyes. Neatly made. Simple linens-sacred and untouched. The sigils on the wall, inlaid with phoenix stone and merlinite, flashing with fire and pure starlight symbolising our ties to ancestral magic, rebirth and unconditional love. My breath caught in my throat. Not from surprise but from recognition. This was how he saw me. How he saw us. Every detail reflected how he wished we could live. Safe. Loved. Together.

'I don't want you to die without knowing me.' my voice steady but raw. The Greeks had no place here but honesty did and I was afraid. He needed to see me. Not the mask I wore in public or the version of me hidden behind a prophecy he had followed. Me. Not the leader, the sister, the priestess or the princess. The woman who had forgotten how to just be. I didn't know what I was asking for but I knew he saw me better than I saw myself. 'Then let me show you how I've kept you.' His voice is quiet, full of reverence. He gestures around us. 'This is where you belong little moon. How I see you. How I pictured our nest to be.'

He holds out his hand to me. An invitation to move closer. My eyes don't shift from his face. My feet bring me closer and the distance between us disappears. He leads me by one hand to the edge of the bed seating me comfortably beside him. No awkwardness between us. No rush. Just movements as natural as breathing. 'I'm tired of sleeping alone in a cold, empty bed.' I admit softly. I was tired of being someone's widow, the people's princess and lonely in a city full of people. Theron's blue eyes shine in their intensity, 'I'm no substitute for Hektor.' 'You are not a choice. You're air in my lungs. A need I can no longer live without.' My response satisfies him and his face clears. He exhaled as if he'd been holding his breath for years.

'Lie with me little moon.' the words are crooned into my ear. Soft. Seductive. I allow myself to flow with it, finding us rearranged with me on my side and him pressed against my back. Still fully clothed his warmth surrounding me. The feeling of being safe all encompassing. The ivy shifts gently in the canopy above us as I close my eyes, 'Don't let go.' His hand tucks my curls behind my ear gently before stroking my cheek with his fingers, 'I won't. Not even when you wake.' He wraps his arm over my waist and I interlace our fingers together after feeling the steady beat in his wrist. There are no further words. He traces his sigil on my palm. I trace mine on his. A silent vow that we belong with each other no matter what life may bring.

Much later a brazier flared before one of the temple walls shimmered like water. My eyes widened. It was not my magic doing this. Theron's arm tightened around my waist, his other hand going for the dagger he had placed under his pillow. *'It's not my magic either.'* He uses our telepathy scanning our safe space for danger. Nostrils flaring trying to pick up the scent of the intruder.

The mirror like wall shifts showing us a cave. Dragons were positioned around the edge. Thea and Nuraya were beside me in water wearing dresses cut in a style I had never seen. Joy intermingled with sadness, lit the faces of everyone we knew including Theron, himself being held back by Alexios and Seraphinus. The scene cuts to a nest without eggs. Two babies lay curled up together. A boy with scales and Theron's hair. A girl with white pinfeath-ers and my curly hair. Above them high on the rock face our entwined sigil etched for everyone to see.

'Are they?' I question softly still not sure if an enemy is playing a trick on us. 'I'm not sure but I think they will be ours.' His voice in my ear calms me. I long to drink in the picture. Two children. Two would unite and bind our clans together for all time.

The wall shimmered again, as if the vision resisted being held too long. As if prophecy had limits and at first all I could see was darkness. The sun rose and set on repeat and each time over a different battlefield. Always the same two armies. The united clans of Thera and an army with horrifying adaptive skills, multiplying over time while the dragon shifters dwindled. They wielded weapons that no one had ever seen before.

Behind me Theron's involuntary roar of pain is music to my ears. If this was to be true he would fight with everything he had to come back to me. A tear runs down my face. I realise it before he speaks the words, 'This is why we'll be separated. To protect them. To survive.' I roll onto my back and stare up into his stricken face the prophetic wall forgotten as our need to hold each other to the present intensi-fies, 'I don't want to part from you. Not now. But we will never really be parted as long as we hold the amulet and the coin.'

His hand clasps mine and as his face softens our hands heat up. He grips mine firmly refusing to let go even though the heat has turned to pain. And as suddenly as it scalded me my hand is perfectly fine hold-ing a ruby pendant set in darkened bronze. He slides it onto the same chain as the coin, wryly noting that the ancients won't mind where the matters of the heart are concerned. 'Hektor gave you the ocean. I give you myself. The ruby is soul forged made from a piece of my heart. No matter the distance. You are my queen. My little moon. If I ever fall, I will still be with you.'

Two perfect tears fell and as they rolled down my face they crystal-lized and hardened into crystals he could carry with a liquid contained within. Pressing them into his hand and folding his fingers over them

I tell him, 'When you are wounded beyond the limitations of human and dragon kind healers, break these open and pour them directly on your wounds. I cannot bear to think of you alone and injured somewhere without aid. You are my everything Theron. Remember our children depend on us finding our way back to each other.' He didn't speak. He didn't need to. His grip said everything as we watched our hours together slip away.

When I woke in the tower I could feel his ruby warm at my throat, pulsing in time with his heart beat and I prayed that he would find the present I had delivered to the caves-a new set of armor. The design unique, reinforced and one of three to be worn that day. I caught part of his thoughts when he found it.

She did not wear a crown. She wore his ruby, and the memory of fire.

Dragon kind would recognise her as their queen. And humans would remember her as the woman who saved a nation.

Troy's united front

Troy's united front

(Deiphobus)

We stood on the plain, the sun casting long shadows over the assembled warriors. The Greeks, with their steel and determination, faced us across the battlefield. To my left, Penthesilea, queen of the Amazons, her eyes fierce with the fire of battle. To my right, Sarpedon and Memnon, stalwart allies in this struggle. But my gaze kept drifting back to the city walls, where Alexander remained, waiting for the signal that our reserves were needed in battle. I needed him with me, but he had a target on his back, not only for the wife he stole almost ten years ago but also for the death of Achilles. It pained me to keep him inside, but it was a necessary precaution.

As we prepared for the coming clash, I turned to Penthesilea. 'Queen of the Amazons, your warriors are the fiercest I've seen. Today, we fight together as one.'

She nodded, her eyes blazing. 'We fight for honour and for Troy. Let them come.'

I moved to Sarpedon and Memnon, who were conferring over a map of the battlefield. 'Sarpedon, Memnon, your strategies have been invaluable. What do you propose for today's battle?'

Sarpedon pointed to a weak spot in the Greek formation. 'We strike here, with all our might. It will break their line and sow chaos.'

Memnon added, 'And my warriors will flank them from the right. They won't know what hit them.'

King Menelaus of Sparta and King Agamemnon of Greece, their presence a reminder of the war's origins but not of its current direction. We met in the center, astride our horses, the space between us charged with the weight of countless fallen comrades. As a man of action, I despised the need for negotiation, but I had been told to try words first before risking any more Trojan blood.

King Agamemnon's voice broke the silence first. 'Prince of Troy, you cry to your neighbors for help. Do you not see this as a sign of your weakness?'

I reined in my horse, my voice steady but with a seething impatience. 'You brought your neighbors to war with you when you arrived. We saved ours for when we needed them most. This war ceased to be about King Menelaus recovering Helena long ago. Now, it is a battle for control of the shipping routes outside the Aegean. Or will you not admit it?'

King Agamemnon's eyes narrowed, but he did not deny it. 'It is true. The Aegean must be secured.'

King Menelaus leaned forward on his horse, his eyes burning with the same fire I had seen ten years ago. 'But I still want my wife back.'

Our words hung in the air, heavy with the futility of peace. I longed to let my sword do the talking, but I knew that this parley was necessary. We turned away, knowing that the next time we met, it would be with swords drawn.

With the failure of our parley, both sides prepared for the inevitable clash.

The battle raged with a ferocity I had rarely seen. The Greeks pushed forward with a thunderous roar, their shields a wall of unyielding iron. We matched them, blow for blow, our warriors driven by a determination born of desperation. The screams of the dying and the clash of swords filled my ears. Mounted on horseback, I could see the entire battlefield, the chaos and bravery of both sides. The flanks of my horse were speckled with the blood of the fallen, each drop a testament to the savagery of the conflict.

Queen Penthesilea was a force unto herself. She rode, guiding her horse with her knees through the melee with a grace that belied the strength of her sword blows. I saw her fall, and for a moment, the world held its breath. She was the last of the great warriors of old. Immediately, a guard of Amazons formed around their fallen Queen, her sacrifice a beacon of bravery that inspired us all to fight harder, to honor her memory with our own valor. In that moment, all fighting ceased. My eyes met those of King Agamemnon's and he nodded slightly. In mutual respect, we all lowered our weapons to honour Penthesilea's courage. The ferocity her tribe fought with belied the tenderness with which they treated their fallen Queen. Sliding her body onto a litter hastily made of their shields, they moved her body from the battlefield.

But the respite was brief. The battle resumed with a renewed intensity, both sides driven by an unrelenting determination to see this through to the end. The ground beneath our feet was stained with the blood of our heroes, our enemies, our brothers, our lovers—blood was blood—and the air filled with the sounds of our struggle. We fought, not just for victory on this day but for the survival of Troy herself.

As the sun dipped below the horizon, casting long shrouds over the battlefield, as if mourning the fallen. Women scurried from one body to the next, looking for loved ones and picking over the cadavers for their belongings. I did not prevent the desecration of the dead Greeks. Why should I? They had not afforded Hektor any courtesy. I would give them all the honour they had shown my brother during the three days his body was missing and his wives desolate with grief.

The poisoned reckoning

The poisoned reckoning

(Alexander)

This isn't war anymore. Not the way Hektor explained it. No clean lines of soldiers waiting for the opposing army to arrive. No amnesty to remove the dead and dying from the battlefield. Men die unaided and corpses rot under the sun. Those we send out to fight have lost their spirit. We are all rotting within. The city contends with air born pestilence. *Have we been cursed by the gods for arguing with each other for so long?* My remaining brothers sit in the war chamber with hollow eyes and gaunt faces. No one toasts at winning a sorty. There's nothing left to toast with. I used to count victories. Now I count the days we survive. Agamemnon no longer wants a clean victory-he wants Troy to bleed out, slow and silent, until all that's left is bone and ash. He'll call it justice. But it's trade routes he wants. Not vengeance. And when he comes, he won't find warriors. Only echoes of a once proud nation. He's circling like a scavenger drawing the net tighter around our city.

This war has never been about Menelaus reclaiming Helena. I know this now. After ten years of fighting even he grows weary of her games. Her words are like honey. She offers advice on matters that she should not be involved with. I have removed anything resembling battle tactics from our room. Maps, scrolls even notes on courage from my mother-I burned them all. Only blank parchment sits upon my desk. Let her read my silence. Her eyes are sharp. Always watching. Always waiting. The silence between her words reveal volumes to me until the truth of her nature screams for the world to hear like a funeral bell tolling for the city she claims to love, and I am no longer that naive young fool who was so easily manipulated. My children and those of my sisters depend on my silence. On vigilance. On burying the truth. She taught me to question. Now I question her every breath.

Shrouded in shadows, I have just watched her steal the god given poisoned arrow that killed Polyxena and Achilles from the war chamber. The arrow hums with old death and the bright possibility of feeding its hunger for more. We had kept its existence quiet out of respect for Polyxena. Somehow she knew. The walls speak to her. Or she makes them. Charming the guards. Claiming I had sent her. Her voice soft, her lies silk wrapped, spreading like tentacles. We are choking because of her. One word would've stopped her. I needed to know who else she had corrupted into helping her this time.

Standing, shrouded by the cloak I had commissioned for her to celebrate the birth of our second son, she sneaks into the stables. 'This place stinks of desperation.' Disgust colours her voice as she adds condescendingly, 'Fitting.' She hates horses. She hates getting dirty. And yet she's here holding my deepest regret in her fist. Her words condemn her as she meets with a myrmidon-conspicuous by his armor. She tells him the arrow's origin story. She tells him of my betrayal. A horse wickers softly in the stall next to her causing her to move closer to the soldier and then she divulges the truth behind Achilles death. His eyes gleam in fury. I should have killed him then. I should have thrown her from the walls. Helena is the danger we have been searching for all this time. I follow her back to the inner palace complex. Slipping from shadow to shadow watching as she busies herself. She doesn't know I heard. She doesn't know her actions will have consequences.

I waited inside the gates, the weight of the world pressing down on my shoulders. The sounds of battle were a distant roar, a constant reminder of the storm brewing just beyond the walls. My hand rested on the hilt of my sword, ready for the signal to lead our host forward. The gates felt like a barrier between the safety of Troy and the chaos awaiting us outside.

Selene and Raya approached, their faces grim with determination, but there was something different about them today. It was the first time I had seen them wearing the armor of Emberis. Their figures clad in dark green tunics and tight leather trousers with sleek dark metal that seemed to absorb the light around them. Selene's cloak was adorned with bright azure and purple feathers sewn around the collar, the same vibrant hues braided through her hair. Azure for the sky goddess she worshipped. Purple for her claim to royal blood. With the change of outfit, Selene's demeanor had shifted to the woman I had always suspected she'd hidden away inside. They didn't speak at first. Their silence was louder than words.

'The goddess blessed me with a vision. This war is being fought across all realms. I saw the sun rise and fall over a thousand battlefields. If you go to fight today my brother, you will not survive the onslaught.' Her voice was tense as if she was trying to delay me from facing what the fates had woven for me.

'Visions are not truth. They are shadows. Echoes. Maybes.' I wanted to fall with my sword drawn not hiding behind a wall where the enemies sought out all our secrets. My own twin had become ensnared in visions. Kassandra followed prophecy. I followed facts.

'If I fall, let it be by choice. Not by fear.' I looked at Selene, the weight of my family and my city bearing down on me. 'Selene, promise me this: if you can, save Helena and my children. I know there's bad blood between you, but my children need their mother.'

Selene's gaze softened, her resolve clear. 'I'll do everything in my power to save them, Alexander.'

The promise hung heavy in the air, a silent pact between us. 'Selene,' I continued, turning back to her. 'There's one more thing. I need you to pass a message to Theron.'

Selene's eyes widened. 'But he's out there, fighting with the Greeks.'

'Tell Theron... tell him that despite everything, there's still a chance for honor in this chaos. We need all the help we can get to save the innocent. Remind him of our pact from long ago.' I paused, the weight of the words sinking in. 'The pact that Hektor made with Theron to protect you at all costs. Kassandra believes you are the key to the future of our people. Kassandra's visions never lie.' I placed a hand on her shoulder, a rare moment of vulnerability slipping through. 'Be safe, my sister.'

I turned toward the battlefield. In the distance, the signal flag fluttered in the breeze. The time for words had passed. It was time for action. I led the charge, my heart pounding in my chest. We fought our way through the Greek onslaught. Chaos surrounded me and I could not see Deiphobus or any of our allies in the heart of the battle. The Greeks continued to push forward with relentless fury. Amidst the fray, I caught sight of an archer, his bow drawn. It looked as if he were using my bow and the arrow Helena had smuggled from Wilusa. His aim was steady. Too steady. The arrow gleamed with memory.

There was a sharp pain in my chest, and I looked down to see the poisoned arrow embedded in my flesh. As I fell, the world around me blurred. Regret washed over me, for my misspent youth and the trouble I had brought to my family's door. But amidst the pain, there was gratitude. Gratitude for the love of my family, for the chance to fight for Troy, for Helena and our children.

The world faded, and with my last breath, I clung to the hope that Selene would keep her promise for I knew Helena never would. Let the gods judge me. Let my children remember me. Let Selene survive.

Helena's true colours

Helena's true colours

(Helena)

Alexander's death did not hit me as hard as it once would have. There was a time I would have shattered but that would have been for show. He had long since lost trust in me, and we had not managed to bridge that gap before he died. I had tried. The man that I had married had turned into a stranger full of cold stares keeping me leashed to his side. Disbelief and sorrow swirled within me, but I couldn't afford to dwell on it for long. Now I was in a precarious position and I was forced to face a reality I had helped create. The chamber was dark. My children play in the next room, their laughter uninhibited. Quieting only when shushed by their nurse. Grief is a luxury I cannot afford. There would be time for mourning when a crown graced my brow once more.

I had sneered at Andromache and Selene. I mocked their grief when they had lost Hektor, but theirs was real. He had loved them in return. Andromache was safe in her role as the mother of the future King of Troy. Selene had loyalty. I had whispers and suspicion. She had a protector, but no one was sure who. He wore no sigils. Moved like smoke and was willing to bleed for her. His men treated her like a queen and yet she wore widows robes. Even in their grief, they were not alone. I was. Meanwhile, Deiphobus was rising in influence, stepping into a leadership role vacated by his fallen brothers. He was no Hektor. But he stood in his brothers place to honour his memory. He was visible. Respected. Available. If I aligned myself with him, I could ensure my safety and maintain my power within the city.

His impulsiveness was a weakness I could work with. The gods knew Alexander had been impulsive when we first met. He had rushed into love the same way he had rushed into battle-unguarded, passionate and strategically clueless. Maybe...just maybe I could still become Queen of Troy with Deiphobus at my side, and failing that, if Troy fell, I would not fall with it. Menelaus sent messages full of pretty words twined around demands for knowledge. Pretty words that claimed he remembered the girl I had been when he claimed me. And yet even he did not call for me so loudly before battle now. Sitting in the shadows, I admitted to myself that my gamble on Alexander had failed spectacularly. The game had changed. And I would not be caught playing the wrong role again.

I knew where Alexander's brother liked to go to think and created a moment for us when he was most vulnerable. It was his favorite spot in the palace—a secluded garden that no one visited and he maintained on his own. It was a place where he could get away from pressing battle plans and endless lists that must be scattered across his desk the way the old ones still were on Alexander's. I must stop thinking about Alexander. He is...was...mine, but not anymore. Not in this world. All of my children deserved the best chance of survival I could give them. Their names would be known-I would see to it and I deserved the best life I could give us. Deiphobus was my only chance in Wilusa so that I would not be traded back to Sparta to end this infernal war.

Remembering I still had a contact waiting for further instruction in the Greek camp, I sent a covert message to Isandros by dropping a bottle over the wall at an agreed-upon location. Glass shatters. So do alliances. But messages can be intercepted and my hand writing was painstakingly disguised so that it would not be recognised. Betrayal. Hardly. I was a woman in a man's world. Even a queen was a pretty side piece to be brought out at state functions and shuffled to the side when something younger caught their attention. Loyalty came at a price. I'd tried to love the husband I had been given to. I had had love and hadn't recognised it for what it was. I had smiled on command. I bore heirs. I was never asked what I wanted. It hadn't mattered. Now I was looking for the best outcome for myself. When the dust settles, I will not be the woman who smiled for love but the one they fear to tread on. I've learned. Thrones are not inherited. They are taken.

My words weave a scenario that Greece cannot ignore-burn the ships. They are rotting on the beach anyway. Pretend plague. Surely illness is rife in the encampment. Wilusa is on her knees. I knew that tunnels existed but no location of the entry or exit. Maybe leaving a gift that King Priam could not ignore would be a way to smuggle soldiers into the city and subjugate it fully. Let them call it a tribute. Instead it would be their doom. Patience would be key. Stealth a necessity. Rubbing my temple with my fingertips, I knew that I had stretched the good graces of my husband of Sparta and his brother to breaking point. Surely if they had a way of bringing chaos and destruction within Wilusa they would be merciful.

The garden was a peaceful haven, filled with bushes trimmed into tall hedges that formed a maze. It was the perfect blend of light and shadow, of passages that drew me through to open spaces with blooming flowers. I was not lost. The moon cast a silver glow on the scene, creating an almost ethereal atmosphere. I had dressed for diplomacy. But the embroidery shimmered like fragile armor hiding my brittle heart. Deiphobus, in contrast, looked worn for his years. He was laying on his back in the heart of the maze, staring up at the stars completely immersed in the stories the heavens told. The burdens of leadership had etched lines into his face, and his eyes, though determined, held a hint of exhaustion.

He didn't turn at first. But his nostrils flared, and I saw the moment he knew. No one else wore my perfume blend and the fragrance entered the space before I did.

'I did not expect you here, Helena. What is it that you wish to discuss?' He turned his face toward me, guarded curiousity in his eyes. I sit gracefully beside him just below his head so that we can speak as equals. Spreading out my skirts to show him I am not armed.

'I,' pausing for dramatic effect he angles his head closer to me. 'I wanted to thank you for looking my ex-husband in the eyes and refusing to hand me over to him today.' Leaving one hand at the edge of my skirts where he could reach out and take it if he so wished. Looking at him from beneath my lashes I used my eyes to gain his interest.

'You have been here for ten years now, Helena. You are part of our family. Why should you leave just because he demands it daily?' Deiphobus's fingers brushed mine as he moved his hand slightly.

'Not everyone could do it with such strength and resolve.' I lightly touched his arm, watching his expression soften at my familiarity. 'You've shown qualities that inspire hope in all of us. Especially now, with everything at stake.' A touch of flattery. A slow bat of my eyelids. I've got his attention. Let him believe this is his choice.

Sitting up his eyes become stern and his face hardens. 'I'm doing what I can. I'm not my brothers, May they rest in Elysium. I will not let Troy fall.' He takes a deep breath, 'Why did you come here Helena?' Trust was a precious commodity and I needed to gain his.

'I came because you saw me as more than a transaction. That alone is rare.' letting my voice catch slightly, feigning emotion I add, 'I've lived behind these walls for ten years. This city. Your culture. Our people. It's a beautiful place to be and I don't want to see it crumble under the boots of Agamemnon.' Adjusting my dress slightly so that the embroidered sigil of Troy normally disguised amongst the pretty embellishments on my dress catches the moonlight. I know he's seen my loyalty and heard the truth that I wanted him to.

'You know how they think. How they move. That makes you valuable. But I need more than sentiment, Helena. If we are to win the war we must be ahead of the game they think they have mastered.' He was right not to trust me. He had good instincts. If I didn't need him so badly I think that maybe we could have been friends.

'I've learned to listen more than I speak, especially when men speak of war. If I can be of use, I will tell you all I know. My place is with the Queen. I hear such interesting tales while sitting by her side.' Letting my fingers brush his again-lightly, deliberately. 'You said you needed more than sentiment. I offer my knowledge of the enemy and of the intrigue within our walls.' Demurely letting my eyes look down to pull off the picture of innocence I wait for his mind to choose the path I had led him down. I waited for him to choose me.

'You speak of things that I need to know. And yet when you look at me like that I forget the world outside this maze exists. No war. No intrigue. I see only you.' His fingers closed around mine, not as a princeling playing at war lord but as a man who'd stopped resisting the temptation of a beautiful woman. His grip was warm, steady and strong. *All the things that Alexander had once been.*

'You show strength and decisiveness in your actions. Be the leader everyone looks up to. Runs to. Feels protected by.' I moved even closer, our bodies pressed together, hands now entwined. My voice was a thread of whisper, one he leaned closer to hear, 'You are that person, Deiphobus. With you Troy stands a fighting chance but my heart does not.'

How easily led men were...a few batted eyelids and carefully chosen words. Breathy pauses and whispered lines had him eating out of the palm of my hand. He was so young. Younger than Alexander had been when I had met him on my private beach in Sparta. Holding the admiring expression on my face I let the emotion seep into my eyes. Eyes he had been searching for the truth. His smile widens at the sight of what he had found.

'We must tread lightly Helena.' He tucks an errant strand of hair behind my ear, 'Alexander is barely across the Hades. I do not wish for his shade to return because he felt the heat of our disrespect.'

Damn Priam instilling his sons with the same regard for the gods that he held. Knowing that he is waiting for a response I answer, 'We must honour his memory, especially around the children, but do not distance yourself. Time is a great thief and I do not want to remember your name in a temple of marble.'

'Then let me be more than a memory.' He frames my face with both hands, words tumbling from his lips like a vow, 'Let me be the man who stays. Let me keep you warm at night. Let me take care of you Helena. You and the children. Maybe one day the gods will bless us with one of our own.'

'I am still in mourning.' I remind him drawing back just enough for appearances. Not rejection. Just a nod to the proprietary lines that I had crossed happily. 'The city must see the grieving widow. That is the mask I wear for them but you...you see me. You have always seen me and you refuse to let go when everyone else would throw me away.'

More children? That would never happen. The maiden and the mother had turned their faces from me.

Before the gates

Before the gates

(Selene)

By the third day, in the middle of the coldest month, the beach lay bare. The once proud armada that had stretched beyond the reach of my phoenix's gaze had been reduced to a third, vanishing under cover of night. Ashes drifted with sand-nature's quiet purge. Predators who had come for blood had left nothing but scars on the landscape. They had burned everything. Only the wooden horse remained standing sentinel over the shells of huts where the kings had gathered plotting our downfall.

I stood on the wall watching as King Priam and his advisors rode out to investigate the encampment. Approaching cautiously expecting an elaborate ruse. In their absence the city held its breath whispering words of hope, confusion and more softly of dread that the conflict was not over. That the Greeks had withdrawn only to gather more allies, regroup and return bolder than before. The silence was unnerving. Prickles of unease ran down my spine. It was Emberis all over again-quiet before the storm, silence before the slaughter.

Ten years of quiet preparation and still-I wasn't ready for what would come next. My hands wouldn't still. I moved from room to room evaluating what mattered enough to me to carry in the small pack Raya had left on my bed-light enough to flee, heavy enough to matter. The ruby pulsed at the base of my throat-Theron's heartbeat steady and grounding. It tapped against my throat keeping me sane as our already precarious life had become deadly.

'*You know what this is little moon.*' His voice in my mind. Steady. Re-assuring. '*You've led behind the walls. Now you'll lead your people through fire.*'

'*What if I'm not ready?*' What if the fire takes them? I've seen this night before.' I reply voice broken, '*I know the cost.*' I didn't know if I could survive losing any more of my family.

'*You are ready my love. This separation is necessary. There is more at stake than human quarrels. You may lose some along the way. But you and your sisters will survive for the future of our kind. For our children. For me Selene.*' His voice is hard, '*You will survive for me because without you I do not have a reason left to fight.*'

Jasmine lingers in my thoughts as his grip tightens-steady, not possessive but anchoring to the present when the past threatens to engulf me.

'*Survive for me, Theron. I refuse to walk through life without you. Hold fast to the future we were shown with our children and the memory of our night together. Live for me. Don't gamble your life for that of another. I need you more than air.*' Words were all we had to offer. But his quiet, unwavering belief in us became my armor for what lay ahead.

I pause at the edge of Thea's room, watching in silence. She methodically sorts through her bundles of herbs. Each pouch is neatly labeled-wound, fever, poison, toxin, trauma. Easily identifiable for quick use. She takes only the bare necessities, leaving behind a heap of silks and jewels without a second glance. She wore them because we made her. Her style is more practical. Her pack is heavy with her tools of her trade. Healing unguents. Tincture bottles wrapped in soft cloth and her dagger is strapped to her waist. Her blond hair is braided around her head off her face ready for action.

'I need to tell you something.' she says, her hands never pausing. 'On one of my trips away from Wilusa I bought us a safe house-far to the north, where no Greek would think to search.' She doesn't smile. She doesn't look up. I wait, knowing this matters. 'We made plans for everyone but ourselves. I bought it so we wouldn't be strangers in someone else's court. We needed a place to regroup. To survive.' I cross the room and wrap my arms around her, holding her close. I reassure her, 'You thought of something I didn't. I'm not angry, Thea. I'm grateful. We'll need that refuge sooner than we think. Who was with you when you bought it?'

'Alexios and Seraphinus.' She lifts her gaze, solemn and steady, reading my face, 'They would have followed our trail to the ends of the earth. Theron is yours. Seraphinus belongs with Raya. They needed to know.' 'You have done well sister.' She pulls away and turns back to her packing. 'Choose one of those jewels for yourself Thea, to remind you of your time in Wilusa. In fact, pack a pouch of them-we may need to sell them one day for coin to survive.' Another weight for my own pack.

I leave Thea's room and return to my own, ready to shed softness for practicality. I was a Queen and I would lead my people to safety. The vibrant clothes I had worn from Emberis would betray me in Troy's muted terrain. A simple tunic and trousers-green and brown lay beside a weathered cloak. Beside the cloak, Raya had placed twin xythia-short blades, wicked and gleaming. I lifted one, letting its weight settle into my palm-balanced, lethal, familiar. She must have forged them for me. They fit my grip like memory. Perfectly balanced. Perfectly mine.

'They think we're cornered.' she says, pausing in my doorway as she adjusts her armor readying for war. She has tempered the metal so that it has a dull sheen to it. A tactical advantage. 'Let them.' I sheath the xythia. 'Their confidence will be their undoing. Is Andromache preparing Astyanax for travel?' I hadn't seen the sister of my heart all day. But we would not leave her to face this hell alone. 'She's ready,' Raya says quietly, her thoughts already on what lies ahead.

The ruby pulsed at my throat in a steady rhythm reminding me that Theron was preparing for battle too. My pack lay open on the bed before me. This had been my home with Hektor. Hektor's armor still stood in the corner-silent, untouched. I let my gaze pass over it, turning instead to my own belongings. I swept the glittering jewels into a pouch and tucked it deep into the pack alongside a second tunic. Plain and durable. Forgettable. I reached for the stone wall, my fingers brushing its rough surface. This place had been my home, as Emberis once was. I whispered my thanks into the stone. Goodbye had no echo, only silence.

'*It is time little moon. Seraphinus waits at the tree's base. Move swiftly. Move silently. Agamemnon's men are creeping from the horse and moving into position all over the city like smoke before a fire.*' Theron's warning fills my mind and one by one we slip from the tower. I lead. Thea follows. Andromache carries Astyanax, still asleep despite the jostling. Raya guards our rear. We will take whomever wishes to flee with us. Beneath the canopy of the tree's shelter, I speak softly but firmly, 'No one gets left behind.'

'My Queen.' Seraphinus calls softly up into the tree-urgency cloaked in reverence. There is no time. One by one we drop softly to the ground. Thea takes Astyanax while Raya helps her down the trunk pointing out the toe holds. Thea scans her surroundings warily picking her way across the open ground leading them to the mouth of the tunnel where they crouch in the silence waiting for us to join them. There is more to her than I knew. I tuck that revelation away-something to examine when we're safe.

In the darkness behind me I see heart break and duty flash across the face of my sister and her beloved. Grief and loyalty-a double edged sword. He offers her a scale and she draws a feather from her brow. Tokens of love and protection. Something to hold through the dark of the night. The ruby pulses at my throat. Glancing down I assure myself that it is tucked securely behind my clothing. Not a beacon for the enemy to find us. Their parting words are sacred between them-I do not intrude. The tree rustles urging me into safety. A final benediction from the sentient guardian that has watched over our laughter and our sorrow. The wind shifts bringing with it the scent of smoke and I turn toward the tunnel. We are crossing into exile, vanishing like mist into legend. I don't look back.

The storm that came unbidden

The storm that came unbidden

(Theron)

We had expected to be unleashed on Wilusa the moment Priam's resolve cracked. They forgot us in the caves. Let the Greeks play their games. We were not part of their trickery. Nor would we answer their call to raze the city to ashes. My scouts reported the remnants of the armada anchored off the coast, poised for a signal to return to shore. They waited. We were not summoned to the party. We came anyway. Our time of vengeance had come. And in its shadow, Selene and her sisters would have the perfect chance to slip out of the city.

We moved like prophecy-scaled, silent and unseen. The Greeks saw only smoke as we moved through the streets with confidence. The city did not see us. It felt us. We had walked every street, shielded every threshold. Now we turned that knowledge into precision. The air was wrong-too still. No dogs barked. No patrols passed. Even the wind held its breath. The scent of fire drifted from the lower town, where the denizens huddled in hovels pressed against the wall. Behind me my shifters struck swiftly and silently. Their blows final. The intruders would never see the morning sun.

Somewhere ahead, Selene leads her sisters to the tunnel Hektor had shown us. It would open up on the banks of the Scamander far from the city. My senses stretched out across our chosen battlefield, searching for her breath, her heartbeat, her memory. A scream shattered the silence. Sandals slapped stone. Armor clashed. Men shouted. Wilusa was waking to its death. We fanned out in groups of three. Moving through the rising storm like a scythe. Spiralling around so that enemies were easily confused. They would parry with one blade only to have another deliver the final blow. No one expected the third blade-dipped in venom donated by the elders of Thera. It was potent, burned cold and all life ended quickly. The internal echo of Selene's vow rings in my ears. *'Survive for me, Theron. I refuse to walk through life without you.'* I would see my mate one last time before prophecy and vision tore us apart. Fates be damned.

The air tastes of ash and betrayal. No one checked the wooden beast for teeth. Priam and his advisors had been duped by a large wooden horse. An offering fit for the gods. A cacophony of human wails pierced our ears, I raised a fist for us to hold fast. Pain rang through our bond. I scanned Alexios and the others-checking for blood, breath and steadiness. They were standing, some bruised. That was enough. Fire danced behind us-embers jumping merrily from one thatched roof to the next. We pulled children frozen in doorways and shielded elders through the worst parts. We did not come to slaughter the inhabitants of Wilusa. We came to protect what history would forget. Fire would cleanse this blot on history's page but the people who had lived the tragedy would never forget it. Tales would be told until legend sank into the annals of time herself.

She has passed this way. A feather-azure and violet crushed beneath sandals. Selene's trail. She was ahead. That was good. It meant that we could shield her path. I inhaled to four. Held. Exhaled to seven. The storm within me stilled. I raised my fist. They moved. Signalers fell. Torches stamped out. Flags destroyed. Patrols scattered in broken pieces across cobble stones. We didn't just fight. We dismantled. No one would follow our path. No one would touch her trail. We erased it with the blood of those who dared. She must live. For our kind. For our children. For our future.

The streets flooded with bodies. Our formation fractured. Fanning out once more, we fight onwards, protecting those who need the help. Fear moved faster than fire. Directing women and children to run towards the tunnel and the location where Lady Selene will meet them. We carved a path through the chaos. We paused. Agamemnon and Menelaus strode up the hill confident in their win. Their finest soldiers pushing citizens back toward the walls of the houses that line the main thoroughfare. No mercy. No hesitation. They walked like victors. My throat tightened at the cost. I sent a flurry of signals backward. We shadowed them on parallel roads, blades drawn moving against the frightened sea of humanity. They had not summoned us. We were the storm they forgot to prepare for.

Unseen Betrayal

Unseen Betrayal

(Helena)

The once bustling city was now a hellscape of smoke and terror. Screams echoed from every quarter. Raw. Relentless. Unending. The city wailed to the gods-a visceral prayer that even in their last moments they could be saved. But the gods were silent. Their game played to the end. Mortals were left to their own devices. Weapons clashed. Everyone fought who could. Men. Women. And children who should never have to raise more than a wooden sword in training. They fought with desperation not discipline. They fought back for escape, not victory. Not as warriors but as survivors.

Keeping my head, I sent the children to Queen Hekuba with their nurse as my focus needed to be with my husband. I had played the role long enough to know when to lean in. Even if I didn't care. I fastened the buckles with practiced ease. Not tenderness...just precision. His armor was familiar. He was not. He was a child still playing at war. Not seasoned like Menelaus nor strategic like Alexander. Shadows slid past the door. Too quiet to be allies. He pushed me behind him, drawing his sword. Reflex on his part. Survival on mine. Gripping his arm, I whispered, 'I have a better idea.' He didn't ask what. He never did.

'There's a hidden corridor behind the tapestry in the next room. Let them chase ghost's while we move.'

'Where does it lead?' Deiphobus shoved my cloak over my shoulders and fastened it at my throat, drawing the hood over my hair with more care than I deserved. We both knew the risk. My face was the symbol that both nations had fought over. My presence in either camp now a provocation. 'Away from here. Through the old palace. Its forgotten. We will remain unseen.' His eyes never left mine. Searching for something I wouldn't give. 'We need to plead for truce. It is the only way we can save the city, my love.' He heard the words. Not the tone. Not the warning. Truth was a luxury and we were out of time. The tapestry was faded like the beauty I had once held in my prime.

He pushed me toward his mother's chambers. Not gently. Not cruelly. Her chambers were the best guarded in the entire complex. She was shrewd enough to see through me. I did not trust her enough not to turn me over to the Greeks herself. I had been the cause of two of her sons deaths and had a hand in all the others. Not that she had been able to prove anything beyond a shadow of doubt. 'Go be with the children. Leave me to my work and if I do not return—leave using the tunnels. Selene will show you where to go.' Selene. Even now she was praised. I was tolerated. Deemed useless enough to hide with the children. I had other plans of my own. Plans that didn't involve hiding. Or waiting.

He saw what he needed to. That was enough. The trap was set. And he was too in love to smell the bait. My face twisted, revealing my true feelings—Selene... it was always Selene. What did she have that I didn't? My conscience cackled into the silence. She was honest. Courageous in the face of danger. Had the ear of the goddess. She was the darling of the court-Why couldn't they trust that I knew what I was doing? Because they were right not to trust me. The corridor ahead was dim. That suited me.

Instead of following Deiphobus's instructions, I shadowed him to where Menelaus was laughing, waving his bloody sword around jovially, celebrating the fall of Wilusa. With a jeer, Menelaus swiftly informed Deiphobus that he had been betrayed. Disbelief cracked across his face. Rage followed. But it was too late. He had underestimated me. That was his final mistake. My task was complete. As easily as drawing breath I traded one crown for another. Just blood and silence. Menelaus didn't trust me but he needed me and he hated me for it. I didn't flinch. I didn't mourn. All eyes would be on me to prove my loyalty to Sparta after proclaiming it to Troy. I would give them nothing. I had mourned Alexander in my own way. Deiphobus had been a placeholder. His death was a punctuation mark to the end of this whole sham. A new game was rising and it would be of my own making.

Menelaus left Deiphobus horribly mutilated for dead, reclaiming me as part of his spoils. Standing amidst their celebrations, my mind grappled with my choices and the outcomes they had wrought. I did not care to know what would happen to the children. Alexander's children. They would not be spared from the endless slaughter. None of the royal children would. If caught, Hekuba, Kassandra, Andromache, and Selene would also be claimed as spoils of war and most likely become high-born slaves for the rest of their lives. Maybe I would insist that they be sent to the edges of our country. Split apart to die in isolation serving in solitude with their tongues ripped from their mouths. Selene's sisters would weep for Sparta. Their tears would heal what our swords could not. And I...I would be Queen of Sparta once more. Only time would tell if Agamemnon and Menelaus would deliver on their promises the way I had delivered on mine. Let the poets write only of the great love match, not of the betrayal that followed. Let the priests curse my name-only the gods knew the truth. I would shape the myth, hiding the truth.

Fire and Blood

Fire and Blood

(Theron)

The heat is unbearable, the smoke thick and choking. But I can't afford to stop. Selene is vulnerable. She waited. That was all I needed. Her belief in me was louder than war. I would not let our last night be a memory. I would make it a promise. Raya and Seraphinus guard her and between them no enemy soldier lives. Trojan defenders trying to protect their city, enemy soldiers intent on bringing it to its knees.

My sword feels like an extension of my arm as I cut down Greek soldiers in my path. Fools. They called to me to join them. Instead they met justice. They called me brother. I answered with silence and steel. The flames cast long shadows on the blood-soaked streets. All life flees before it now. Except for us. We were born of the flame and made it our weapon. The tunnel was close. So was she.

Buildings collapse around me, the debris creating treacherous alleys. Greek soldiers ambush me. Word somehow spreading that we are no longer fighting together. My blade moves before thought. They came at me with fury. I answered with purpose. My duty is to my own people. Not puffed up kings hell bent on destroying nations to gain access to whatever glittering resource they hold possession of. My armor and clothing are smeared with blood—both my own and that of the soldiers I have fought. My face is streaked with sweat and soot, marking me as a warrior emerging from the depths of chaos. This hellscape is my playground.

I can do nothing for the royal children lined up, frozen in place on the battlements in their night clothes. Shocked awake and scared witless. Mothers scream for their children. Restrained by their captors wailing their despair. Turning my face from the scene in front of me I push forward stoically. If choosing Selene is a crime I will gladly pay the price for all of eternity. Maybe I will. I did not curse the gods. They were not my gods. Rhythmic thumps as the children are pushed. Sudden silence as the world holds its breath. Seven children lay with their heads smashed open. Seven children who would never see the sun again. And they called me a beast. Humans were cruelest to those of their own kind. I bore witness. That was punishment enough.

Locating the entrance to the tunnel Seraphinus, Raya and Selene are all fighting. She does not keep her hands clean while others fight to defend her. Ruby hidden. Hair braided back. Blood streaks her forehead and she summarily cleans her xythia on the enemies clothing before sheathing them. She wears layers of practical clothing suitable for a trek through the mountains. She fights without armor. Without restraint. Relief washes over me. Our eyes meet. Acknowledgement. Respect. Relief. Her actions are those of a warrior queen. My warrior queen. Admitting these words to myself is easy—uttering them in front of our clans would be much harder. Never before had there been a bond formed between shifters of two different species. We were anomaly and miracle. A bond no elder had ever dared imagine. We were needed. We were the prophecy incarnate.

'Selene.' For a brief moment the world ceases to exist. Carnage could wait. I would have this moment with her.

'Wilusa is falling.' Her silver eyes glow with deep sadness. Tears swim but do not fall. 'How many have come this way?' I pull her close directing my question to Seraphinus. 'Twenty.' He answers. A red and gold feather peeks from the edge of his armor. A scale on a chain graces Raya's neck. Twenty souls. We had sent more. The gods had taken their share. Feeling our hearts fall into sync, I focus on Selene pressing my lips to hers. All sound ceases. Nothing else matters but the beautiful being I cradle gently with my hands. Her mouth tastes like warm berries on a summer's day, a surprising sweetness amidst the chaos. I press my body against hers, pinning her to the palace wall, feeling the warmth of her through the layers of clothing. I pour everything into that kiss, knowing that she will understand my message of determination, hope, love, and fear. This moment is ours—it is a promise and a farewell. We were no longer legend in waiting. We were legend in motion.

We break apart reluctantly, breathless. '*We need to go,*' she says, her voice barely more than a whisper, brushes my mind, her words for me alone, '*Come find me, Theron. Claim me for your own in front of your people and mine. My sisters approve of this match. Their approval is all I need.*' She wasn't asking for a promise. She was giving me something to hold on to.

I nod, slowly releasing her hand. 'Stick to the route. We'll be right behind you.'

We both knew I wouldn't. The words are for the survivors hunkering down in the tunnel. I tap at the base of my throat where the ruby rests on hers, silently reminding her we would see each other even when we were apart.

With a final, longing look, she turns and is absorbed by her people already in the tunnels. I watch her form disappear into the shadows, my entire being aching and filling with emptiness with each step she takes away from me. She had her duty and I had mine—I would guard her to my last breath. But duty calls, and I turn back to face the oncoming storm.

We were sacrificing much, but through the amulet and the coin, we would be bound. Not by law, but by legacy. Not by blood, but by choice. Our bond is strong, and until I see her again, it will remain so. Prophecy foretold this. Selene, Raya, and Thea were the heart of the prophecy...the last of Phoenix kind and their choices would be crucial in the days to come in navigating the chaos and ensuring as many people as possible would be saved. Exchanging charged determined looks with Seraphinus, we turned our backs to the tunnels. If any wished to pursue our females, they would have to go through us first.

I witness acts of heroism and sacrifice—Trojan soldiers stand with us holding the line to allow others to escape, civilians risking their lives to save their neighbors. My shifters display their abilities to protect the vulnerable. No longer hiding their teeth beneath a mortal exterior. Assigning some to usher the fleeing refugees into the tunnels and others, such as Gwydion, the opportunity to cause some real damage to those who would follow. We coordinated our efforts, showcasing the strength of our clans to the world. Let them come. Let them try. We would answer with fire. Let the gods watch. We had heard their words. We were ready.

With a final glance at the tunnels where Selene has disappeared, I redistribute my shifters to hold the line. Humans and shifters work together the way Selene, Hektor and I dreamed of. Smoke curled around our scales like a benediction. The fate of the future of Wilusa and our kind rests on our shoulders, and we will not falter.

In shadow and in song

In shadow and in song

(Selene)

The tunnels are dark, cold, and dripping with an unidentifiable slime that coats the walls. Every so often, a drop splashes onto someone's shoulder, eliciting a stifled gasp or shiver. The faint, musty smell of decay lingers, a reminder of the years these passageways have existed unnoticed beneath the palace. I can almost hear the echoes of the past—the smugglers who once used these tunnels to keep our city alive, moving silently in the shadows, just as we do now. Along the walls, arrows and discreet symbols guide our way. A promise etched in soot and silence. A double edged sword to lead us safely to the banks of the Scamander River. Traps had been laid for those who would be foolish enough to track us.

A child's whimper echoes through the narrow passageways, quickly hushed by a protective parent. The sound pulls at my heartstrings. A stark reminder of the innocence caught in the crossfire of our struggles. I could not shield them from the nightmares that would haunt their dreams but I could follow the path and get them to safety. Stationed along the path are Raya's chosen handmaidens, those she has trained personally to execute this evacuation. Their silent vigilance reassures me. Ready to act. Ready to protect those in their charge. They stand as silent sentinels, their presence a reassuring constant in the dark.

Hurried footsteps pound the dirt, and whispered prayers are passed backward, being added to along the way. The prayers weren't for the goddess's ears. They were talismans to hold onto. The rhythmic murmurs are like a lifeline, a fragile thread connecting us all in our shared desperation and hope. Fear and determination permeate the air as we gather at the Scamander in the dark, waiting until the very last survivor exits the tunnel. We do not cross into safety. We cross into myth buried beneath layers of legend. I waited for the last soul not because I had to, but because I could not bear to leave anyone behind again. Their fears were mine along with their hopes. Xythia drawn, I silently dared someone to try their sharp edges already dipped in Greek blood. Let the world forget our names.

The firelight flickers across the faces of the refugees, casting deep shadows that accentuate their exhaustion and fear. Their eyes held questions I could not answer. The youngest children cling to their parents, their wide eyes reflecting in the flames. The older ones, forced to grow up too soon, wear expressions of grim resolve. They understand the stakes, and their bravery humbles me. We are all bound by the same fate now, united in our struggle for survival.

'Keep moving, and stay quiet,' I urge, my heart beating loudly in my own ears. The Greek army would give chase. The long trek was ahead of us, through mountain passes, on narrow pathways, both treacherous and unforgiving. Every step forward was one more away from Theron. My eyes raised to the stars fading in the early morning light. Inhaling slowly to center myself I silently beg for their help. The stars did not answer. But they watched over us with a soft light that calmed my nerves. I had been born to rule from a throne not lead my people into exile. And yet, I had led my family for the past ten years in exile from Emberis. I had the knowledge, Raya the skills and Thea the healing touch. We were not beaten. We were far from it.

'I want you to separate into groups of no more than ten, including children,' I instruct, with all the grace and resolve I can muster. Striding forward, I cut through the growing group directly into the center. I did not shout. I did not need to. 'We have negotiated with the temples along the way. Please choose your deity wisely as they can only sustain a small number of refugees. They will feed you, clothe you, and hide you until you can find a new home or a home will be chosen for you. We do not have the luxury of time. Move now.' My words are a lifeline, and I can feel the survivors clinging to them, pushing forward despite their exhaustion and fear. I watched them divide into three columns. They looked to Raya, Thea and I as if we were their salvation. We did not offer salvation. We offered survival. Our salvation belonged to the goddess.

30 people out of a city of thousands. My heart sinks. I wanted to save so many more. The reality of our situation is a bitter pill to swallow. Every face in the crowd represents a life, a story, a future that hangs in the balance. I can see the toll it has taken on them. Lines of worry etched deeply into their faces. A haunted look in their eyes. Some murmur their gratitude, others beg to be part of whatever group I choose. They could not. My sisters and I would not remain at the temple our group ended up at. We had sanctuary waiting elsewhere. They looked to me to lead.

The weight of leadership presses heavily on my shoulders. I glance around at the faces of those who have put their trust in me, hoping that I am strong enough to bear this burden. They did not ask for perfection. Andromache quietly reaches out to squeeze my hand in solidarity, holding Astyanax close to her body underneath her cloak. Her silent support is a balm to my frayed nerves, and I draw strength from her presence. Raya's sharp eyes constantly scan the area, ever alert for any sign of danger. Her unwavering focus a result of her warrior training.

Thea, with her calming aura, whispers promises of safety and a brighter future to the youngest and most frightened. Her soothing words and gentle touch bring a semblance of peace to those who need it most. We cannot afford to show weakness now; every moment counts, and every decision could mean the difference between life and death. Chivvying them into the order of the temples along the way, Raya indicates she wants me at the front of the column. Every grouping was a gamble. Even now I was not sure that we did not harbour a spy in our midst. Our entire network could crumble. I did not feel brave.

'Everyone is looking at you to lead the way forward,' she says, direct as usual. 'You are a Queen, Selene, and you are a Princess of Troy. Do your damn job and lead your people.' Her words are a harsh reminder of the responsibility that rests upon my shoulders. I was not ready. Drawing my cloak tighter around me, I take the pack Thea hands to me and shoulder the heavy burden that has been left to me alone to save as many lives as possible. The weight of it seems to grow with each passing moment, but I steel myself for the task ahead. I would lead them not because I was chosen but because I remembered the cost of indecisive leadership.

As we move out, we move silently through the early morning stillness. The path ahead is uncertain, but we are guided by the dim light of the moon and the distant glow of the burning city. We did not speak of what we left behind. Three lines of women covered in ash moving forward with a single purpose. Survival. We walked between two lights. One fading. One burning. Shades existing between the sun and the moon. The cool air is a welcome relief from the oppressive heat of the flames, but it also carries a chill that seeps into our bones, a reminder of the harsh realities we face.

I glance back at the column of refugees, their faces illuminated by the early dawn. Each one of them has entrusted their lives to us, and I am determined not to let them down. Raya and Thea move with quiet efficiency, their presence a steadying force for those who follow. Together, we form a united front as we always have. Ruler, warrior and healer. Sisters. Survivors. They did not follow us because we had a plan. They followed us because we were survivors just like them.

Part Six

Epilogue: Hope for the future

(Theron)

It is almost over. The city a conflagration lighting the sky for all to see. The pride of Troy overwhelmed by the tenacity of the Greeks and the result of one woman's greed. The fire did not discriminate. It devoured marble and memory alike. Parts of the palace still stood especially around the tunnel entrance. Acrid smoke stings my nostrils. The cacophony of human sound fading in the white hot anger of the cleansing fire. The time for war had passed. This was erasure. I had seen cities fall. But this was different. This had been her home.

My shifters rested while Alexios, Seraphinus and I stood guard. We would not let the secret of our mates escape fall into the hands of those who wished them harm. Fire salamanders swum through the air. Twining around our bodies playfully. Enticingly. They had been birthed in the midst of this destruction. They danced for joy to celebrate new life from old. Their heat did not burn. For us they were the equivalent of a pet house cat. I wanted to keep one. To share with Selene the joy that could be gained from its purity. Such a creature is not meant to be caged. Silently wishing them well I send them on their way chasing my flame filled breath down the corridor. Their departure a necessity. They could not heal the injured and dying. Greece had taken enough from us this night. One of my shifters lay dead and another too injured to move.

Yet they continue to remain relentless as Agamemnon and his men sweep through the flames checking each room in this corridor not re-alising we were waiting with blades at the ready. Agamemnon himself steps forward, his face contorted with rage, demanding to know what we are doing in this corridor and why we are keeping it closed to his soldiers. He is furious with our impassive expressions.

'What is the meaning of this?'; Agamemnon roars, his voice echoing off the walls. 'Why are you blocking the way? Open this tunnel imme-diately and let my soldiers pass!'

I remain calm, my gaze unwavering. 'No. I don't think we will. My clans are done working with you and your egotistical desire to rule the world. You don't own us. Do you know the exact wording of the oath our ancestors made to each other? Once we have the token we are no longer bound to obey your words. And guess what, little king—we have the amulet and the coin.'

His fury does not match my own at the loss of two of my family members. I'm not about to tell him that the coin is no longer in Wilusa. I had a duty to all my family including my little mate who needed as much of a head start as I could give her by stalling them here.

Agamemnon's eyes narrow, and he draws his sword with a sneer. 'You think that little trinket will save you? You are traitors, and you will suffer for your betrayal.'

I laugh, a deep, menacing sound. 'I have something better.' Focus-ing my power, I project a vision into Agamemnon's mind—teeth and claws, sharp and deadly, ready to tear him apart.

Agamemnon turns several shades past white and breaks out into a sweat, his bravado crumbling before my eyes. 'What... what are you?' he stammers, stepping back in fear. Connecting the dots in his own mind, I shift slightly, smooth scales covering my forearms, smoke curl-ing out of my nostrils. 'Dragon. Shifter.' I emphasize, letting the reality sink in. He had seen the man. Now he saw the myth. Every second he stalled was another heartbeat for her freedom and I would have her safe.

A shout draws my attention. Seraphinus is locked in a fierce duel with Isandros. The Greek warrior produces a weapon we have never seen before. My eyes widen. They have adapted. It has begun. The fight that we had witnessed in the temple. The weapon cuts through Seraphinus's scales like butter, causing him to roar in pain. Blood pours from his wound in rivulets. What the hell kind of weapon was that? Nothing the mortals had could affect the shifters this way. His natural healing isn't kicking in. I could not save him. Not yet. Not without risking everything.

Isandros pulls Seraphinus close, hissing in his ear, 'You're dead, and so are your children's children's children.' With a final, vicious shove, he pushes Seraphinus back, creating space between them. He doesn't flinch. His pain is visible but he watches Isandros's every move with a steady gaze.

Seraphinus parried the next strike, but Isandros moved with ruthless efficiency, pressing his advantage. Seraphinus didn't falter. His jaw tightened, and his grip on his sword remained unwavering. 'I will never let you harm them,' he growled, his voice steady and fierce despite the exhaustion I knew he felt. He would not fall. Not yet.

Isandros lunged, his blade aimed straight for Seraphinus' heart. 'You're too late. Your fate is sealed.' I mark his face in my mind. He's a dead man when we catch up with him. A silent vow. A promise etched in stone.

Seraphinus parried the strike, pushing Isandros back with a force that seemed impossible for someone in his condition. 'Not if I have anything to say about it,' he retorted, his words filled with raw determination. Scales dulling from whatever was on that blade.

I fought harder, desperation fueling my every move. The weight of Isandros's words hung heavy in the air, a reminder of what was at stake. Seraphinus was fighting not just for himself, but for all of us. I couldn't let him do it alone.

Finally, I broke through the line of soldiers and made it to their side. 'Finn, I've got your back,' I shouted, positioning myself beside him, ready to face Isandros together.

'And I have your's.' Alexios shouts in my ear. Together we make up the three sides of a triad ready to scythe through the enemy.

Seraphinus glanced at me, a flicker of relief in his eyes, but his focus never wavered. We stood back to back, ready to take on the monster who threatened our very existence.

There's panic in my best friend's eyes as he looks from his arm to me and then back again. He's injured and distracted—a bad combination for the battle we're fighting. Seraphinus staggers, blood pouring from his wound. Desperation surges through me. I grab him and shove him toward the tunnels. Alexios closes the gap blocking Isandros's next strike with steel. The rhythm of the triad held even though one point was injured.

'Go! Find Selene and ask Thea if she has something that can help,' I commanded. 'Be my eyes. Guard my mate. Live for yours.'

Seraphinus stumbled into the tunnels, his steps unsteady. As he disappeared from view, I turned back to face the Greek onslaught, my determination hardening into steel. I would hold the line. I would keep my promise even though the odds had just risen sharply against us.

Through our deep bond as nest mates, Finn projected his delirious thoughts into my mind. His vision blurred, and he struggled to stay conscious, believing I was with him on the trail, guiding him to safety. The walls seemed to close in, the sounds of battle growing distant in his mind. I couldn't guide him physically. But I could anchor him. I could hold him to this plane of existence until he could reach help.

'The woman Nuraya—she is your mate,' Finn muttered, his gaze unfocused. His face hardened as he continued, addressing me as if I was beside him. 'What of it? Is it not enough that we sacrifice everything so that you can be a complete imbecile to our Queen? The woman you have been calling out to every night for ten years. My own mate faced dangers on the killing fields in the dead of the night so that you could be assured that she was safe and well! I will watch her back and see her safe. I will ensure that the Queen is well hidden from those who wish her harm.'

He did not know of our shared existence through the amulet and the coin. In his delirium this was not just a rebuke. It was a reminder. Of who I was. Of who I had failed to protect.

His words cut deeper than any blade. Even in his weakened state, Finn's dedication and sacrifice were clear. I understood the weight of his words and the truth they held. I had shamed myself for not claiming her in front of our people, and for that, I would pay the consequences for years to come.

Dawn of the Phoenix rising

Dawn of the Phoenix rising

(Nuraya)

The tower of smoke rising high in the air stood as a beacon to the terror that had consumed Wilusa, marking the devastation left in the wake of Troy's fall. The smoke, initially thick and black, was full of particulates and ash from the burning city, creating an impenetrable, opaque cloud. As time passed, the smoke began to cool, turning into a whitish-grey color, becoming more transparent and cloudy. It lingered as a ghostly veil over the landscape, a stark reminder of the devastation that had taken place. We had covered many schoinos in the first few days, keeping our promise to the people we had managed to save, leaving each temple one group less than when we arrived there. Scanning the horizon for trouble, I kept an eye on the group we were traveling with. My eyes never rested. Each movement, each whisper of wind could be a threat or omen. I counted heads, I counted breaths. I counted the few goats we had acquired. I had lost one. I would not lose another.

Thea was exhausted. Her usual smile long gone. Finn had stumbled into our encampment. Scales dull. Lips blue. Eyes bright with pain. He had masked the pain from our bond. When the mask dissolved I hit the ground when he did. They had laid us together on the same litter.

I had woken after a period. He had not. Thea had fought for his life tending him day and night. Life is precious and he was family. My family. My tears and my blood infused him with enough energy to heal. Just enough regenerating power to wake up but not enough to change his cell make up. This was a toxin. She had identified that much. We still didn't know enough to produce a working antidote. He needed my blood and tears daily. It wasn't enough but it was all I had to give. Despite the unknown injury he moved with surprising agility, determined not to slow us down. He felt the danger surrounding and chasing us as much as I did. The enemy was hiding in the smoke beyond the blind spot of every reflective surface just out of sight but not out of mind.

My eyes drifted to Selene. At first, she had shown immense courage in leading our people away from Wilusa. Then she began to withdraw into herself the same way she had after Hektor's death. The haunting emptiness that threatened to consume her visible on her face as we fought tooth and nail to keep Seraphinus in this world. 'I have led those going to temples to their safe houses.' she spoke into the silence, 'There is no one left but family and I will not lead our family to their doom.' Her hand clasped firmly around the ruby at the base of her throat. I had seen her break before. This was different. 'You lead sister.' My hand grasps her shoulder, 'I will shoulder decision making but you lead.' She didn't argue. She didn't cry. She simply nodded and kept walking.

As we made our way through the rugged terrain, the night grew colder. The wind whipped around us, carrying the scent of burning wood and distant salt from the sea. We gathered together for a brief respite, huddling close around the small fire for warmth. Rogue Greek soldiers still roamed the countryside looking for refugees. We were not safe yet. Andromache, focused on the weakening Astyanax, stayed a bit apart from the group, her worry etched deeply on her face. I feared her son was not long for this world, and if he died on the road, would she lay down beside him and never move again? Andromache had been a shell of herself and visibly flinched each time her eyes caught the tower of smoke.

I took a deep breath, feeling the weight of the responsibility on my shoulders. 'We need to discuss our next steps,' I began, my voice steady despite the turmoil within. 'We are heading to Pompeii, where the priestesses we sent ahead from the temple of Eiliethyia have established a new order. They are known as the House of the Phoenix.' Thea's school had been more successful than initially thought. The villa had been teeming with life. Not a place for peaceful recovery. We wouldn't find rest there and we needed to find new identities in a world whose eyes were firmly fixed on Wilusa.

Selene nodded, her eyes reflecting a mix of hope and resolve, though there was a distant look in them. 'The priestesses have established a temple there, and they are dedicated to rebirth and renewal. It is a place where we can find sanctuary and rebuild. Pompeii is far enough from our enemies and provides the anonymity we need.' I met her gaze, steady and sure. Despite her disinterest in the daily details she had agreed to our next course of action.

My eyes find Finn, leaning against a tree ever watchful, his strength slowly returning despite the green veins of poison still evident on his arm. 'I sent word ahead and have heard from the sisters of the House of the Phoenix that they have arranged a cover story for you to continue to watch over us as a freed gladiator turned temple guardian. What do you think?'

He considered my words carefully. 'It allows me to remain close to you.' Remembering his duty, he included my sisters with an apologetic grin. 'With your majesty's permission, of course, I will remain watchful over yourself and Thea as well.'

Selene straightened her back and spoke bluntly, 'I am no Queen. Titles no longer hold the same weight they once did. I lead because I promised to do so, but my heart is in Wilusa. Each step I take away from Theron tears at our bond.' Her silver eyes settled on me, an expression of deep regret on her face. 'Raya, you must lead us to our new home. I cannot.'

I felt a pang of empathy for Selene, understanding the depth of the bond she shares with Theron. Her plea was raw and honest, reflecting the immense pain she must be enduring. Stepping forward, I placed a reassuring hand on her shoulder. 'I will do what it takes to get us there,' I promised her. 'There you must rest Sister. He will come when he can. He has not broken one oath yet.'

Finn pushed off from the tree and joined us, lightly tugging on my braid as he passed me. Locking eyes, we shared a moment of silent understanding. He would stand beside me, be my shield, and have my back as needed. The journey ahead would not be easy, but we were united in our purpose.

As the fire crackled and the group settled into a quiet lull, Finn motioned for me to follow him a few steps away. 'Raya,' he said softly, his eyes reflecting the flickering flames, 'there's something I need to tell you.'

I nodded, sensing the seriousness in his tone. 'What is it, Finn?'

He took a deep breath, his gaze unwavering. 'Your sister. Her majesty the Queen. She cannot abdicate her throne. It is passed by blood. You may lead momentarily but she will remain the Queen.'

I met his gaze evenly, 'I have no interest in wearing a crown. Selene is soul sick. Her bond is fraying with distance. She needs time.'

'She needs Theron.' He's blunt and I treasure that about him. His words cut through the palace courtesies. 'But until she is ready. We rise, together.'

A spark of warmth and determination ignited within me. Little did Finn know he had just uttered the creed of the Royal Guard of Emberis, a promise that we would survive, make it out alive, and thrive in new situations. The words carried the weight of our history and the hope for our future.

Suddenly, a distant noise made us both tense. We listened intently, hearts pounding, but the sound faded into the night. Finn's expression hardened with resolve. 'We'll make it through this, Raya.'

Returning to the group, I exchanged glances with my sisters. As the first light of dawn began to break through the velvety darkness that had surrounded us, I spoke words indelibly engraved on my soul that Finn had uttered unwittingly, 'We rise.'

Afterword

Afterword

The story behind the fall of Troy has always fascinated me. As a child I wondered if one woman could be considered so beautiful that anyone would be so easily manipulated. I wondered if she could be considered so innocent if she left behind children in Sparta. I wondered if there was an underlying power play set in motion by the united Greek states. Were the gods really involved or were they conveniently blamed for human nature. Why should all the attention fall on Alexander or Paris (as some texts refer to him as) and Helena when other relationships were affected by their actions.

Then the movie and television series were released and I felt all the feels. I agonised with Briseis who didn't understand her place after she was taken to Achilles tent (neither her princess nor her priestess rank protected her and she gave up her dignity), with Andromache and Hektor, and even some what Achilles himself because Brad Pitt made his pain real to me. I mourned with King Priam when he begged for the body of Hektor. Each life a thread in a story that has captivated the world for centuries.

I can only hope that I have given this legend the due attention that it deserves.

Playlist for Shadows of Troy

Playlist for Shadows of Troy

Sam Tinnesz & UNSECRET-We need a hero
Imagine Dragons-Warriors
Sam Tinnesz feat Yacht Money-Play with fire
Beth Crowley-Warrior
Sting-Fields of Gold
Fallout Boy-Centuries
Christina Perri-A Thousand Years
Enya-Only Time
Linkin Park-Castle of Glass
Alanis Morrisette-You Outta know
League of Legends-Legends never die
Coldplay-The Scientist
Jeremy Renner-Love and Titanium
Zedd feat foxes-Clarity
Fireside Melody Craft-My Father's savage daughter
Sam Tinnesz Far from Home-the Raven
Voiceplay ft Linkin Park-Heavy is Crown
Zayde Wolf-Born Ready
The Everlove-Monster
Adele-Rolling in the deep
Smash into Pieces-All eyes on you
Beatles-Here comes the sun
Fort Minor-Remember the name
Billie Eilish-Everybody wants to rule the world
Leonard Cohen-You want it darker
Twentyone Pilots-Doubt

Rag n Bone Human
Two Steps from Hell-Heart of Courage
Livingston-Traitor
The hanging tree
Pentatonix-The sound of silence
Halocene-My Immortal
Livingston-Half Life
Linkin Park-In the end
Linkin Park-Numb
Gnus Cello-Reflections of Light
Smash into Pieces-Heroes are calling
Eagle-Eye Cherry-Save Tonight
Alex Warren feat Ella Henderson-Carry you home
Two Steps from Hell-Protectors of the Earth
Imagine Dragons-Demons
Two Steps from Hell-Dragon rider
For King and Country-Burn the Ships
Zayde Wolf feat. Ruelle-Walk through the fire
Wicked (the movie version)-Defying Gravity
Queen-We will Rock You
Anahata-Savage Daughter
Emimem-Lose Yourself
Halocene-This is our war
Peyton Parrish-I'll make a man out of you

Resources

Resources

Troy

https://www.realcityoftroy.com/2021/04/

Troy: excavation - Livius

Helen of Troy | Legend, Family, & Worship | Britannica

Polyxena - Wikipedia

Briseis - Wikipedia

Philoctetes in Greek Mythology - Greek Legends and Myths

Deiphobus - Wikipedia

Origins and Introductions: Troy and Rome in Medieval British and Irish Writing | Celts, Romans, Britons: Classical and Celtic Influence in the Construction of British Identities | Oxford Academic

Britain's Trojan History - Historic UK

Troy 2004 Movie

Troy: Fall of a City 2018 Television seriess

The Iliad-Homer

The Odyssey-Homer

Britain's Hidden History

Unique Artifacts Reveal The Ancient City Of Troy Is Much Older Than Previously Thought - Ancient Pages

Skeleton Of Last Trojan Discovered – Ancient City Of Troy May Have Been A Religious Sanctuary – Archaeologists Say - Ancient Pages

University of Cincinatti-Troy VII

Christogenea-classical records of Trojan-Roman-Judah

providencejournal.com-A lost ancient city built by Trojan War Captives has been found news.artnet.com-The Ancient City of Tenea Only Existed in Myths-Until a Team of Archeologists Found the Real Thing in Greece

ancient-origins.net the Aenid, Troy, The Sea Peoples and Migrations to the Tyrrhenian Sea

macair.com-Aftermath of the Trojan War and Returns of the Achaean Leaders

johnchaple.co.uk Britain's Hidden History Prince Brutus

Greece

The Cult of Athena: Worship Practices in Ancient Greece - Greek Mythology

Paris in Greek Mythology - Greek Legends and Myths

Why Was The Spartan Army So Successful? - Ancient Pages

King Menelaus Of Sparta: Husband Of Helen Of Troy And Key Figure In The Trojan War - Ancient Pages

Cassandra: Greek Goddess Who Foretold Cursed Prophecies - Ancient Pages

Agamemnon - Wikipedia

Achilles - Son Of King Peleus And Leader Of The Nereids - Ancient Pages

mythologian.net/agamemnon-greek-hero-life-death-facts-myths/

maicar.com-Ajax, the Achaeans, Achilles

Mythical creatures

Dragons in Greek mythology - Wikipedia

Phoenix (mythology) - Wikipedia

Dragons And Dragon Kings In Ancient Mythology - Ancient Pages

Mythical Fiery Bird Phoenix In Mythologies Of Many Ancient Cultures - Ancient Pages

greekmythology.com/Myths/Phoenix

igentry.blogspot.com-Interesting Facts About Phoenix Bird

gbtimes.com/legend-chinese-phoenix

Britannica.com – Fenghuang

About the Author

About the Author

M. J. Wright is a writer, artist, and community volunteer based in Raymond Terrace, NSW. Whether writing young adult romance, new adult romance, sci-fi fantasy, or historical paranormal fiction, her stories span timelines and worlds, but always return to the quiet strength of survival, love, and self-discovery. *Shadows of Troy* is her fifth book—a story born from the need to escape, to imagine, and to explore the age-old question what if...

When not writing, M. J. Wright enjoys escaping into the mythical world of *Hogwarts Legacy*, crocheting, and tending her garden.

You can find her online at Facebook under MJWright2024, where she shares glimpses of her creative process and upcoming works. Alternatively, she can also be found at her own website at https://mjwrightauthor.square.site/

Coming Soon

Coming Soon

Tales of Irrawang

In a town stitched together by service, the Rotary Club is more than a weekly meeting—it's where stories unfold, friendships deepen and change quietly takes root.

Mark, a fifth-grade teacher and club president, holds the reins with quiet determination. Jake, the town policeman, and Sam, the carpenter and volunteer firefighter, bring youthful energy and heart. Hannah, a newly arrived author, challenges the town to think more inclusively. Ravi engineer's solutions with quiet precision, while Tom the baker carries the weight of legacy. Debbie overshares, but her loneliness fuels connection. Emily reports the town's heartbeat, Grace fights to save her farm, Helen builds the case for a multipurpose centre, David keeps the tech running, and Elise dreams big—if only she knew where to begin.

Through interwoven tales of resilience, humour, and hope, *Tales of Irrawang* offers a glimpse into a community where Rotary values aren't just spoken—they're lived.

June 2026

Anniversary Edition of *The Broken Child*

In a world where women are rare and should be revered, Marianna de Montmercy is neither cherished nor protected. She is forgotten—pushed to the margins like everything imperfect in this fractured society.

Ten years after its first release, *The Broken Child* returns in a commemorative edition: new cover art and bearing a fresh chapter that stirs the prophecy still waiting to be fulfilled.

Dystopian, mythic, and emotionally unflinching, this edition marks the beginning of a new cycle. For those who remember Marianna's silence and those meeting her for the first time...the story is not over...

Who is the child of the prophecy?

August 2026